No Dummy

"And bless the food we consume to the nourishment of our bodies and to—"

"*Ooohh.*" A loud collective gasp and assorted cusswords rose from folks in the audience who hadn't bowed and closed. Heads popped up. My gaze darted back to Kenny Strickland. The bass case now lay unzipped with the sides flapped open. A tiny Nike stuck out. I'd seen those gag stuffed legs poking out the back doors of eighteen-wheelers on the highway. The little blue jeans and tennis shoes made it look like a child's leg was caught in the door. Kenny's expression combined confusion and anger. He grabbed the shoe and yanked. A small but complete body tumbled onto the stage. Kenny flinched, then keeled over flat on his back. Other musicians rushed over. Two of them fanned Kenny as he lay spread-eagled on the floor. The scene reminded me of an old Three Stooges routine. Other folks must have thought it was a joke, too, because some of the audience laughed.

The guitarist placed his fingers against the carotid area, looked up, and solemnly shook his head. My breath caught in my chest. I realized the figure might not be a dummy. Not a joke. A real body . . .

Hey Diddle Diddle, the Corpse and the Fiddle

FRAN RIZER

BERKLEY PRIME CRIME, NEW YORK

THE BERKLEY PUBLISHING GROUP
Published by the Penguin Group
Penguin Group (USA) Inc.
375 Hudson Street, New York, New York 10014, USA
Penguin Group (Canada), 90 Eglinton Avenue East, Suite 700, Toronto, Ontario M4P 2Y3, Canada
(a division of Pearson Penguin Canada Inc.)
Penguin Books Ltd., 80 Strand, London WC2R 0RL, England
Penguin Group Ireland, 25 St. Stephen's Green, Dublin 2, Ireland (a division of Penguin Books Ltd.)
Penguin Group (Australia), 250 Camberwell Road, Camberwell, Victoria 3124, Australia
(a division of Pearson Australia Group Pty. Ltd.)
Penguin Books India Pvt. Ltd., 11 Community Centre, Panchsheel Park, New Delhi—110 017, India
Penguin Group (NZ), 67 Apollo Drive, Rosedale, North Shore 0632, New Zealand
(a division of Pearson New Zealand Ltd.)
Penguin Books (South Africa) (Pty.) Ltd., 24 Sturdee Avenue, Rosebank, Johannesburg 2196,
South Africa

Penguin Books Ltd., Registered Offices: 80 Strand, London WC2R 0RL, England

HEY DIDDLE DIDDLE, THE CORPSE AND THE FIDDLE

A Berkley Prime Crime Book / published by arrangement with the author

PRINTING HISTORY
Berkley Prime Crime mass-market edition / March 2008

Copyright © 2008 by Fran Rizer.
Cover art by Sawsan Chalabi.
Cover design by Rita Frangie.
Interior text design by Laura K. Corless.

ISBN: 978-0-425-22091-7

BERKLEY® PRIME CRIME
Berkley Prime Crime Books are published by The Berkley Publishing Group,
a division of Penguin Group (USA) Inc.,
375 Hudson Street, New York, New York 10014.
The name BERKLEY PRIME CRIME and the BERKLEY PRIME CRIME design
are trademarks belonging to Penguin Group (USA) Inc.

PRINTED IN THE UNITED STATES OF AMERICA

10 9 8 7 6 5 4 3 2 1

This story is dedicated to the memory of Randall Hylton—an honorable man, a dear friend, and a musical genius.

Acknowledgments

Special appreciation to Jeff Gerecke, my agent, and to Katherine Day, my editor, for leading Callie into print.

Thanks also to Gene Holdway and Mark Harvell, for bluegrass and musical expertise, and to Lucy Ballentine for sea island research. No, she is not Loose Lucy!

Chapter One

The sweat trapped in the bottom of my bra was making me crazy. I slipped a hand under my "Bluegrass Rules" tank top and pulled out the elastic. Water trickled down my midriff, and I flapped the fabric to create a little breeze.

Cousin Roger of radio WXYW stood on the outdoor stage, sopping perspiration from his forehead with a red bandana while he prayed into the microphone, "Heavenly Father, be with us as we break for lunch and bring us back for some more of this fine music and . . ."

I didn't mean to. I promise I didn't mean to, but I peeked. Glanced around to see who had their eyes closed. My friend Jane, sitting to my left, had her eyes squeezed shut. Like it mattered. Politically correct folks call her visually handicapped, but I, Calamine L. Parrish, call a spade a flipping shovel. Jane is blind—completely, totally, politically incorrect blind.

The fellow on my right had his eyes open. His hair was as bushy as Kramer's on the old *Seinfeld* show, and he ogled me like SpongeBob SquarePants making the big eyes. He was grinning and staring at the skin I exposed when I flapped my shirt. Like he'd never seen a bare navel!

I snatched the top down and looked up at the stage, which was elevated several feet above the ground. Three of the pickers—Dean, Arnie, and Van—stood motionless behind Roger, heads bowed, eyes closed, sweat dripping off their noses. *Dalmation!* Kenny Strickland, who played the stand-up, doghouse bass, had already unplugged his equipment and was steadily packing it up. During the prayer.

I try not to curse, not even kindergarten cussing, but Kenny almost made me say *shih tzu.*

Tacky, tacky, tacky. Kenny Strickland had sung three gospel songs during Broken Fence's set, and now he plodded back and forth behind Cousin Roger as he beseeched God's blessings on the festival. Granted, Kenny wasn't up at the front where Roger was praying into the center vocal microphone, but he was plenty visible. He carried his personal amplifier and cords to the back of the stage and placed them near his instrument case, lying against the worn-looking, dark blue velvet curtain at the rear.

Most outdoor stages don't have any drapery at all, but Happy Jack Wilburn had cleared part of Surcie Island and built the campground and stage area for this festival last fall about the same time the county remodeled the cafetorium at St. Mary Elementary School. The same school that now has new burgundy curtains. The same school where Happy Jack's mother is principal.

Kenny reached down to pick up the empty case, grabbed it, and strained. Wouldn't budge. He pushed it over and unzipped it.

Puh-leeze. What kind of wimp can't pick up a pile of cloth? I hoped someone had filled it with rocks. Would serve Kenny right, what with him being so disrespectful to God and Roger. Ex-cuuze me. That wasn't a hundred-watt idea. The case had been onstage since Kenny emptied it and left it there at the beginning of the show. It had been in sight of everyone in the audience since then, so I wasn't the only one who'd have seen if somebody put something in it.

My eyes returned to Cousin Roger, and I tried to concentrate on his words.

". . . and bless the food we consume to the nourishment of our bodies and to—"

"Ooohh!" A loud, collective gasp and assorted college-level cusswords rose from folks in the audience who hadn't bowed and closed. Heads popped up. My gaze darted back to Kenny Strickland. The bass case now lay unzipped with the sides flapped out.

"What happened?" Jane's eyelids popped open beneath her rose-tinted sunglass lenses, but of course she couldn't see the tiny Nike sticking out of the case. I'd seen those gag stuffed legs for sale at the truck stop in Beaufort, and I'd seen them poking out the back doors of eighteen-wheelers on the highway. With the little blue-jean and tennis shoe hanging out, it looked like a child caught in the door. Not humorous to me, and an artificial limb protruding from the bass case during prayer was just as bad, if not worse.

Kenny's expression combined confusion and anger. He grabbed the kid-sized tennis shoe and yanked. A small but complete body tumbled onto the stage. Kenny flinched, then keeled over flat on his back. *Phlap!*

Roger had stopped praying and turned to see what was going on. "What the . . ." he said, but everybody was talking, and I doubt most folks heard the graduate-level third word. The other musicians rushed over. Two of them fanned Kenny as he lay spread-eagled on his back. Reminded me of an old Three Stooges routine. Other folks must have thought it was a joke, too, because some of the audience laughed.

The tall, gray-haired guitarist knelt beside the mannequin. Dean Holdback. I'd played banjo at bluegrass jams with him at Lou's Pickin' Parlor back when I lived in Columbia. Dean placed his fingers against the carotid area, looked up, and solemnly shook his head. My breath caught in my chest. I realized the figure might not be a dummy. Not a joke. A real body.

A muscular bald-headed man in a green T-shirt with "Staff" printed on the back in all caps climbed onto the stage and bent over the small form, held the wrist, and touched the neck as Dean had. He stood and stepped to one of the microphones. "Is there a doctor here? All security officers report to your stations," he announced. "Everyone else, remain seated," he added when several folks in the audience jumped from their seats.

A few of them rushed toward the stage to get a better look. Others headed toward the path to the campground, following that age-old teacher admonition to get away when trouble starts. They were stopped by more staffers who looked like bouncers standing around the music arena. In a firmer, louder voice, the guy onstage repeated, "Remain seated. Return to your seats!"

Jane's fingernails clawed into my arm. "Girlfriend, if you don't tell me what's going on, I'll hit you," she said. That's how Jane and I are. Always polite to each other.

I leaned over and cupped my hand between my lips and Jane's ear. "I think there's a dead body on the stage," I whispered. "It looks like a little boy."

"Callie Parrish, I swear. Corpses follow you around ever since you started working at the funeral home. I guess somebody's been murdered, and you'll solve the crime."

"Not this time, Jane. I'm not getting involved."

That was my second unintentional fib of the day.

Chapter Two

The audience remained seated, kept in place by the staff members posted around the area like guards. There were a lot of verbal complaints, but no physical challenges against the mandate to remain in our seats. One man in the back kept screaming that he'd paid money and he wanted to hear bluegrass music. I turned around and recognized the shouter. He was Billy Wayne Wilson, who'd been a year ahead of me in high school.

The plastic webbing of my lawn chair scorched my bare legs below my shorts, and I squirmed.

My friend Jane remained still. She sat with her legs crossed under the skirt of her purple vintage hippie dress. Her rose-tinted sunglasses and red bangs contrasted brightly with the artificial yellow sunflowers on her broad-brimmed straw hat and her shocking pink cubic zirconium earrings. Jane's long hair fell to her waist in the back, look-ing fresh and dry, while my blonde hair dripped sweat, and my shirt clung to me like I was in a wet T-shirt contest. Kramer Hair kept glancing at me. Well, really at my bosom. I don't have much of my own in that department,

so what he actually saw was the result of my inflatable bra.
But he'd never know the difference, that's for sure.

Jane began tapping her foot. She had her iPod earplugs
in her ears, and I figured she was listening to Patsy Cline.
In some ways, Jane is about as modern as a girl, or I guess
"woman," since she's in her early thirties, could be. But her
taste in music and movies tends to be outdated, and she
likes retro hippie clothes, too. She inherited most of the
clothing from her mother, who claimed to be the "first and
last" hippie in St. Mary.

I wished I had a book with me. I'd brought several mysteries to read, but they were all back in the Winnebago.

Sheriff Harmon and several deputies arrived not long
after Dr. Johnny King, a mandolin player from Beaufort,
examined the short body. Jed Amick, the county coroner,
whose beaky face and lanky body always make me think of
Ichabod Crane, showed up about half an hour later.

Cousin Roger and the Broken Fence pickers, including
the revived Kenny Strickland, sat on the front edge of the
stage. The sheriff stepped to the microphone and announced, "I'm Wayne Harmon, sheriff of Jade County. My
deputies will need to talk with each of you before you're allowed to leave this area."

Someone called out from behind me, "You mean the
campground area, don't you? Can we go to our campers?"

Sheriff Harmon shook his head no and continued, "We
want you to remain where you are until a deputy takes your
statement. After that, you may go to the concession stands
at the back of the arena. You may visit the portable johns
on the path to the campground, but don't go to your campers.
Return to your seats here."

"What about the show?" the same voice called. "I want
my money back."

"Mr. Wilburn will give you details about the festival as
soon as possible. For now, just stay where you are until
we've taken your statements."

Billy Wayne still tried to argue with Sheriff Harmon,
and several others joined in his complaints. They were too

hot. They wanted food and cold drinks. They wanted to go to their campers. They wanted their money back. They wanted music. They wanted to leave. I was glad Daddy wasn't there. He would have been one of the loudest complainers. I craned my neck around to look at Billy Wayne. When he jumped up and headed toward the stage, several men in green T-shirts ran to him, but the man who stopped him was real law enforcement. Billy Wayne struggled, and several other officers helped handcuff him. Sheriff Harmon stood silently as they walked away. When it was over, he spoke.

"Let me tell all of you that because you were here when this happened, every one of you can be considered a material witness. If you have a problem following my directions, we can question you back at the county jail."

Dean Holdback's eyes locked on mine when I looked back at the stage, and he smiled in recognition. He slid off the edge of the stage and walked to me. "Callie, good to see you." He offered his hand to shake, but I gave him a little hug.

"Welcome to Jade County," I said with a smile that I hoped wasn't *too* friendly. I liked Dean a whole lot, but he wore a wide gold band on his left hand. I motioned toward Jane. "Dean, this is my friend Jane." I touched her on the shoulder. "Jane, I want you to meet Dean Holdback, the guitar player with Broken Fence." She looked blank for a moment, then reached up and pulled the iPod plugs out. She turned off the music and offered her hand. Dean grasped it, and held it what seemed like a long time to me, but it didn't appear to seem awkward to the two of them.

"Dean's from Columbia. I met him at a Friday night jam at Lou's Pickin' Parlor up there," I added.

"Your group sounds great," Jane said and grinned. "And, no, I wasn't listening to my iPod when your band was playing. I turned it on while we've been sitting here waiting." She nodded toward me. "Callie says there's a child's body on the stage. What's going on?"

Dean knelt on one knee in front of us. He leaned close. "It's not a child. It's Little Fiddlin' Fred."

"Little Fiddlin' Fred?" I gasped. "What's he doing here? Is he really dead?"

"Oh, he's dead, all right. I thought he was before I checked his heartbeat. There's a short metal rod of some kind sticking out above his lip. And blood. His shirt's covered with blood."

"We couldn't see that from out here," I said. "All we—"

"A homicide," Jane interrupted. "Everywhere Callie goes, there's a dead body."

Dean chuckled. "You're not accusing my favorite female banjo picker of killing Little Fiddlin' Fred, are you?"

"No. Callie's solved a couple of murders around here, but she's already promised me not to get involved in this one."

"Little Fiddlin' Fred wasn't shown on any of the advertisements," I said. "Was he supposed to perform?"

"Who's Little Fiddlin' Fred anyway?" Jane interrupted.

"Fred's one of the best fiddlers in bluegrass." Dean leaned even closer. "He just joined up with Second Time Around. That's a big step up because Second Time Around is an internationally known band. Played Europe and Japan last year. Fred came in this morning. His first gig with them was supposed to be the opening act tomorrow."

" 'Little Fiddlin' Fred.' Why do they call him that?" Jane asked.

"He's a dwarf. A member of the Little People of America," I added, just to let Dean know that I knew the proper term.

While we talked, deputies took statements from other members of Broken Fence, and as they finished, the musicians walked toward the back of the arena. Headed to the concessions or portable restrooms. Sheriff Harmon had cordoned off the back of the stage with yellow crime scene tape and was huddled at one end with Coroner Amick and Jack Wilburn, owner of the campground and promoter of the festival.

"Dean, did you hear the commercials on WXYW for this weekend?" I asked.

"Yeah. Are you thinking about that line they used that this festival would be full of surprises?"

"Yes, that's exactly what I was thinking. This isn't some kind of stunt like *Candid Camera*, is it?"

"No, Callie, that's really Little Fiddlin' Fred lying dead onstage with some kind of metal sticking out of his face."

"Did you say there's a piece of metal?" Jane said. "Callie found a broken needle in a corpse's neck last year."

Dean shook his head. "This isn't a needle. It's a short handle of some kind right above his top lip." He paused. "There's a first time for everything, and this is the first time Broken Fence has had a dead body onstage during our set."

"The first ever Sugar Pie Bluegrass Festival on Surcie Island," I said, "and the grand opening of Happy Jack's Campground."

"The first festival I've ever been to," said Jane.

"The first time Broken Fence has been on a trip in our band bus," said Dean.

"Band bus?" I squealed. Those guys had talked about wanting a band bus for as long as I'd known Dean.

"Yep." Dean grinned. "Finally gave up our day jobs, bought a bus, and gonna hit the circuit full-time this summer. First time out and we open the show with a dead body in Kenny's instrument case. That seems like a bad omen."

A forensics van pulled up. Technicians began processing the scene and photographing Fred's body lying against the heavy curtain at the rear of the stage as deputies interviewed people in the arena. They started at the back of the audience and worked their way up to the front row, which was only Kramer Hair, Jane, and me.

Having grown up in St. Mary, I knew the officer who talked to Kramer Hair. Deputy Smoak was a friend of some of my five brothers during their teenage years. I assumed he didn't remember me because he introduced himself.

"I'm Deputy Jim Smoak," he said, "and I need to ask you a few questions, so I'd appreciate it if you'd step over here with me." He led me away from my lawn chair. I left Dean talking to Jane.

The deputy asked for my name and address and wrote them on the paper on his clipboard. On television and in the mystery novels I read, there are generally two officers, one questioning while the other writes. But this wasn't television or a book; it was real life on a sea island off the coast of South Carolina.

"Miss Parrish, were you here from the beginning of the show?"

"Yes, sir. As a matter of fact, my friend Jane and I brought our chairs up from the campground and sat down at least thirty minutes before the show began."

"Did you see the bass player arrive?"

"Yes, sir. I watched the Broken Fence band members set up. They came onstage through the curtains at the back. I guess the steps must be back there." The officer nodded. "They did a sound check to make sure all of the microphones were working."

"Did you actually see the bass player take out his instrument? Or was it out of the case when he came onstage?"

"I watched Kenny unzip the cover, remove the bass, and leave the case crumpled at the back of the stage near the curtain. About the same place it is now. I didn't stare at it while Broken Fence played, but I think I would have noticed if anyone bothered it." I hesitated, then added, "And there wouldn't have been room for a body in there with the instrument. The case is exactly sized and shaped for a bass."

"When did you become aware that something was wrong onstage?"

I confessed that I'd been peeking during the prayer and been puzzled that the case seemed heavy when Kenny tried to lift it.

"Did you attempt to distract attention from the stage by exposing yourself during the prayer?"

"What?" Buh-leeve me, I wasn't expecting that question.

"You lifted your shirt during the prayer. Were you trying to draw attention to yourself so people wouldn't notice what was happening onstage?"

"No, sir." I knew who told him that. The guy with the

Kramer hair. I explained that I was just hot and fanned my tank top for air, not realizing that anyone would be watching me during the prayer.

When Deputy Smoak finished writing, I read over the papers and signed my statement. "You can go to the food stands for something to eat if you want, but Sheriff Harmon doesn't want anyone to leave this area until all statements are taken." He laughed and added, "And Callie, keep your clothes on in public."

"I thought you didn't remember me."

"I remember you, and I remember your friend Jane, too. She's blind, isn't she? I don't guess I should ask what she saw."

"She's blind, but she's very in tune with what goes on. Sometimes she seems to hear more than I see."

Smoak and I walked over to Jane. She sat alone because another officer was questioning Dean up near the stage. I told Jane I'd get us something to eat while she spoke with the deputy.

"I want root beer or Dr Pepper," Jane said. Like I didn't know her preference in soft drinks.

There was no question where I needed to go first. Jane and I had arrived early in my brother's Winnebago motor home, parked in a good site on the side of the campground nearest the performance arena, and left the air-conditioning on. I hoped to slip into the Winnebago, use the restroom, and have a few minutes of cool comfort, but a deputy stood guard just beyond the portable johns on the path to the campground.

Portable restrooms are wonderful things for shy people at public performances where there are no bathrooms, but puh-leeze, I'd rather hide behind a bush than go into one of those tin can outhouses. But since the deputy wouldn't be any more likely to let me go into the bushes than go to the Winnebago, I had no choice.

As usual, there was a fan at the top of the little metal building, but it was still stifling hot, a little smelly, and made me think of being locked in an abandoned refrigerator.

Portable restrooms used to make me think of vertical caskets, but since I got locked in a casket last fall, I now know that caskets are even worse for living people than portable johns.

The deputy nodded at me when I stepped out of the little cubicle. I headed back up the path to the concessions at the back of the listening arena, opposite end from the stage. Lots of times at small festivals like this, the foods are hamburgers and hot dogs prepared by civic groups like the Lions or Optimists to earn money for local charities, but Happy Jack had arranged commercial concessions.

Bob's Best Barbecue out of Charleston and Marie's Grill from Beaufort both had movable stands they set up at carnivals and fairs. Bob's operated out of a trailer and Marie's from the back of a customized truck.

Between the two was an unpainted plywood stand, obviously built on the spot. An extension cord ran from a nearby power pole and hung from a hook in the ceiling. A posterboard sign proclaimed this stand, such as it was, to be Gastric Gullah. I'd never heard of the establishment, but South Carolina Low Country descendants of West Africans are called Gullah and have maintained much of their culture, especially since many of them were somewhat isolated on sea islands. I understand a lot of the Gullah language, though I don't speak it well. I love Gullah food and definitely would have wanted something from Gastric Gullah, had it been open.

The smell of barbecue was heavy. The hog population is depleted considerably on the Fourth of July in the South, and a lot of barbecue is eaten all through the summer, but it wasn't my choice on this unseasonably hot April day. I stepped up to the line at Marie's Grill.

Dining awnings were erected over six picnic tables identical to those I'd seen at each campsite when I'd parked the Winnebago. I don't know how much good canvas ones would have done in the heat, but these were the plastic kind, and the shade was deceptive. No cooler under that plastic than out in the open, maybe even hotter.

When I asked to borrow my brother John's motor home and bring Jane to a bluegrass festival this wasn't what I'd expected. I'd known it would be hot, but the heat was record breaking for April, and I could hardly wait to get to the front of the line. The man behind me nudged my back. Like I could make the line move faster. Buh-leeve me, if I could have hurried things up, I would have. I tried to ignore the nudger, but he tapped me on the shoulder. I turned around. It was Kramer Hair.

"Whass up?" he said.

"I beg your pardon?" I answered in a witchy school-teacher tone, uglier than anytime I ever spoke back when I taught kindergarten.

"I'm sorry if I hurt you," he said. His hair wasn't his only Kramer characteristic. He was about the same size and had similar features. He wore baggy khaki pants with front pleats and an orange and blue Hawaiian print shirt with the top three buttons open. He'd missed the opportunity to complete his ensemble with flip-flops and instead wore penny loafers with no socks. Penny loafers with shiny silver dimes.

"Oh, no, that little bump didn't bother me at all," I said.

"That's not what I meant. I'm apologizing for not calling you after I got your telephone number."

"What are you talking about?" I said. "I don't know you."

"We met at the Myrtle Beach Convention Center a couple of Thanksgivings ago. You gave me your number, and I promised to call, but I never got around to it. I've got a sister, so I understand how that hurts a woman's feelings."

What kind of come-on was this? Thanksgiving at Myrtle Beach is a big annual indoor bluegrass festival, and I've been there a few times, but I hadn't given this guy my number.

"Listen, mister. I've got five older brothers, so I know all about pickup lines, and yours isn't one of the better ones. I've never seen you before."

"Don't get all huffy about it. You'd really like getting to know me"—he smirked and winked—"if you know what I mean."

Thank heaven I reached the counter just then. I turned my back on the nincompoop, bought two hot dogs and drinks, then headed back to tell Jane about the fellow in line at the refreshment stand.

Chapter Three

"**Y**ou'd better thank me for this," I said, handing Jane her chili dog and Dr Pepper. "I had to put up with the biggest creep I've ever met at the concession stand. The one who told the deputy that I exposed myself."

Since I hadn't told Jane about Kramer Hair, I expected that comment to pique her interest, but she was more concerned with her hot dog than my words. She sniffed. "You got extra onions, didn't you?" she asked.

"Of course, mustard, chili, and extra onions. Just the way you like it."

She held the hot dog to the side and raked the onions onto the ground. She fingered through the chili and picked out every little piece of onion. When she was finished, Jane wiped each finger with her napkin and began eating.

"What's the matter?" I asked. "You always want onions."

"Not today." She grinned. "Dean and I are having dinner together, and I don't know when the sheriff will let me go to the camper to brush my teeth."

I sat down and unwrapped my own hot dog. "Dinner?" I

asked. "I don't think we'll be let out of here by suppertime. The only three food stands are Marie's Grill, Bob's Best Barbecue, and something called Gastric Gullah, which isn't open yet. Your dinner date will probably be another hot dog or barbecue, and you know you hate barbecue."

"Callie, you brought me to this miserable oven of a festival. Now I've met someone I enjoy talking to, so why are you being so catty? Did you have something going with Dean in Columbia? Do you want him yourself?"

"Dean's a nice guy, and I don't have a problem with your talking to him, but don't get too interested. Jane, there's a big gold band on his left hand and through the years I've known him, I've never seen him come on to any female."

"I know about the wedding ring. I felt it."

"Been holding hands with a married man?"

"While you were gone, he helped me find the restroom. He guides by holding hands, instead of touching my elbow like you."

"Sorry," I snapped. "Next time you need help, I'll hold your hand." I lightened up. "Where's Dean now?"

"He left with a guy named Jack who needed his help with something."

"Probably Happy Jack Wilburn. I'll bet he's fit to be tied. The weather was bad enough to ruin this festival before Little Fiddlin' Fred got killed. Now the sheriff won't let in any more customers. I think the Sugar Pie Bluegrass Festival is doomed."

"You don't know the half of it. I heard someone tell Dean that Sheriff Harmon is not letting anyone leave the campground or festival area, and he's set up a roadblock at the bridge and isn't letting anyone else on the island. I'm sure that's going over great with people who live here and won't be able to get home from work."

"Not too many people live on this island. It's small and was totally undeveloped until Jack Wilburn built Happy Jack's Campground."

"Even one person would be too many if I was the one person Harmon blocked off the road to my home."

I laughed. "Jane, you don't even *go* to your job. You work from the comfort of your home." Because of her blindness, my friend experienced difficulties with dependable transportation to and from work. She's a night person anyway and has earned her living the past two years working evenings as Roxanne, a 900 number telephone sex "conversationalist," as she calls herself. I don't think much of Jane's job, but she thinks even less of my touching dead people working as the cosmetologist at Middleton's Mortuary in St. Mary, our hometown about twenty minutes away.

We ate silently for a few minutes before I added, "I'm sorry if I seem negative about you talking to Dean. I know you're grown. I just don't want you to get all excited about somebody who's probably just being . . ." I almost said, "kind," but I caught myself and said, "nice." Jane would have interpreted the word "kind" to mean that Dean felt sorry for her.

"No problem-o. Just don't get in my face because I like Dean. I'm definitely grown." Jane paused and thrust her chest forward, emphasizing the magnificent cleavage that had magically popped out while she was in middle school. At thirty, well, almost thirty-three, I was still waiting for the magic pop-out and covered that I was boob-challenged with inflatable bras from Victoria's Secret.

I finished my slaw dog and Coke, then offered Jane some premoistened wipes to clean her hands. Their lemon scent would help with the onion odor on her fingers.

Being in the mortuary business, I shuddered when I glanced at the back of the stage and saw that Little Fiddlin' Fred's body still lay there. Forensics technicians were doing their thing, and I know they don't move murder victims as quickly as we try to pick up our mortuary clients, but the weather was *way* too hot for a corpse.

I was surprised to see Deputy Smoak removing the

crime scene yellow border that had encompassed the entire
stage area. He tossed the wadded tape to the back of the
stage and, pulling a new length off the yellow roll, he ran it
across the full width of the stage about halfway between
the mics at the front and the body at the back. Surprising.
But the next thing that happened was astonishing.

Happy Jack Wilburn drove up in a big supercab Dodge
truck loaded with wood. He and several musicians, including Dean Holdback, placed a set of premade wooden mobile
home steps at the front of the stage and began unloading plywood and two-by-fours. After considerable sawing and
hammering, they created a plywood back wall across the entire stage directly in front of the yellow crime scene tape.
Now the stage was only half as deep, and the audience
couldn't see what was going on behind the plywood partition. The men moved the steps around the corner to the side
of the stage.

Grasping the center vocal microphone, Happy Jack
pulled it close to his lips. He cleared his throat and said, "I
apologize for the heat and the tragedy. Sheriff Harmon
says to tell you that you can go to your campers now, but
nobody will be allowed to leave the campground yet. The
music starts back right here onstage at six o'clock this evening, and we're going to dedicate this festival to Little Fiddlin' Fred."

Some guy in the audience yelled, "He's dead, ain't he?"
Like Fred had been lying still all that time just resting.

"Yes, Little Fiddlin' Fred, who was supposed to perform
with Second Time Around for the first time tomorrow
morning, has passed away."

I almost chuckled at Happy Jack's euphemism. "Passed
away" is Southernese for "died," but it sure seemed an inappropriate word choice for the corpse at the back of the
stage behind that wooden partition. I assumed the new wall
was meant to protect the public from watching what went
on back there.

"That's why," Happy Jack continued, "the Sugar Pie
Bluegrass Festival will be dedicated to Little Fiddlin'

Fred's memory. There'll be some adjustments in the program this evening, but the show will go on, and I hope to see every one of you back here at six o'clock this evening for more great bluegrass music."

Chapter Four

"**What** are you ladies camping in?" Dean Holdback asked as he joined Jane and me on the path to the campground. He grinned and took Jane by her hand.

"I borrowed my brother's Winnebago motor home for the weekend," I answered.

"Then you have air-conditioning?"

"Oh, yes," Jane said. "It has everything, even a shower."

"Good," Dean said. "I didn't want the two of you sleeping in a hot tin can or a tent tonight."

"John's motor home is really nice," Jane said. "Would you like to see it?"

"Certainly. Do you want to see Broken Fence's new band bus?" I saw the cringe on Dean's face the minute he said "see." When I first met Jane, I did the same thing every time I used a sight word, but I learned long ago that she wasn't bothered by those terms. Jane's usual good-bye was "See ya later."

When we reached the campground, Dean said, "Looks like I'll see your motor home before you see our band bus. One of the guys must have taken it." A puzzled expression crept across his face. "Don't know where it can be. The sheriff's not letting anyone leave the campground."

I pulled the key for the Winnebago from my shorts pocket, unlocked the door, and we stepped single-file into wonderful coolness. The driving area with steering wheel and two big high-backed swivel seats sat to the right of the single door. Fully self-contained, the cooking range, oven, microwave, refrigerator, air-conditioning, and lights could be run from the generator, but each site at Happy Jack's had electrical hookups, so I'd just plugged in the RV. Left of the door was the galley area with a table and sitting booth, tiny double sink, and kitchen appliances.

Upholstered in blue and gray, the interior had looked and smelled new when we picked up the Winnebago from John. Now it smelled much worse than the portable restrooms on the path between the music arena and the campground.

"Whew!" I said. "That's not exactly aromatherapy, is it?"

"Did you put that purple stuff in the toilet like John told you to?" Jane asked.

My turn to cringe. The last thing my brother said before he drove off in my old Mustang was, "Be sure to put the purple deodorizer in the commode before you use the bathroom, and add some each day. Just read the directions." I was so excited about bringing Jane to her first festival that I'd forgotten about it. Now we'd invited Dean in, and the place smelled. Ex-cuuze me. It stank.

Dean didn't seem bothered. "Where's the purple stuff?" he asked. "We use it on the band bus. I'll put it in for you." He guided Jane to the bench seat by the table.

"John handed me a new bottle just before he left," I answered. "I think it's in the overhead cabinet in the back over my bed."

Dean walked from the front driving and kitchen area back through the narrow hall with the refrigerator on his left and door to the bathroom on the right. His head almost touched the ceiling. I followed him, explaining, "That's not a wall at the end of the hall. See that handle. Just slide it to the right and the door goes into the wall."

"A pocket door," Dean said as he slipped it open and stepped into the back area of the motor home. Blue comforters covered the single beds on each side of the narrow floor space. Like anyone would need covers even with the air-conditioning on. Little doors opened to storage areas above each bed.

"Look in the cabinet on the right," I said and realized that there was no way both of us could stand together in that constricted walkway. I went back to the kitchen area and sat at the table across from Jane.

"Found it," Dean answered and turned around with the bottle of purple stuff in his hand. "This will take care of the problem in no time." He opened the door to the bathroom and I heard the gurgling as he poured in the chemical deodorant and then flushed the toilet.

Dean squeezed in beside Jane and stuck his feet out into the driver's area. There was no way those long legs would fit under the tiny table.

"Would you like something to drink?" I asked.

The question was directed toward Dean, but Jane answered.

"A beer," she said.

"I didn't bring any beer," I said. "Most bluegrass festivals are nonalcoholic. How about a Dr Pepper? I brought you plenty of those." I walked back to the refrigerator and opened it. The door was directly across from the bathroom, and the purple stuff was already working. The unpleasant odor had disappeared.

With a Dr Pepper in one hand, I asked, "How about you, Dean? I've got Coke, Dr Pepper, and generic root beer."

"Got any Diet Coke?" Dean asked.

"No, but I have orange juice and bottled water."

"Water's fine," he said.

"Anybody hungry?" I asked. "I've got Moon Pies."

Jane laughed. "Callie always has Moon Pies," she told Dean.

"Yeah, I'll take one. Haven't had a Moon Pie since last time I was at Lou's Pickin' Parlor. Is that where you discovered them?"

"No, I ate Moon Pies all the time growing up. If Daddy or one of my brothers took me to a store, they always bought me a Moon Pie."

"A Moon Pie and an RC Cola?" Dean questioned.

"Nope," I answered. "Moon Pie and milk. Daddy didn't let me have soda when I was little. Only let me drink milk and juice."

"Where are you from, Dean?" Jane said.

"Originally from North Carolina. Why?" Dean responded.

"You said 'RC Cola.' Around here, we roll our *r*'s, and it sounds like 'R-roh-C' Cola."

I passed out drinks and put the box of Moon Pies on the table for people to help themselves. Jane and Dean talked as though I didn't exist with her telling him about her years at the school for the blind and him telling her about his music.

After about ten minutes, I stood and said, "I'm going for a short walk. Be right back."

Good grief! I hate being ignored. I'd cooled off in the motor home, and besides, I've got a wide streak of nosiness, and I wanted to find out if Little Fiddlin' Fred's body had been picked up yet.

Walking along the path from the campground to the stage area, I tried to think of a way that Little Fiddlin' Fred could have been murdered and put into Kenny Strickland's bass case. I really wanted a chance to talk to Kenny about it. The whole thing was like a locked room mystery with the watching audience serving as the walls. Some people might say the body was put in when folks closed their eyes for the prayer. I knew better. My eyes had been open.

Speak of the devil—I spotted Kenny standing among the plants a hundred feet or so off the path with a woman I didn't recognize. I'd met Kenny's wife at a festival several years back, and this female was her size, but Mrs. Strickland's hair hadn't been as dark as this woman's. That didn't mean it wasn't his wife. Some of us ladies change our hair color frequently. I'm one of them.

I'd stepped off the path to approach Kenny and his companion, but I backed off when I realized they were arguing. I couldn't distinguish their exact words, but the shrillness of their voices and expressions on their faces made it obvious that they weren't enjoying a friendly talk. I hurried back to the path and to the stage area.

The chairs were just as we left them in the music arena, but everyone must have taken off to their campers like Jane and I did because there was no one around.

Curiosity got the best of me. I edged back until I was standing where I could see behind the stage. Yellow crime scene tape surrounded the steps at the back. Sheriff Harmon stood with a group of deputies and technicians.

One of the deputies whom I didn't know noticed me and started toward me with a *You're not supposed to be back here* look. Sheriff Harmon glanced up at the officer and saw me standing beyond him. He said something I couldn't hear to the deputy, who stopped and headed back to the sheriff. As I turned to go back to the front of the stage, the sheriff called to me, "Callie, bring the hearse around here."

"Huh?" I swear that's exactly what I said. Before I quit teaching, when my students answered me with "huh?" I told them the only question to which that was an appropriate answer was "What's the answer to nothing?"

Sheriff Harmon spoke as he came toward me. "The body is onstage at the top of those stairs. We'll need the hearse around here."

"I don't have the hearse." I stammered when I said it. My bosses at Middleton's Mortuary, brothers Otis and Odell Middleton, don't like the word "hearse."

Just then, Odell pulled to the back of the stage in our newest "funeral coach." He left the engine running when he stepped out, body bag in hand. Sheriff Harmon and I walked over to Odell. The first words from his mouth were,

"Callie, what are you doing here? Otis said you weren't working this weekend."

"I'm not. I took the weekend off to bring Jane to the bluegrass festival."

"Did you come to play your banjo?"

"Not onstage. Might jam some later if it cools off and anybody starts parking lot picking. Hard to tell what will happen after this." I waved my hand toward the taped-off area.

Sheriff Harmon interrupted. "Sorry, Callie. I thought Otis had sent you with the hearse. When forensics finally told me to call for body removal, Otis said he was tied up in a planning session and Odell was out."

"Hyumph." Odell makes that raspy sound when he's teed off. "Sheriff Harmon, when Middleton's won the bid from Jade County to transport corpses, I assured you that the fact we're a small operation would never be a problem." He looked at his watch. "I think it's almost a thirty-minute drive from St. Mary, and you called less than thirty minutes ago. On top of that, it took me ten minutes to convince your deputy to let me through the roadblock at the bridge to the island."

Harmon chuckled. "Yeah, maybe I should write you a speeding ticket for getting here so fast."

Odell laughed, too. He pulled a handkerchief from his pocket and sopped sweat off his bald head. He and Otis were born identical twins, but when they'd started going bald, Odell shaved his head and Otis got hair implants. Odell's love of barbecue has also put about forty pounds more weight on him than his vegetarian brother.

"Callie," Odell said, "since you're here, how about helping me with this?"

"Sure," I said and reached for the body bag, but Odell held it tight.

"No, I'll bag him. You back the funeral coach up to the steps." *Dalmation!* Dead bodies are my business, but the Middleton brothers protect me, and I seldom see a victim of violent death before Otis or Odell embalms and restores the body. Though I would love an excuse to go to Charleston and sneak by Victoria's Secret, I'd never been sent to take a corpse to Charleston for autopsy. The brothers occasionally let me pick up a body from a hospital or nursing home but never after dark and never from an accident or homicide.

I got my South Carolina cosmetology license through vocational ed in high school, then earned a degree in early childhood education at the University of South Carolina in Columbia and stayed there teaching kindergarten during my marriage. The divorce was finalized about the time I realized that I didn't want to spend the rest of my life with little people who wouldn't stop talking, wouldn't lie down for naps, and wouldn't stop asking "Why?"

Ex-cuuze me. I don't mean that kind of little person. Little Fiddlin' Fred was a card-carrying member of Little People of America, but I meant the five-year-olds in my kindergarten class. Though, sure enough, someone had stopped Fred from talking and made sure he'd be lying down—permanently. I thought back to the article I'd read in *Bluegrass Now* magazine. I'd never seen Fred perform except on television, but he'd been a great fiddler and a pretty good comedian, goofing around a lot on stage. In the magazine interview, he'd teased the female writer and come across as a big flirt.

When I moved back to St. Mary, my redneck daddy wanted me to live with him and whichever of my five older brothers happened to be between marriages or relationships at the time, but I lived with Jane a short while, then got my own place and started working at Middleton's Mortuary as a cosmetologist and girl Friday. The Middletons offered to send me to embalming school, but there's no way I'd want to do that. I'm perfectly happy beautifying my clients, who never talk back and never refuse to lie down.

By the time all those thoughts had raced through my mind as I sat backed up to the steps in the funeral coach with the air-conditioning set on high, Odell and Deputy

Smoak opened the back of the vehicle and slid the body bag in. The bag was adult-size and the body didn't seem to half fill it. I wondered why Odell hadn't carried it by himself until I thought about Little Fiddlin' Fred's photos in both *Bluegrass Now* and *Bluegrass Unlimited* magazines. He was diminutive and had short arms and legs, but his chest and arms looked muscular in the photos I'd seen. He probably weighed a lot more than a child his height would have.

"You want a ride? I can drop you off in St. Mary on my way to Charleston," Odell said as he opened the driver's door for me after slamming the back of the funeral coach.

"I'm sorry," Sheriff Harmon interrupted, "no one who was here this morning is going to leave until I say so."

"Okay, but I really don't like Callie hanging around here with a murderer on the loose." Odell turned from the sheriff to me. "Don't do any amateur sleuthing. One of these days, that nose of yours is going to get you in trouble."

Since my past snooping had caused me more problems than I care to admit, I didn't argue with Odell, nor with Sheriff Harmon when he called, "Be careful," as I headed around the deputy posted at the side of the stage.

The officer who'd tried to stop me earlier snapped, "Don't come any further."

Good grief. First he didn't want me near the crime scene. Now he wasn't going to let me leave it.

Thank heaven I tried to think of some snappy response before I answered because the deputy wasn't even talking to me. The Kramer-haired creep was trying to go behind the stage. It almost looked like they were dancing, with Kramer Hair leaning and stepping side to side while the deputy followed his moves like a basketball guard, repeating "No, you can't come back here" over and over.

"Why'd you let her go back there then?" the nincompoop demanded and pointed at me.

"They needed her to drive the hearse," the officer responded.

"What?" Astonishment popped his eyebrows up, re-minding me even more of Kramer on the *Seinfeld* show.

"Get out of here before I cuff you," the deputy said.

The intruder made a giant slide to his left, did a hundred-and-eighty-degree turn away from the deputy, and stepped beside me as I reached the front of the stage.

"Hey, are you still mad at me?" he asked as he touched me on the shoulder.

"I'm not angry with you. I don't even know you, but I'd advise you to keep your hands to yourself." I shrugged away from his touch.

"You really do look like someone I met at a bluegrass festival in Myrtle Beach." He grinned. "Allow me to intro-duce myself. I'm Pulley Bone Jones." He shook my hand vigorously, grinned, and added, "Now that you know me, can I buy you a drink?"

"What?" I snapped with the hateful tone I usually reserve only for my brothers when they've been on my last nerve.

"Any kind of sody pop they sell at the snack bar. You've got my curiosity up. I want to know why they let you drive the hearse."

At a party, I wouldn't have given this guy the time of day, or night, for that matter, and I certainly wouldn't have let him buy me a drink. In broad daylight, a Coke didn't sound bad at all.

"I only have a few minutes." I paved the way for a fast escape if I changed my mind. "But we can have a Coke if you like." Good grief, here I was with the biggest creep I'd ever met. Guess I was feeling a little left out with Jane so wrapped up in Dean.

Bone and I sat on a bench beneath another plastic awning, though it didn't do much to cut the awful heat, may have even intensified it. But the ice-cold Coke tasted great, and I felt safe enough sitting across from Pulley Bone Jones in public in broad daylight.

"What did you say your name was?" he asked.

"You haven't asked, and I haven't said, but my name is Callie. Where'd you get the name Pulley Bone?" I expected some amusing story about making a wish over a giant turkey bone at Thanksgiving.

"Just call me Bone. Tell me why the cops let you go backstage, and then I'll explain my name."

"I work for the mortuary that will transport Little Fiddlin' Fred to Charleston for the autopsy. Sheriff Harmon thought I was here on business, but I came for the music."

"You work for a funeral home?"

"Sure do."

"You don't seem like that kind of person." He slurped the bottom of his Coke.

"What do you mean? I don't look like a blonde Morticia?"

"No, you just don't look like you'd be in a racket like that."

"Racket? What do you mean?"

"Everybody knows funeral homes gouge people when they're weak with grief."

"Not where I work, we don't."

"Excuse me while I get a refill. Want one?" He reached for my cup and stepped over to the Marie's Grill register.

When he brought back our drinks, he continued as though there'd been no pause in the conversation. "Look what you read in the papers. Funeral homes selling skin and tissue off of bodies without the family's consent. Forcing expensive embalming that isn't necessary."

"I suppose you think everybody should be cremated."

"That's crooked, too. Like that place in Georgia where they just dumped the bodies out in the woods and sent families ashes that weren't even human, much less the ashes from their loved ones."

"Cremains," I said. "That's what you call the ashes from cremations, and that was one out of thousands. I work for Middleton's Mortuary in St. Mary and we run an honest business. Furthermore, we have our cremations done in Charleston and we never sent anyone to that place in Georgia."

Enough was enough. I'd tried to be nice to this guy, but

no more. First, he'd been rude to me that morning. Now he insulted my profession. I stood and turned to leave, but as I did, curiosity got the best of me. I asked, "And what kind of business are you in?"

"I'm a dowser."

"A what?"

"A water witch. That's why folks call me Pulley Bone. I do most of my dowsing with a forked branch off a hackberry tree."

"I've never heard of a hackberry."

"It's in the elm family, but I do just as well with dogwood when I find a Y-shaped branch and whittle it to the right size and shape."

An attractive brunette lady walked up and Bone turned from me. He stood and hugged her. It took a few moments for me to realize this was the same woman I'd seen talking to Kenny Strickland on my way from the campground. Bone whispered something in her ear.

I walked away. Headed back to the Winnebago to be ignored some more.

Bone looked over the woman's shoulder and called, "You're welcome for the Coke," and I realized that I'd been every bit as rude as he'd been. Maybe I needed to jog along the beach, rev up some endorphins to make me act nicer.

Chapter Five

On occasion, rare occasions, I take my dog, Big Boy, running, but most of the running I do is simply a matter of running out of circumstance. My thought of jogging on the beach seemed too much like real running and didn't last long. What I really wanted to do was read. I was about halfway through one of Maggie Sefton's mysteries and was eager to see how it ended.

Not that knitting or crocheting or weaving or sewing has ever held my attention very long. In fact, when I got divorced, I learned to crochet, thinking I'd make a great big afghan for my bed. I've still got it, all sixteen square inches, and my divorce afghan will probably be the same size when Donnie's been out of my life twenty-five years. I don't read Maggie Sefton's books because of my love of needlework but because her mysteries are *great*!

The problem was the book's location. Not where the story took place; where I'd left the novel. It was in the Winnebago with Jane and Dean. I didn't want Jane to think I was checking up on her, and I had no desire to sit there like a lump on a bump while they gushed over each other.

I walked through the campground to the beach and sat on the sand. The heat was stifling and tempted me to slip into the water in my shorts and tank top, but I've lived on the coast all my life. An abnormally hot day this early in spring didn't mean warm water. Those waves would be cold.

The Atlantic, almost a teal blue, lapped up against the white sand. I've seen on television that oceans and beaches can look very different. I've never seen the Pacific Ocean, never seen any ocean except the one I was looking at, come to think of it, but I've always loved the colors of the Atlantic. Birds flitted through the sky. My favorites are seagulls. They're larger than some of the others, and they flap their wings slowly enough to let you watch the movement before holding them still and soaring through the blue sky.

When I was a teenager, Beaufort had a fund-raising event to support sports. Daddy paid for Frank and me to go up in a hot air balloon. I'll never forget how it was to look down on Beaufort and St. Mary. The islands off the coast looked like little specks from the air. When I went back to school, I asked the teacher to show me maps. We counted thirty-five sea islands stretched along the coast of South Carolina and Georgia. Sitting on the beach now, I wondered, *Did I see Surcie Island on that map years ago or was it too small to show?*

If I couldn't have my mystery book, I wished I had Jane's iPod. Not really. Most of what she has on it are old songs and a whole lot of Patsy Cline. Jane likes to sing along with Patsy Cline, and Jane absolutely cannot carry a tune. Know that saying about not being able to carry a tune in a bucket? Buh-leeve me, if someone gave Jane a bucket with a tune in it, she'd spill it out.

Ever since I quit teaching kindergarten and moved back to St. Mary, I'd been promising Jane to take her to a bluegrass festival. We were both ecstatic to learn about the festival on Surcie Island, fewer than twenty miles from where we live. When the weather turned so hot the week before, I'd almost postponed our trip, planning to attend another festival later, but since I had my brother John's motor home with air-conditioning, we came anyway. Now there'd been a murder. I get enough of death and dying on my job at the mortuary. I didn't need it on my R&R time.

Who would have killed Little Fiddlin' Fred anyway? Did he have an enemy from the past? Could the murder have been random? No way! Drive-by shooters sometimes kill randomly, but Fred's killer had pulled a locked room crime onstage in front of an entire audience, even if the audience was small.

Thinking of drive-by shootings put my mind on guns. I grew up hunting with my daddy and five older brothers. At my apartment, I have a double-barrel shotgun and a rifle in my bedroom closet as well as a .38 revolver in the drawer of the bedside table. If Fred hadn't been singled out for some personal revenge and the killer was some loose psycho, Jane and I could be in danger. What good did my weapons do me back in St. Mary?

"Callie." *Dalmation!* I hoped that loud male voice wasn't Pulley Bone Jones.

I looked away from the water and saw Jane and Dean heading my way. Dean was calling my name, and sure enough, he guided Jane by holding her hand.

"I'm right over here," I shouted.

"We've been looking for you," Jane said as they approached me.

"Yeah," Dean said, "with what happened this morning, I don't think it's a good idea for either of you girls to wander around by yourself."

I bristled just a little. "I wasn't 'wandering around.' I came down to enjoy the beach."

"So long as you're okay," Dean said in a consoling voice as though he realized I wasn't happy with him. "We haven't seen you around Lou's Pickin' Parlor in a couple of years," he continued. "Did you and Donnie move down here?"

Jane laughed. Long and loud. "Callie got rid of that hound dog and moved back home."

Dean looked at me with an expression that could have

led to condolences, but when he saw the smile on my face, he changed tactics. "Are you happier?" he asked.

"Definitely."

"Good! Still teaching school?"

"No. I'm using my cosmetology license working at Middleton's Mortuary."

"Do you like it?"

"Most of the time."

"Good again." He paused. "Kenny took the band bus, hoping to get off the island before the roads were blocked, but he didn't get to the bridge before they closed it, so the bus is back. Do you want to see it?"

"Sure," I said as I stood. Dean offered his hand and helped me up. We walked back to the campground with him holding Jane's hand on one side and mine on the other. I'd known Dean long enough that it had no effect on me. I figured he was helping "the ladies" walk on the sand, which tends to drag against feet sometimes.

Jane's eyes aren't deformed in any way, though they have no expression. Her rose-colored shades are a fashion statement, not to hide her blind eyes, but regardless, there's no feeling in them. I gauge Jane's mood by her walk. She was walking real happy. I'd never try to take a man from Jane, but Dean was married, and not available to either of us, so I didn't feel guilty about his holding my hand. Yeah, but Jane would have been furious if she'd seen me, so I pulled my hand away from Dean's.

Dean's "new" band bus had been previously used, maybe by lots of bands, but a magnetic sign beside the door proclaimed it the traveling home of the Broken Fence bluegrass band. We took a quick tour and while the bus wasn't as fancy as the Winnebago, it had most of the amenities; they just weren't as new or pretty. In addition to four bunk beds in the back, two on each side of an aisle, there was a gaucho couch in the front. The curtains and carpet were worn, but serviceable.

Dean showed off the bus as if it had been a McMansion,

but the other band members were busy consoling Kenny, assuring him that it wasn't his fault Little Fiddlin' Fred's body had been in his bass case. I wondered if they knew that for sure. Kenny paced back and forth in the tiny kitchen area of the bus, saying, "I can't believe it. I can't believe it. I'll never put my Kay bass back in that case."

Dean told him, "Don't worry about it. I doubt you ever get that case back. It's evidence."

"Evidence of what?" Van asked.

"Of whatever happened to Little Fiddlin' Fred," Dean said.

"Maybe it was a natural death," Kenny suggested.

"Come on, you saw all that blood on his shirt. And there was something metal sticking out above his lip. I don't think law enforcement is treating it at all like a natural death." Dean's comment didn't help Kenny. He sat down on the couch, looking as though he might faint again.

"What did you tell the deputy?" Van asked.

"What do you mean what did I tell him?" Kenny answered. "There wasn't anything to tell him. I unpacked my bass, played the set, then found Fred in the case when I started to pack up."

"Did the sheriff find you?" Arnie said.

"The sheriff? I didn't know he was looking for me." Kenny's skin paled even more.

"He said he had some more questions."

I wanted to ask Kenny if the woman I'd seen him arguing with was his wife and to tell him about Bone hugging her, but Kenny didn't look capable of handling any more questions, from me, from the sheriff, or from anyone else.

I was ready to get out of there.

"Come on, Jane," I said. "These guys have to perform tonight."

"No, no," Dean said and took Jane's hand again. "Stay here with us." It didn't take much convincing for Jane to decide to stick around. I returned to the motor home and had a quick shower, two Moon Pies, and a reading rest on the bed with my book. I've never been much for napping in the daytime, but I call lying down with a mystery novel a "reading rest," and that refreshes me more than what Jane calls "power naps."

Chapter Six

My stomach lurched.

Dean had brought Jane back to the Winnebago just in time for her to brush her teeth before we walked to the stage area at six o'clock that evening. Broken Fence planned to practice for a while. Now Jane and I were sitting in our lawn chairs on the front row, the same place we'd been earlier.

To me, a dead man had just climbed the steps and walked onto the stage. He now stood a few feet behind Cousin Roger. Not Little Fiddlin' Fred, and I don't mean the guy was stiff like rigor mortis or anything like that. He just looked amazingly like someone I knew. Someone who was dead.

"Ladies and gentlemen," Cousin Roger said, "for months, WXYW has been promising you that the Sugar Pie Bluegrass Festival will be full of surprises. Unfortunately, we started off with a horrible, tragic shock. Sheriff Harmon has asked me to tell you that you may continue to come and go from your campers, but he still says no one is to leave the campground."

Voices behind me called out questions like, "Is Second Time Around going to play tomorrow?" and "Does the sheriff have the right to do this to us?"

The underarm wet spots on Cousin Roger's light blue shirt reached down to his heavy leather belt with its big silver buckle. "Yes, the sheriff has the right to do that. If you doubt it, just go over to the jail and ask Billy Wayne Wilson. He's cooling his heels behind bars. And yes, Second Time Around will perform tomorrow. Our sponsor Happy Jack has taken measures to let the festival continue. The band scheduled to open tonight didn't get in, but we've adjusted the schedule and will begin this session with a real treat. I promised this gentleman that I'd introduce him only by his stage name. Please put your hands together and welcome—the Great Pretender!" I punched Jane in the arm and pulled the iPod plugs from her ears.

The man was lean and tall. Very tall. He wore black slacks, a blue-and-white-striped shirt, red vest, black bow tie, and an Abe Lincoln stovepipe hat. The wire-rimmed glasses and gray beard were familiar, too. He carried a Gibson acoustic guitar, and he wore banjo picks on his thumb and first two fingers.

Without saying a word, he stepped to the center microphone. His long-fingered hands picked "Wildwood Flower." I recognized the full thumb-picking style with the thumb beating out the dominant base line while the other fingers picked the melody. First we heard the song in Johnny Cash's voice and style, then in Mother Maybelle Carter's, and finally we heard it as Elvis Presley might have performed that old bluegrass standard. The audience erupted in applause, accompanied by catcalls and whistles.

"Thank you, thank you very much," the man said in an Elvis voice. "As Cousin Roger said, I'm the Great Pretender. I was pretending to be Randall Hylton pretending to be Johnny Cash, Mother Maybelle, and Elvis Presley." His voice changed to the pitch and tone I remembered belonging to Randall Hylton. "Now I'm gonna pretend to be

Randall Hylton being Randall Hylton." He played and sang, "Room at the Top of the Stairs," which was written by Hylton and made into hit recordings by both Ralph Stanley and Charlie Waller.

I've seen lots of Elvis imitators, and many bluegrass performers show strong influences from the greats, but this was the first time I'd seen a grasser outright imitate another bluegrass performer. Playing someone's material in that person's style and even dressing like him.

Folks in the audience who'd never seen the real Randall Hylton perform probably didn't realize that the Great Pretender was a dead ringer for the great performer who died in 2001. Good grief! Did I say that? I mean, did I even think that? Glad I didn't say it out loud. Calling someone a "dead ringer" for a dead person is tacky, tacky, tacky.

Some folks would call this kind of imitation disrespectful, but I'd seen Randall Hylton perform live lots of times at Lou's Pickin' Parlor and at festivals. I knew that the performer who wrote and sang "The Jeffrey Dahmer Song" wouldn't have been offended. He would have laughed.

Hylton's humor was never X-rated, but it wasn't always what some folks might call in good taste. "The Jeffrey Dahmer Song" is sung to the tune of "I've Got Friends in Low Places," and the first line is, "I've got friends in crawl spaces."

Now that I was past the shock of the Great Pretender's appearance, I settled back in my chair to enjoy the performance.

Bluegrass music audiences usually have at least one yeller. Not a screamer. A yeller. Screamers ooh, aah, and swoon. Yellers holler out messages. I wasn't the only one in the audience who was familiar with Randall Hylton's routines. Someone behind me shouted, "Hey, Great Pretender, you're mighty tall. How tall are you?"

I mouthed Randall Hylton's classic response right along with the Pretender. "Five feet, eighteen inches."

Jane leaned toward me. "How tall is he?" she asked.

"Looks to be about the same height Randall Hylton was: six feet six inches," I said, "and he's dressed like Hylton, too."

"Who's Randall Hylton?"

"He was a performer and songwriter. Had over a hundred and fifty songs recorded by other artists. Wrote lots of gospel songs, love songs, train songs, and story songs."

"Why do you talk about him in the past tense?"

"He died unexpectedly a few years ago."

"Was he killed at a festival like Little Fiddlin' Fred?" Her tone was hard to determine. Not really shocked, but close to it.

"Oh, no, Hylton had an aneurism, died in a hospital in Tennessee."

Talking to Jane about Randall Hylton reminded me of some of his funny material. I've always thought there's more comedy in country music than in bluegrass, but some grassers do get a chuckle now and then. Hylton usually got belly laughs.

Being a southern bluegrass gal, I've yelled out at festivals and concerts myself.

"Can you do 'Big Foot'?" I shouted.

I remembered the first time I heard Randall Hylton perform "The Legend of Big Foot." I was pretty shy back then, but I roared with laughter when he sang about a female Sasquatch putting the make on him, patting his thigh and batting her eyelashes. As the Great Pretender did the song, he looked and sounded just like Hylton.

Jane leaned toward me again. "How many people are playing?" she asked.

"Only one," I answered.

"The music sounds like more than one person."

"That's because he's thumb-picking," I explained. "It's a kind of finger-picking guitar style that originated in Mehlenburg County, Kentucky. Mose Rager, Merle Travis, Chet Atkins, and Randall Hylton were known for thumb-picking."

"I never heard of any of those people except the Hylton fellow the Great Pretender is imitating."

"Well, thumb-picking is well-known enough that there's an international championship contest every year."

"Are you sure there's only one player? Are you fooling me? It still sounds like at least two guitars to my ears."

"It's not your hearing. Thumb-picking weaves the music so intricately that it sounds like more than one instrument to almost everyone."

"Who else plays that way?"

"Do you remember your mother's old records by the Everly Brothers?"

Jane sang, "Bye, bye love. Bye, bye happiness." Of course, she wasn't on key. She never is. Thank heaven she stopped singing and asked, "Is that who you're talking about?"

"Yep," I answered. "Their dad, Ike Everly was a well-known thumb-picker."

"How do you know all that stuff?"

"If you'd grown up with my daddy, you'd know it too."

I leaned back, expecting to hear more of the Great Pretender, but Lewis Fox and the Whet Strap Boys took their places behind the Pretender, and I knew there wouldn't be much more thumb-picking.

"I'm gonna go backstage and talk to that guy," I told Jane.

"Backstage? I thought you said the back is closed off."

"I mean I'm going to catch him coming off the stage on the steps they added at the side."

The Great Pretender received a huge round of applause at the end of his show. Guess the folks were ready for some lighthearted, even silly, fun after the way the festival got started.

A few autograph collectors were waiting at the bottom of the steps to talk to him. He kept his guitar hanging from the strap around his neck, set his guitar case on the step, and grinned. I hung back and listened as Lewis Fox and the

Whet Strap Boys started off with "Rank Stranger" while the Pretender talked with fans. On closer look, he didn't resemble Randall Hylton as much. The gray beard and hair were either premature or dyed. His face was younger. Hylton died in his fifties. This guy looked to be in his midtwenties, maybe even early twenties.

When the Great Pretender and I were the only two left at the steps, I said, "I really enjoyed your act. It was truly like seeing an old friend again."

His eyes lit up. "You knew Randall Hylton?"

"Not well, but I saw him lots of times and even went to dinner with him once in Columbia. Well, not just him and me. The South Carolina Bluegrass Society took him out to eat when he came to town to perform, and I went with them."

"I've been playing guitar since I was six years old." He put his guitar into the hard case that he'd set on the step while he signed autographs. "I saw Randall Hylton when I was twelve, and he just blew me away with his thumb-picking and all the stuff he could do that I'd never seen before. I bought one of each of his tapes and CDs. Randall Hylton kept me out of trouble through my teens. I was too busy practicing my guitar and trying to master thumb-picking to get into drugs or alcohol."

"You're really good. Randall Hylton would be proud to know he influenced you."

"He died in March of the year I planned to catch up with him at some festival that summer and see if he'd listen to me pick and maybe give me some advice. I cried. I just went off by myself and played my guitar and cried about a man I'd never even spoken to." His eyes moistened as he said the words.

Good grief! I never know when my training for working in the mortuary will come in handy. I reached up and put my hand on that tall shoulder and patted him, just the way I do the bereaved at work. He leaned over enough to let me know that it was okay to put my arm around him. I gave him a little hug, then stepped back.

"I never eat before I perform, and I'm starving," he said. "Would you join me for a sandwich or something? I'd really like to talk to you some more."

"I want to talk to you, too. Let me tell my friend where I'm going."

"Oh, you're here with your boyfriend?" he asked.

"No, I'm here with my female friend."

He raised an eyebrow.

"I didn't say 'girlfriend,' " I added.

"Would be your business, not mine."

I led him around to the front, introduced him to Jane, and told her we were going to the concession area.

Jane said, "Take your time, girlfriend."

Chapter Seven

Sitting at one of the picnic tables beneath the plastic awning at Bob's Best Barbecue, I pulled a couple of napkins from the dispenser and tried to sop the perspiration from my face in a ladylike manner. It was seven o'clock, but the sun wouldn't go down for another hour or so. Gastric Gullah was still empty.

The Great Pretender had suggested food, but all I wanted was a cold drink. (Okay, I confess. I ate a few more Moon Pies while I was reading that afternoon.) He went to the window and ordered. When he returned, I accepted my cup with thanks and sipped the iced tea as he dug into a barbecue sandwich and Pepsi.

"Mr. Pretender," I began and laughed. "May I call you Great, or do you go by another name offstage?"

"Andrew Campbell," he answered between bites. "Call me Andy. And what shall I call you besides Blondie?"

"Just call me Callie," I responded, wishing that I looked better. At my best I'm not bad-looking, but I couldn't be too pretty at the moment after sitting in the heat through his act and wiping all my makeup off with the sweat.

"Callie. That's an unusual name. Is it for real or a nickname?" He dabbed barbecue sauce from his lip with a napkin.

"It's a nickname."

"For what?"

If it's possible to blush on top of a sunburn, I'm sure I did. Probably turned as bright as a ripe tomato.

"You don't want to know," I said and sipped the last of my iced tea through the straw.

Andy took the cup to the serving window for a refill, but he asked again when he returned, "What's your real name?"

"It's embarrassing," I answered and took another swallow of tea.

"You never have to be embarrassed around me," he said in that melodious voice.

"My daddy was drunk when he named me. I have five brothers and he was trying to think pink, think feminine. He named me Calamine Lotion Parrish."

The Great Pretender Andy laughed so hard that cola sprayed from his mouth onto the table. He grabbed napkins and wiped up as he continued to chortle.

"I'm sorry. I can see why you might not want to share that with everyone, but you can tell me anything, anytime. What did your mom think of your name?"

"She never knew. My mother died when I was born. I grew up with my dad and a house full of brothers."

Andy's face crumpled. "I am so sorry," he said and reached to pat my hand. I didn't say anything. After another bite of his sandwich, Andy continued, "Where are you from, Callie? You seem familiar to me."

"I grew up in St. Mary, moved away for a few years, but I'm back living in my hometown again. I work for Middleton's Mortuary."

Andy choked a little, took another long drink from his Pepsi, and said, "You're a mortician?"

"No, in Funeralese, we call my job cosmetizing. I do makeup, hair, nails, and whatever is necessary to make the deceased look pleasant for the bereaved."

"Wow! You really do talk Funeralese. I've got an uncle who runs a funeral home in Lexington, South Carolina, and he talks just like that. When I was in high school, I used to get paid minimum wage to sleep on the premises when they had a body, but I sure wouldn't want to do that for a living."

"Are you from Lexington?"

"Yep. Grew up there and it's still my home base, but I'm hoping to stay on the bluegrass circuit from now on." He leaned toward me. I couldn't help noticing his dark brown eyes through the wire-framed glasses. "You said you saw Randall Hylton in person. Tell me honestly what you think of my act. You don't think any of it's disrespectful to him, do you?"

"No, I don't, and the act is good. I enjoyed it very much, and I'm sure his fans as well as folks who never saw Hylton in person will appreciate it, too."

"I've been working on writing songs and creating new jokes, but I love doing Hylton's material, and I haven't written anything good enough to put with it. I—"

Andy was interrupted by the dark-haired woman I'd seen arguing with Kenny and later being hugged by Bone. This lady was all over the place! She leaned over Andy's shoulder. He stopped talking and looked up at her. I hadn't seen her too clearly before, but this time I took a close look.

Pretty with long, curly black hair and dark, bright eyes, she had gorgeous cheekbones. Her figure looked young in her jeans and crimson off-the-shoulder blouse, knotted just above the jeans to accent her slender waist, but the crow's-feet around her eyes and smoker's wrinkles around her red-lipsticked mouth showed her to be at least ten years older than me. I'm almost thirty-three, and I'd guess she was midforties.

Good grief! I hadn't cared about Bone, but I was interested in Andy and resented the interruption. Who was this woman? Was she following me around, waiting for me to talk to a man so she could steal his attention? Ridiculous! I'm a lot of things, but I'm not usually paranoid.

"Melena," Andy said as he stood and turned to embrace her. Buh-leeve me. The last thing I need is some guy who has a girlfriend, but the next thing he said was, "I'm so sorry about Fred."

The woman wiped her eyes with a napkin, but I noticed there were no tears. Really she just meticulously patted gently to avoid mussing her makeup.

"I just don't understand how anything like this could happen," she said. "Everybody loved Fred."

Andy offered the woman his seat and suggested he get her a sandwich. She declined the food, but asked for a cup of black coffee. It was hotter than a Fourth of July bonfire and she wanted coffee?

"Callie"—Andy motioned toward me—"this is Melena Delgado. She's Little Fiddlin' Fred's wife."

"Widow now," the woman corrected and patted her eyes again.

"Yes," Andy said, "I didn't think of that. It's hard to believe I talked to Fred this morning and now he's gone."

Melena's eyes widened. "You saw him this morning? What time?"

"Early. Right after I got here, probably around eight."

"Oh." She continued wiping around her eyes where there were no tears that I could see. "I wasn't here that early." She smiled.

"I'll get your coffee," Andy said, obviously a little uncomfortable. I couldn't blame him. I know from my work that people mourn in many ways, but this woman showed no grief. She didn't seem to need much comforting, but I offered my condolences anyway.

"I'm so sorry about your husband," I said.

"I just don't understand it. He was murdered, you know."

"No, I didn't know, but I assumed it was homicide from the way the police have taken over the back of the stage and asked us not to leave until further notice."

"I'm from the Low Country, over at Adam's Creek, but I came down from Burlington, North Carolina, where we live now, to surprise Fred and see his first performance with Second Time Around tomorrow. I wasn't expecting the shock when Happy Jack told me Fred is dead."

"Everyone was stunned," I said.

"He was killed with a tuning fork." She turned and smiled at Andy as he placed a Styrofoam cup of coffee in front of her and sat down beside her.

"With what?" Andy asked.

"A tuning fork."

"Does anybody ever use one of those anymore? Everyone's got electronic tuners these days," Andy said.

Melena sipped coffee. I couldn't understand how anyone could drink hot steaming liquid in the heat. Jane and I drink coffee in the summertime, but only indoors with air-conditioning.

"I don't know many people who even own a tuning fork these days, but the one used to kill Fred had been sharpened, so it wasn't meant to be used for tuning anyway," Melena said. "The distance between the prongs was almost exactly the space between his nostrils."

"Sharpened?" I echoed her word.

"A tuning fork is shaped like a U with a handle on it," she said. Like I wouldn't know that. I have a couple of tuning forks myself, but I nodded as though I'd never seen one.

"The prongs of the U had been sharpened and rammed up his nostrils through the nasal cavity," she continued. "He died instantaneously, like when mercenaries kill by slamming the nose so hard that it shatters the bones into the brain."

Andy's eyes widened behind his glasses. "How do you know that?" he questioned.

Melena sipped her coffee and ignored him.

"He asked," I said, "how do you know that Fred was killed with a tuning fork and the prongs had been sharpened?" My tone sounded as sharp as the prongs may have been.

Melena's eyes darted around, and for the first time since she'd joined us, she appeared stressed.

"Uh, I don't know," she said.

"Then why'd you tell us that's how he died?" I didn't mean my words to be a demand, but they were.

Andy put his arm around Melena's shoulders and cut me a disapproving look. "It's okay," he softly consoled Little Fiddlin' Fred's widow, sounding exactly like an undertaker.

"I'm just so glad that Fred didn't suffer," Melena stammered. "I don't know exactly how I know about the tuning fork. I must have overheard the sheriff or one of the forensics people talking about it." Her shoulders shook slightly, as though she were shivering.

A yellow and black butterfly flitted by. Melena reached out and closed her fingers over the wings. She opened her hand, and the butterfly flew away.

"A male monarch," Melena said.

"A male?" I questioned. "You mean you could actually see his little—"

Melena giggled. "Oh, no, I didn't see his boys. The wing markings are different on males and females. Not on all butterflies, but on monarchs and a few others."

I couldn't see my own face, but my expression must have been total amazement.

Melena explained, "I was studying to be an entomologist when I met Fred."

"Sharpened?" Andy said and took the last bite of his sandwich.

"What?" Melena asked, as though a butterfly had erased her husband's murder from her mind.

"For someone to sharpen the prongs of a tuning fork and force them into a person's head is an unusual way to kill somebody," Andy said.

"I just hope they catch him soon." Melena sipped her coffee. "So we can all get out of here."

I tried. I promise I tried, but I couldn't resist. Otis and Odell would have been so proud of me. "Mrs. Delgado," I said, "they've sent your husband to Charleston for an autopsy, but if you need a local funeral home to handle sending him to North Carolina for burial after the postmortem, please call Middleton's Mortuary in St. Mary. We're very near, and we'll be glad to take care of everything for you."

"I hadn't even thought about where to have the funeral. Are you a Middleton?"

"Oh, no, I'm Callie Parrish, but I work at Middleton's, so I can assure you that Mr. Delgado would receive the best care." I almost said that the charge for the casket would be less because Fred would fit into a child's unit, but thank heaven I caught myself. Thoughts about Melena being a rather tall woman and Fred being so little invaded my mind, but I'd read enough to know that little people—the politically correct term for midgets and dwarfs—frequently marry full-size spouses. Anyone who doubts that should watch the *Maury* show. Besides, I'd heard that Fred had a reputation as a ladies' man and loved all sizes.

"I'll remember the name Middleton's," Melena said and turned to Andy, dismissing me. "I caught your act," she said to the young man; then she blinked her eyelashes before purring, "You're even better than the last time I saw you." I swear that's exactly what she did. A widow for less than a day and probably at least twenty years older than Andy, she fluttered her eyelashes at him. I grew up in the South, but I don't think I'll ever be a Southern Belle. I'm not a natural Magnolia Mouth, and I'd probably barf if I ever batted my eyelashes at a man.

"Thanks," Andy responded.

"I was wondering if you have a manager," Melena continued.

"No, I'm just handling bookings myself." Puh-leeze. The man turned to putty and his head swelled up like a basketball right in front of my eyes. I mean that figuratively, of course.

"With Fred gone . . ." She paused to wipe around her eyes again with a napkin. I knew the moisture was perspiration, not tears, but Andy's expression exuded sincere sympathy. "My days are going to be empty and long without all the chores I did for Fred. Not just bookings, but performance clothes and other details. I took care of all of Fred's needs. I'd like to talk to you about managing you."

Well, I never! (Actually, I have, but not recently.) Seemed to me she was acting more concerned with empty nights than empty days. I considered removing myself from this flirtation, but Melena's little act was cut short by Kramer Hair rushing up to us.

"Melena, I've been looking all over for you," he gushed.

"Hey, Bone, I need to talk to you." Melena batted her eyelashes at Andy again and ignored me completely. "Oh, Great Pretender, please excuse us," she said with the emphasis on "Grea-a-a-a-t." Melena walked away with Kramer Hair, and Andy turned back to me as though I'd just reappeared.

"Now, where were we?" he asked.

"I'm on my way back to check on my friend Jane," I said, stood, and headed toward the listening arena.

Chapter Eight

A dead fiddle player. An obnoxious water witch. Air temperature that felt like ninety degrees long after sunset. Not the least hint of a breeze. Any of those should have been enough to burn out my pleasure jamming with a bunch of pickers in the midst of the campground at almost midnight, but I was happy as a pig wallowing in a mud puddle.

Jane, along with Bone and a few spectators I didn't know, sat in lawn chairs near seven of us standing in a circle, playing old bluegrass tunes, wearing out "Cotton Eyed Joe" along with our callused fingertips.

Parking lot picking is a bluegrass tradition. Also called "jamming," it doesn't have to take place in a parking lot. We stood in a clearing near the center of the campground. I'd brought my banjo but sat by Jane when I came over from the Winnebago. Three members of Broken Fence in the group—Dean, Arnie, and Van—flattered me by inviting me to pick. They didn't have to ask twice.

I glanced behind me at Jane and tried to see through to the motor home. I'd left the door unlocked, thinking I'd be able to see it from the clearing, but Spanish moss on tree branches draped gauzy veils between the clearing and the parked RVs. The good news was, there wasn't a cloud in sight, and the stars and full moon brightened the night, giving me a clear view of the Great Pretender standing right beside me. Thumb-picking, finger-picking, or flat-picking as the song demanded, that stud muffin sounded as hot as he looked.

A fiddler I didn't recognize stood across from Andy and me. Tall, though not nearly so tall as Dean and Andy, he had very black hair and a craggy face. There was something a little spooky about the expression in his eyes, but he was one of the best fiddle players I'd ever heard.

Dean Holdback was singing the last verse of "Little White Washed Chimney" when someone touched my left arm. I shrugged, pulling away to free my hand, to move from a G to a C chord, when I saw Jane had come up behind me using her cane and was trying to get my attention. I leaned my head toward hers but kept playing.

Just as the song ended, Jane said, "I want to go to the camper. Gotta use the bathroom." Everyone in the group heard her, but Jane didn't care. She isn't at all squeamish about bodily functions. Just about touching things.

"Can you wait a few minutes and we'll go in for the night?" I asked as Dean stepped out of the circle and walked around to us.

"Stay and pick a few more, Callie," he said. "I'll escort Jane to the Winnebago and back here."

Jane's face lit up, and a little red flag popped up in my brain. The attraction between those two felt electric. Jane was wise to the ways of the world, and Dean was a grown man, but I'd seen him around for several years and never saw him come on to any woman. He was married, and his mistress was music. If he ever strayed, I figured it would be serious for him. Jane was inclined more toward flings than commitment, but rejection would devastate her. The chemistry between them was strong enough to lead to a big explosion, and I didn't want to be around to pick up the pieces of either of my friends. I wavered for a moment, considering what to say.

It wasn't necessary. Jane took Dean's hand and told me, "Give us the key."

"You don't need it," I answered. "I left the door unlocked in case you wanted to go back early."

"You didn't plan to guide me?"

"Thought you might use your cane."

"Wooded areas aren't exactly like traveling in town. I'm good, but I'm not magic," Jane said.

"I think you are," said Dean, and they walked away.

Arnie Stands called the key for "Blue Moon of Kentucky" and kicked it off. His powerful tenor voice serenaded folks in the next county.

Earguhhh!!! A scream blared over Arnie's singing.

For an instant, I thought it was a peacock. When those birds court, their cries sound exactly like a woman being murdered. I know. My daddy used to raise peacocks. Excuuze me. Another unintentional fib. I've heard many a peacock in the throes of passion, but I've never actually listened to a person being murdered.

Aruhhh!!!!

Not a peacock.

Jane.

Bone jumped from his chair and dashed toward the campers. I took off right behind him, banjo flapping against my chest as I ran. Thank heaven for the cushion of my padded, inflated blow-up bra.

What had Dean done to Jane?

Whatever it was, when Bone and I reached them, they stood on the ground just outside the open camper door with Dean patting Jane's back and trying to soothe her with soft words.

"Jane," I called. She stopped shrieking and pointed toward the motor home.

"He's in there," she gasped.

"Did someone attack you?" I asked as Bone bounded up the step and into the Winnebago.

Before either of them had time to answer, Bone barreled out the door, leaped to the path, and collapsed into a heap.

There are lots of cute euphemisms for throwing up, but Bone wasn't tossing his cookies. Not hurling. Not barfing. He vomited. Long, loud, retching puke.

"What's wrong?" I said and stepped toward the door.

"Don't think you want to go in," Dean warned. Still patting Jane, now on the shoulder.

"It stinks," Jane said. "I asked Dean to come in and pour more purple stuff in the toilet. I opened the sliding door to sit on my bed while he did it, and . . ." She burst into hysterical sobs.

"And what?"

"I touched it," she howled and collapsed in Dean's arms. While he was busy holding her up, I stepped into the camper.

Buh-leeve me. The stench was unbelievable. Daddy had one great-aunt who lived way out on a sea island and still had an outhouse when I was a little girl. This was a hundred, no, a thousand, a million times worse.

Jane's fussy about touching things. I always figured it was because her fingers are so sensitive from reading braille. That didn't really seem sensible though. Like many other visually handicapped people, Jane only used her right index finger when reading braille. Maybe her fussiness about touching things was because she didn't always know what her fingers were going to find. Then again, it might have been just one of Jane's idiosyncrasies. Whatever the cause, Jane was hysterical about whatever she'd felt. What had she touched? A piece of poop? It smelled like the toilet had overflowed, even backed up from the sewage tank. I expected water and human waste on the floor, but the carpet was dry. I looked toward the rear. The pocket door was open.

I saw what lay on the bunk.

The camper reeked of sewage, all right, but the odor came from the bedroom, not the bathroom. It's not uncommon for the sphincter to let loose at death. I knew this from reading mysteries, even before bodies became my business.

He'd been garroted with what looked like a cut-off piece of a thick E string from a bass fiddle. Twisted tight at his neck, the ends were knotted on capos, which had been used for handles. A prepared weapon like the sharpened prongs of the tuning fork. Premeditation.

The face bulged dark blue. Discoloration occurs as a corpse decomposes, but there was no odor of decomposition seeping through the fecal smell. He couldn't have been dead more than an hour or so anyway because I'd showered and changed my sweaty clothes in the camper while Dean and Jane went to the snack bar between the end of the festival performances and the beginning of parking lot picking.

Ex-cuuze me. Once again, I was getting my exercise jumping to conclusions like a character in a Magdalena mystery. Maybe the victim had been killed somewhere else and moved to the motor home.

At first, I didn't recognize the swollen face and open eyes almost popping from their sockets. His mottled purple tongue protruded between huge, misshapen lips. Not postmortem bloating. The hands were normal in size and color. The swelling and blueness resulted from the manner of death.

The face of brutal strangulation.

The face of a man who'd pranced around the stage packing his equipment during a prayer. He wouldn't be so disrespectful again. I wondered if the bass string around his neck had been one of his own, had once been in the same case where Little Fiddlin' Fred was found.

I backed away, down the narrow hall. Sirens shrilled before I reached the camper door, stepped out, and leaned against the side of the Winnebago for support against the weakness washing over me.

John's beautiful motor home would be impounded by the sheriff's department. I sometimes bragged that I neither took nor gave guilt trips. Donnie, my ex-husband, would argue that I didn't take them, but I sure gave them. John's my most affectionate brother, but he'd figure out some way to blame me for this happening in his camper. The "some way" would probably be my leaving the door unlocked. Not just foolish, but dangerous on an island with a killer running loose. I'd soon be on a *walking* guilt trip, because John would hold my Mustang ransom until the sheriff released the Winnebago and I'd paid for enough expensive professional cleaning to make it smell new.

Puh-leeze. Here I was worrying about my brother's motor home when I should have been thinking about poor Kenny Strickland lying dead on Jane's bed and the grief his fellow band members were sure to feel.

Morning had dawned by the time Sheriff Harmon dismissed me. He'd interrogated each of us who'd been in the motor home after Kenny's death several times.

Over and over, he asked, "Callie, did you touch or move the body?"

"No," I repeated and finally shot back a question of my own. "Why is that so important?"

"He's lying faceup with no signs of a struggle. It's hard to picture someone being strangled that way without putting up a fight unless the killer was behind him, and if he was choked from behind, he should have fallen forward and been found lying on his face. I know you don't have any qualms about touching a corpse. Are you sure you didn't flip him over to be certain he was dead? You can admit it if that's what happened."

"Flip him over? You've gotta be kidding. I can't flip a man his size over by myself."

"You turn them at the mortuary, don't you?"

"Sure, but I have mechanical lifts at work. I can't just grab an adult body by its feet and turn it over."

"Okay." Harmon changed the subject. "You can go now, but don't leave the campground."

"Speaking of leaving," I responded, "when can I have the Winnebago back?"

"I'm not sure. It's a crime scene and I have more technicians coming here tomorrow. After that, we'll take it in and hold it for evidence."

"Evidence of what?" I snorted. "Evidence that Kenny Strickland died? Your forensics technicians have already hauled out sacks and boxes of stuff."

The sheriff gave me a withering look, but didn't say anything.

"And," I continued, "Jane and I need our clothes out of there."

"Nothing comes out."

"Come on, Wayne," I begged, calling him by his first name to remind him that he'd known me all my life. "You don't have to let me go in. Can't you bring our suitcases out to us?"

"Nope. Unless you want to wait and help Otis or Odell when they pick him up, you can go to bed now."

"If I help bag the body, can I bring out my clothes?"

"No way. Go on and get some sleep, Callie." The sheriff smiled.

"Good idea. I'll catch a ride off the island to the nearest motel."

"Afraid not. You won't be allowed to leave the campground."

"Guess you expect me to sleep on one of the picnic tables," I snapped.

Harmon didn't say another word. Just walked away.

Dean and Jane came over when they saw the sheriff move away from me. Andy joined us and said, "You're welcome to sleep in my truck, but I'm embarrassed to offer it. I call it my Silver Pigeon. It's an old gray Toyota with a camper shell on the back, but no air-conditioning."

"Oh, no, thanks," Jane said. "Dean's invited us to sleep in Broken Fence's Golden Eagle."

"Golden Eagle?" I asked.

"That's what they named their new band bus."

"Not really new, but new to us," Dean corrected. After all, Jane couldn't see the wear and tear on the bus, but I'd seen it. "We've got some repairs and decorating to do."

I've known musicians to name their guitars—Randall Hylton called two of his Michelle and Lakeisha. But naming vehicles? Andy's Silver Pigeon and Dean's Golden Eagle. Shades of Stephen King's *Christine* or flashbacks to adolescence?

"Thanks, Andy," I said, "but air-conditioning wins out." I wiped sweat from my forehead with the back of my hand.

"You, too, Andy," Dean offered. "I had no idea you didn't have cooling. We've got four bunks in the sleeping area, and you can use the couch up front. I usually sleep in the reclining driver's seat anyway because my legs are too long for the bunks or the couch. The girls can have mine and Kenny's bunks." His eyes glistened. "I wish we could go back upstate and be there for Kenny's wife, but since we have to stay here, please accept the invitation and the air-conditioning."

As we walked to the bus, I tried calling Daddy and John on my cell phone. I'd actually remembered to charge it and bring it, but there was no signal. John is my oldest brother, my sweetest brother, my most understanding brother, but he was gonna blame me big time for his motor home being impounded. I felt like crying, but I was too tired.

Chapter Nine

Sun blazing through worn burlap curtains woke me. I knew from the brilliance that it wasn't early morning. In college, a promiscuous friend complained that she never knew where she was when she awoke. I'd never had that problem. Dated Donnie all through college. After my divorce, I abstained because sleeping around wasn't good for a teacher's reputation. By the time I quit teaching, I realized that relationships need to have meaning for me. Have I ever been intimate with anyone other than Donnie? To paraphrase the military: Don't ask, and I won't tell.

That's a long way around to a short statement. This was my first time waking up with no idea where I was. Confusion and fear blurred in my mind. I looked around. Across a short aisle from me were two empty bunks, one over the other. I was lying on the same level as the top one, so I assumed I was lying above a similar bottom bed. I leaned over and peeked. A lower bunk, but no one there either.

The mental fog cleared and memory kicked in. Kenny Strickland dead in my brother's motor home. The offer to sleep in Broken Fence's band bus. Crawling up to the top bunk wondering if I'd ever get any sleep with Arnie and Van snoring like two freight trains just across the aisle. Must not have been as loud as I thought. I'd dropped out of consciousness from the moment my head hit the pillow. A dead man's pillow. I'd slept in Kenny's bunk while Jane slept in Dean's—without him, I hoped.

"Callie," a voice called from the other side of the worn burgundy velour curtain that partitioned off the sleeping area.

"Right here," I said.

"Are you dressed?"

"Yep, still got on what I wore last night." I did, too. Had on my inflated bra under a wrinkled T-shirt and my new panties with the padded tush under white shorts. The new panties have just a little foam rubber right over the bunky cheeks. The saleslady told me they would "lift" and "define" my somewhat flat derriere. Actually, they were new yesterday afternoon when I put them on. I'd brought four pairs, but they were in my luggage in the Winnebago. Thank heaven for pantiliners!

The curtains parted, and Andy stepped in holding out a cup of coffee. "Fixed it the way Jane said you like it. Do you really always use cream and four scoops of sugar?"

"Sometimes three, sometimes four." I took a sip from the mug. Perfect. "It keeps me sweet."

"Everyone else has gone to the music arena to see Second Time Around. Jane and Dean said to let you sleep, but I thought you might not want to miss the show."

"What time is it? Have they started?"

"Almost eleven, but we can catch it from the beginning if we hurry."

I handed him the coffee and began climbing down from the bunk. Andy set the cup on the floor and reached out to help me. Daddy calls me Pollyanna because I always try to see the positive side of any situation. Now I was glad the sheriff didn't let me get my clothes from the camper. I would have removed my underwear and put on a sleep shirt. As it was, I still wore my blow-up bra beneath my

T-shirt. Right above where Andy put his hands to lift me down.

I washed up in the tiny bathroom and redressed in the same clothes. When I came out, Andy handed me a sausage biscuit wrapped in a napkin. "Compliments of Dean—Jimmy Dean, that is—and the Golden Eagle's microwave," he said in a John Wayne voice.

When Andy and I reached the stage area, most people were sitting about where they had yesterday with their chairs in nearly the same spots. Familiar faces in familiar places, except for Jane and Bone. Her chair had been moved to the second row with Dean, Van, and Arnie. Bone's chair was gone.

I heard mumblings among the audience. Some complained that everybody should get their money back. Others were still excited to see Second Time Around. There was also speculation about what the band would do without a fiddler.

Cousin Roger introduced the band. "And now, bluegrass lovers, the group many of you came especially to see. Put your hands together for—Second Time Around!"

He waved toward the steps at the side of the stage. The musicians climbed up and took positions. Comedians run on and off a stage, but bluegrass pickers move rather somberly, careful not to bump or drop an expensive instrument. Second Time Around's been playing a good while. Their name came from the fact they originally played under another name, split up, played with other bands, then re-formed their original five-piece group: guitar, banjo, mandolin, bass, and fiddle. Today there were only four of them. No fiddle player.

They jumped right into "Waiting at the Station" without any stage patter. From that, they segued into "Hot Summer Nights." The audience roared approval with applause and yells.

"Wey-ull," the banjo picker said, "we're not going to talk much about what has already happened here. We came to play some music for you. The next song we're gonna do is an old Country Gentlemen favorite, 'Uncle Pen.' Problem is that we gotta have a fiddle for that number, and as you know, we sadly lost our new fiddler yesterday."

Silence. I don't know what he expected the audience to do. They certainly wouldn't cheer or boo.

"But the show must go on, and we've got a fill-in for you. Please welcome"—he waved toward the steps—"Aaron Porter."

A fiddle in one hand and bow in the other, a lanky man in a black suit climbed the stairs. He wore a purple silk shirt and a lavender necktie with fiddles painted on it. He had a head full of jet black hair, obviously tinted because nobody with as many wrinkles as he had could have that shade naturally. That's not a criticism. I, for one, am glad that the good Lord led people to create the rinses, tints, and dyes that enable us to change our hair whenever the mood strikes. I noticed that Aaron's head tilted a little toward his left shoulder even before he tucked the fiddle under his chin.

The crowd went wild. Aaron Porter was the original Second Time Around fiddler, all the way back to the first band. He was also the tall, dark-haired man I'd seen standing across from me the night before. Not expecting him to be at the festival, I hadn't recognized him then in his jeans and denim shirt. I should have known him by his fiddling.

Aaron Porter had begun his career playing jazz saxophone in New Orleans, moved to zydeco fiddle, then switched to bluegrass about the time Second Time Around's first band formed. Word was out that he'd retired in Virginia and wouldn't be playing anymore. Little Fiddlin' Fred was to have replaced him, but the legendary Aaron Porter now stood onstage taking the place of his replacement. Was it fortune, coincidence, or some less pleasant reason Aaron Porter just happened to be here to take Little Fiddlin' Fred's place?

I pushed that nasty thought out of my head. Good music

makes a body feel good. Erase that. It makes a body feel great! Bluegrass music takes a person away from problems, even though song themes are often sad. Second Time Around seemed determined to make this part of the festival memorable for their performance, not for the deaths of two bluegrass musicians.

"Uncle Pen" was the hardest, fastest, tightest performance I've ever heard.

Cousin Roger ran back onto the stage, looked up at the sky, and said, "I see Charlie Waller up there applauding right along with this crowd."

"Who's Charlie Waller and where is he?" Jane asked.

"He was the lead singer with the Country Gentlemen. He's deceased. Cousin Roger was looking up at the sky like Waller was watching down on us." I paused. "Who knows? He might be. They talk about a rock 'n' roll heaven. Maybe Bill Monroe, Carter Stanley, Lester Flatt, Charlie Waller, and the other greats like Maybelle Carter who have passed on are in bluegrass heaven."

Jane laughed. "Did you say, 'have passed on'? I thought you hated that term."

"I do on the job, but I'm not at work right now."

The next song was "Sea of Life" with Aaron Porter on vocals. Second Time Around had the audience in the palms of their hands. The music got better and better, lifting the small audience to new heights. The applause seemed endless and deafening, though the crowd probably didn't add up to fifty people. The only way Aaron Porter could have been more impressive was if he'd balanced his fiddle on his nose like Roy Acuff used to do on the Grand Ole Opry.

By the time the band finished, my head and heart were so full of music that I couldn't think of anything at all, much less murder. I was overwhelmed like I am when I go to a Claire Lynch concert, and she is my *absolute* favorite singer!

Second Time Around was a hard act to follow, and I guess none of the bigger, better-known groups wanted to fill that spot, so Cousin Roger introduced the Pine Tree Sisters.

Jane and Broken Fence stepped up behind me. "I'm going with Dean," she said, and they headed toward the concession area.

Chapter Ten

"**Whass** up?" Bone said to me as he unfolded two lawn chairs and set them beside me. Melena stood beside him, Styrofoam coffee cup in one hand, a denim bag in the other. It wasn't exactly a purse, more like a medium-size tote. He motioned her toward the chair.

"Welcome to the hootenanny," I joked as they sat down.

"Yeah, the Pine Tree Sisters aren't exactly Bill Monroe, are they?" Bone said as he slumped down in his seat and stuck his legs out in front of him.

"More like the Kingston Trio in drag," Melena said. "Maybe they'll do 'Hang Down Your Head, Tom Dooley' next."

The three young women onstage wore old-timey button-up shoes, floor-length gingham dresses, and ruffled pinafore aprons. Bouffant curls that I'd bet were extensions or synthetic hairpieces blossomed out from white bonnets. Their three guitars provided instrumentation, and old folk songs filled their repertoire. There are people who love their music. I'm not one of them.

"I was thinking about going to the camper for a nap, but

I'm waiting for my friend Jane to come back," I commented.

"Where is she?" Melena asked.

"Went for a walk." I don't know why I didn't tell them Jane had gone off with the Broken Fence band. I guess I didn't really think it was any of Melena's business.

"Isn't she blind?" Bone asked. "Can she manage with just a cane on this strange turf?"

"Oh, she does very well, but she's with Dean Holdback."

"Broken Fence?" Melena asked.

"Yes, Dean's the tall one."

"Have you heard these girls before?" Bone nodded toward the stage.

"Yes, and when they do their tribute to Stephen Foster, I'm leaving whether Jane's back or not. Their version of 'Oh, Susannah' has no resemblance to bluegrass."

"Don't tell me if it ain't 'Dueling Banjos' and 'Rocky Top,' you don't think it's bluegrass." Bone grinned. He dropped his cigarette on the ground and rubbed it out with the toe of his boot. Guess the sand had scuffed up his penny loafers the day before.

"I've told you not to do that," Melena scolded, bending over to pick up the butt. She dropped it into her Styrofoam cup. Must have had a little coffee left because it made a tiny plopping noise.

"Yeah, and the signs say I can't smoke here, but I do anyway, don't I?"

I ignored them and answered Bone. "No, I don't think bluegrass has to be 'Dueling Banjos' or 'Rocky Top,' and nobody else does these days. Now some folks think a song had to be in *O Brother, Where Art Thou?* As for me, I grew up with a daddy who listened to Flatt and Scruggs, Bill Monroe, and the Stanley Brothers."

"And what did your mom listen to?"

"I have no idea. She died when I was born."

Bone looked down. I was surprised the nincompoop even knew when he committed a faux pas. Then again, I was just as guilty for speaking so flippantly about death in front of a woman whose husband died the day before.

"Sorry," Bone mumbled and glanced up at the stage. The Pine Tree Sisters began another Stephen Foster number. "You ladies come over to the trailer with me. I wanna show you something," Bone said.

Good grief. Like I wasn't on to him already. "What do you want to show us? Your etchings?" I asked in a sarcastic tone.

"Callie, I wouldn't invite my sister along if I planned to show you my etchings." He slipped me a wicked grin with arched eyebrows. "Although I do have some excellent etchings if you're interested." He winked at Melena. "Sister, you wouldn't mind staying here while I show Callie my etchings, would you?"

"I didn't realize you two were related," I said.

Melena stood and said, "Come on, I'll protect you from my little brother."

I looked up at the stage. This set would probably last another half hour, and I wanted to learn more about Melena and Little Fiddlin' Fred. What was the connection between them and Kenny Strickland? I wasn't investigating, just curious. Well, really just nosy, as usual.

"Okay," I said and followed Bone and Melena to the path to the camping area. "Were Kenny Strickland and your husband good friends?" I asked Melena.

"They knew each other, but so far as I know, their only connection was at performances. We didn't visit socially." Melena pulled a glass mason jar from her tote and peered into it while we walked. She smiled. The bereaved act in mysterious ways. This was the first time I'd seen a recent widow carrying around dead lightning bugs. At least, that's what I thought they were. There were no holes in the lid of the jar. As a child, my brothers helped me catch lightning bugs, and I remembered that when I forgot to set them free, they died if no one had punched holes into the cap.

Bone cut off my questions with "Hurry up" and a faster

walk. The travel trailer he headed toward wasn't quite the
smallest one I'd ever seen, but it came close. I'm not expert
at estimating length, but it probably wasn't more than thirteen or fourteen feet long. Bone opened the door, and cool
air whooshed out at us. Melena and I followed him in and
sat at a table booth to our right. She tossed her Styrofoam
cup into a little trash can under the table.

Bone opened an overhead cabinet above the stovetop.
He brought out a package of small paper cups, the kind
dentists use when they want you to spit, and a large
familiar-shaped bottle. He placed three cups on the table,
then set the full liter bottle of Original Mint Green Scope
beside them. Melena grinned, screwed the top off the bottle, and poured about an inch of the green liquid into her
cup. She handed the Scope to me and said, "Here, help
yourself."

Puh-leeze. What kind of weirdos were these people?
They showed little reaction to the murder of Melena's husband, who also happened to be Bone's brother-in-law, and
now they sat down to share mouthwash?

While I gaped in wonder, Bone poured himself a cupful.
Melena sipped, but he threw his down his throat like a
shooter. They were *drinking* Scope.

"No, thanks," I said.

"Come on, a little one won't hurt," Bone said and
poured about half an inch of green liquid into my cup.

"Okay," I said, "but I'm not going to swallow it."

Melena and Bone laughed. "Like the president who
didn't inhale?" she said.

I picked up the bottle and read the label. "It says here
not to swallow it."

Bone burst into raucous guffaws. "Take one little sip,
Callie."

One little sip. The burn made me gasp and a bit of the
fiery liquid slipped down my throat. "Gin!" I shouted and
spewed the rest out.

"What did you think it was?" Melena asked and took
another small drink.

"I should have known better, but I honestly thought it was mouthwash. Figured you two were crazy."

"It's mint gin," said Melena, "looks like Scope, so if it's put into a Scope bottle, nobody gets busted for open containers under the car seat or for liquor at dry festivals. If we had mouthwash in that bottle, we'd wind up with some major problems if we swallowed the glycerin in it."

Bone laughed and said to Melena, "You and your science." He turned to me. "If you don't like gin, how about an Orange Blossom Special?"

"What's that, besides a great song?"

"Orange-flavored vodka in a Citrus Listerine bottle."

"I'll pass on that, too. I really thought you two had flipped out drinking mouthwash."

"I wasn't trying to trick you." Bone poured more into his cup and tossed it back. "I assumed you'd know I was offering you a drink. Guess that explains your confused look."

"I'm not a teetotaler. I drink sometimes, but gin has never been my choice."

"Bet you're bourbon and Coke," said Bone.

"No, I like—" I didn't get to finish the sentence because someone banged on the door and flung it open. A short brunette woman wearing short shorts and a halter top stood on the step with a large garment bag. Behind her, a slim, gangly fellow in running shorts tried to balance several pieces of luggage and a box.

"Whass up?" Bone greeted them. "Come on in."

The brunette stepped through the door, followed by the man. Melena stood. "I'm going back to catch the last of the Pine Tree Sisters," she said.

The woman reached out and touched Melena's arm. "We heard about Fred," she said. "I'm so sorry." She air-kissed Melena beside her cheek.

"I think I'm in denial," Melena replied. "I just can't believe he's gone. I guess it will really hit me when the authorities let us leave here and release Fred's body to the family. Well, to me as his wife. I'm just glad he didn't suffer. It'll seem real when I start dealing with plans."

"It's just terrible," the woman said. She turned toward me. "I'm Sarah."

"Callie Parrish," I said.

"Sorry," Bone said. "My manners aren't always the best thing about me." A villainous leer. "The best thing about me is much better than my manners. Callie, allow me to introduce you to"—he gestured toward them as he called their names—"Sarah Phillips and Ron Reuben. They're one of the surprises for the festival." He handed each of them a paper cup and added, "Want to freshen your breath?"

Melena and I stepped out as the couple held their cups out to the Scope bottle. She headed toward the path to the music arena, and I walked beside her. "Too bad about last night," she said. "Did you know Kenny very well?"

"Not well enough for him to be in the motor home. I don't understand it at all."

"Well, I don't understand why anyone would murder my Fred."

"I don't mean to offend you," I began, knowing that any statement beginning that way usually *would* offend, "but I work with bereaved people on my job, and nobody seems to be reacting to these two deaths the way I expected. I'm surprised that bands are playing at all today."

"Until we can leave this island, I'd rather listen to anyone—except the Pine Tree Sisters—than sit and worry."

"You missed a really good performance by Second Time Around, but I guess seeing them today would have been painful, knowing your husband was supposed to be up there with them."

"Oh, I would like to have seen them, but that sheriff had me cornered for another statement." She paused and stared at an insect flitting around a bush with yellow flowers. She reached into the denim tote, pulled out the mason jar, and unscrewed the lid. She slid the top to the side but didn't completely remove it, held the jar up, and quickly closed it when the bug flew in. She dropped the jar back into the tote and smiled at me. "Sorry for the interruption," she said, "but that was too good a catch to ignore." We continued walking.

"You collect insects?" Well, duh . . . that was my reply.

"Everywhere we go. I've got an extensive collection."

"Good you have a hobby . . ." I began, thinking I'd tell her it would help to keep busy while she was grieving—or whatever.

"It's more serious to me than a hobby. I've collected insects as long as I can remember, starting with lightning bugs before I started school. I used to just catch the insects and mount them on boards with stickpins. Now I usually kill them with fingernail polish remover or some other chemical before sticking the pins in them on displays."

"Fingernail polish remover? Why not use bug spray?"

"The acetone in the remover kills them more quickly and gently. Have you ever watched a roach die after spraying it with one of those canned sprays?"

I promise, I tried not to lie, but I couldn't stop myself. I just didn't want to discuss roaches struggling and waving their little legs and antennae as they died.

"No," I said, just as though I'd never even seen a roach, alive, dead, or dying.

We'd reached the end of the path, but we stopped and stood talking at the edge of the music arena.

"I hope to someday discover an insect never before captured. Even then, I'll never stop collecting, but I always kill specimens as quickly and painlessly as possible."

"Yeah," I mumbled.

"If I do find an unknown insect, I plan to name it after Fred. Like I said, I think I'm in denial or shock or something. Fred and I were married over twenty years, and we spent those years traveling together and working for a break in his career." She wiped her eye with the back of her hand. I wasn't sure, but that could have been a real tear on her cheek. "Did you know Fred had signed on with Second Time Around?"

"Yes, Dean Holdback told me that."

"The tall guy in Broken Fence?"

"That's the one."

"Well, Fred and I worked hard to get him into the big time, spent every minute on his career, every dollar on fiddles and music equipment. Finally he got his break and someone broke it."

"That's what I was talking about. Not to hurt your feelings, but I'd think after all those years, your reaction to his murder would be more than grief over his career."

Melena's eyes narrowed. "Who told you?" she demanded.

"Told me what?"

"Was it Bone? Did Bone tell you?"

"I don't know what you're talking about."

"Bone told you that Fred and I were separated, didn't he?"

"No, I didn't know that."

"I wanted to keep it quiet for a while, and now that he's dead, I'd just as soon nobody ever knows. We would never have divorced anyway, but he wanted a separation, and that's why I didn't come down here with him. I decided to surprise him at his first performance with Second Time Around, but he never even knew it." Melena's hands trembled and she sniffled. "Please don't tell anyone," she begged.

"Of course not. That's none of my business."

"I don't know what to do now." Melena resumed walking toward her chair. "I mean after we get out of here and I have Fred's funeral. I quit college when I met Fred, and I'd like to go back to school, but I don't know how well I'd do competing with young brains, and my scholarships are all gone. Then again, if I found the right talent to manage, I could put someone else at the top like I did Fred."

I tried. I promise I tried, but I couldn't resist asking, "Someone like the Great Pretender?"

"Yeah, with the right management, that man could go to the top."

"Melena," I tried again, "what's the connection between your husband and Kenny Strickland?"

"None really. We all knew each other from festivals and venues, but they never performed together or anything like that."

"I was trying to find a connection for Fred's body being in Kenny's case and for Kenny being murdered right behind him in another macabre musical way. It's gotta be the same killer."

"Sorry, I can't help you. I don't have any idea why anybody would kill either of them. I barely knew Kenny Strickland."

We sat down, without another word, to listen to another Stephen Foster tune. Melena's statements didn't quite jibe with what had appeared to be a heated argument between her and Kenny when I saw them earlier. The separation aside, I still couldn't understand why Melena wasn't more upset about her husband. Or why she denied knowing Kenny well enough to fuss with him. My reverie was interrupted by Roger thanking the Pine Tree Girls and announcing, "Take yourselves a fifteen-minute intermission and get something cold to drink 'cause this next act's gonna have a surprise for you!"

Just then Dean and Jane came up, carrying three bottles of Dasani water, saving me from the decision whether to go to the snack area during the break.

"Hey." Dean nodded at me, then assisted Jane into her chair. "Gotta go get ready for the stage." He handed me a bottle of water, opened the other two, gave one to Jane, and half emptied his in one long gulp.

"Where have you been?" I asked Jane and then realized how it sounded. "I'm sorry," I said. "You *are* grown."

"I didn't ask you where you went. Dean and I came back before, and you weren't here." Jane's tone clearly told me she wasn't in a good mood.

"Remember the creep I told you about? He was Little Fiddlin' Fred's brother-in-law. I've been talking to him and his sister." I whispered so Melena wouldn't hear.

"You've been investigating?"

"No, just talking."

"Does the widow look like someone off *Seinfeld*, too?"

"No, she's older, but quite pretty. Dark hair and eyes."

"What's she wearing?"

"Shorts and a red peasant blouse tied at her waist."

Fifteen minutes later, Lewis Fox's bass player, carrying a bass case similar to the one that had held Little Fiddlin' Fred's body, followed Dean, Arnie, and Van onto the stage behind Cousin Roger.

"Now, back for your listening pleasure, here's Broken Fence." The band broke into "Colleen Malone" before Cousin Roger completed the introduction. At the last note, Dean stepped up to the vocal mic.

"As most of you've probably heard, Broken Fence suffered a tragic loss last night. Our bass player and friend Kenny Strickland died. He'll be missed, and we considered canceling further appearances here, but since no one is allowed to leave, we know Kenny would want the show to go on. Please welcome"—he waved toward the bass player—"Norm Hunter of the Whet Strap Boys."

Norm waved at the crowd. Dean introduced Arnie on mandolin; Arnie introduced Van on banjo; and Van stepped up to the center mic. "We'd be remiss if we didn't introduce you to the tallest guitar player in bluegrass, Dean Holdback. We keep Dean in Broken Fence because we can always find him in a crowd." Dean curtsied. The crowd cracked up at six feet eight inches and well over two hundred pounds of man curtsying.

Chapter Eleven

"**And** now . . ." Van turned toward the others. "Can we get a drum roll out of these stringed instruments?" The three other musicians tapped their knuckles in percussion on the wooden bodies of the guitar, mandolin, and bass. "You were promised surprises at this festival," Van continued, "and we have one for you right now."

Reverend Cauble, a lay preacher I knew because Otis and Odell often hired him for funerals of deceased who had no minister, climbed the steps and walked over to Dean. I figured he was roasting in his black suit, the same one he wears at the mortuary. What kinda deal was this? A memorial service onstage? Appropriate, but hardly something to be introduced as a "surprise."

"Dearly beloved," Cauble intoned. That's the only word that fits how Cauble talks. He intones. "Though we've had two tragedies at this festival, we are now going to celebrate a joyous occasion."

The band broke into an acoustic bluegrass version of "Here Comes the Bride," and from the back of the arena, a man and woman approached the stage. The man wore a light blue seersucker suit, pink carnation boutonniere, white buck shoes, and a cream-colored straw hat. Looked like a character out of William Faulkner or Tennessee Williams.

The woman's white dress was traditional bridal, long sleeved and full skirted with a six-foot train dragging along, kicking up a dust storm. She carried a bouquet of pink and white roses and carnations enveloped in baby's breath.

The bride stumbled as they walked side by side with arms linked, but the groom caught and supported her as they climbed the steps on the side and walked to Cauble in the middle of the stage. Broken Fence stepped respectfully into a semi circle behind the preacher.

The vows of the brief nondenominational wedding ceremony were obviously written by the couple. They included reference to the couple meeting at a bluegrass festival and the preacher prayed that their love and marriage would last as long as bluegrass music is around. When Reverend Cauble announced, "I now pronounce you husband and wife," he added, "Ronald, you may kiss your bride."

The man dipped the woman so far back that her head almost touched his knee. He lifted the veil and flipped it back over her head. He planted a long, loud, smoochy kiss on her, then stood her upright. The woman shook visibly. I wondered if the heat had gotten to her. Would she faint?

"Ladies and gentlemen," Dean said, "I present to you Mr. and Mrs. Ronald Reuben." When the couple turned toward the audience and bowed, I realized that the bride and groom were Sarah and Ron from Bone's trailer. "Mrs. Reuben will now toss her bouquet for some lucky young lady in the audience." Dean motioned toward Sarah. She bent and bowed her knees, held the bouquet between her legs like a four-year-old basketball player making a free throw, and tossed the flowers into the air.

The bouquet flew straight at me. I reached up, only to be knocked aside as Melena leaped into the air like a Dallas Cowboys cheerleader with arms and legs splayed back in parentheses. She snagged the bouquet right before it reached me and clutched it to her chest as her feet touched the ground. Her grin was total joy, the excitement of the win. Suddenly, her expression changed to something unidentifiable—shock, horror, maybe embarrassment. She threw the flowers into the air as though they were hot potatoes. Melena sank back into her lawn chair and broke into loud sobs.

The bouquet landed in Jane's lap. She lifted it and held the blossoms to her nose. "Roses," she said, "roses and baby's breath with carnations."

"What did she say?" Melena asked through her sobs.

"She said roses and baby's breath and carnations," I answered.

"How'd she do that?" Melena sniffled up her tears.

"Fragrance."

"I can understand knowing roses by their odor—but carnations and baby's breath?"

"Oh, Jane's good at that," I said. "She can identify almost anything by smell. She recognizes people by scent, too. Changing colognes doesn't even confuse her. She can tell it's me no matter what I'm wearing."

Commotion on the stage tore my interest away from Melena. Sarah and Ron were having their first dance, clogging to "Rocky Top." The faster the band played, the quicker their feet flew. I consider myself a pretty good dancer, but no way could I have kept up with those two. Sarah's legs were flying when she stepped off the front edge of the stage and tumbled onto the dirt in front of Jane and me.

I jumped from my chair to help Sarah, but Ron leaped from the stage and landed on both of us. Staff ran over and pulled us all to our feet. I slipped back to my lawn chair and brushed the dirt off my legs. The bride's and groom's clothes were wet with sweat and filthy with dirt, but I have to say they'd both freshened their breaths extensively. The whole area smelled like a distillery.

Jane sniffed and said, "Gin. Definitely gin and mint." She turned toward me. "You told me no alcohol was allowed at this festival."

"Not supposed to be," I answered, "but some folks sneak booze in anyway." I leaned closer to her. "Pulley Bone Jones has mint gin in a Scope mouthwash bottle in his camper. That's what the bride's been drinking."

Just as I mentioned his name, Bone arrived carrying a collapsible chair. "Whass up?" he said before he motioned his sister to move over, then set his seat up between Melena and me.

He'd overheard what I told Jane because he leaned across me and asked her, "Would you like some of my special mouthwash?"

"Would you repeat that?" Jane said. Her expression was quizzical.

"I asked if you'd like some special mouthwash."

Jane's face lit up with surprise. "Boner?" she whispered in a soft, seductive voice.

The surprise on Jane's face was no match for the shocked look Bone wore.

"Roxanne?" he said. "Are you Roxanne?"

I'd warned Jane over and over this would happen. Someday one of the callers on her 900 line would turn out to be someone we knew. In this case, someone we met turned out to be a regular client. She'd mentioned this guy she called "Boner" to me as one of her steadiest clients.

"Callie, will you change places with me?" Bone asked.

We switched chairs so that we were lined up Jane, Bone, me, then Melena. I wondered where Andy was. Would he be the next act? Would he come out and sit on the other side of Melena so she could talk more with him about becoming his manager? Aaron Porter put an end to that fear. He came through the middle of the crowd carrying an orange canvas-backed director's chair and set it up beside Melena.

"Hello, Mrs. Delgado. I've been wanting to tell you how sorry I . . ."

I tried. I promise I tried to keep my mind on the music and not listen to the conversation on either side of me. I succeeded in ignoring Aaron and Melena, but I couldn't help dipping into Jane and Bone's talk.

Jane's words were hard to hear. She spoke softly. Bone probably thought he was whispering, but I could hear him. "You lied to me, Roxanne. You said your hair was raven black, but I love the red."

Broken Fence kicked off "Love Me Darling, Just To-night," and I didn't hear Jane's response.

"It shouldn't be awkward," I overheard Bone say. "I feel like we know each other"—he smirked with what he considered a flirting smile, which was wasted on Jane since she couldn't see it anyway—"intimately."

"No, no, I understand you're not a . . ." Bone's volume dropped and I didn't hear the last word, but buh-leeve me, I could guess what he'd said. He grinned. "Only on the phone, you say? Do you have a cell phone with you? I'd love to call you right now."

I quit pretending not to be listening and laughed. "Outta luck, Bone," I interrupted. I pulled my phone from my shorts pocket and held it out to him. "I haven't been able to get a signal on this thing since we got here."

"Shoulda remembered that from when I worked here with Happy Jack and at that new crab restaurant they started building on Flower Island." He leaned toward me and asked, "You can't hear our conversation, can you?"

"Some of it."

"I really like Roxanne—I mean Jane," he said, "but I don't want to embarrass her."

"She's not easily embarrassed, but she doesn't like discussing her work, and she's not here to work."

I'm not sure if Jane heard what Bone and I said, but she probably did. "Boner," she said, "we can talk later. I'm really tired and I'd like for Callie to take me back to the bus for a nap."

Bone jumped up and touched Jane's arm. "I'll walk you to the campground," he said.

"No, I said I'll talk to you later. Callie, please go with me." She stood and put her cane in front of her, moved it left and right much faster and more forcefully than her usual way, and whapped Bone in the shin with it. "Sorry," she mumbled as I stepped beside her and led her away from the music area. I tried unsuccessfully not to grin.

About the time we reached the path to the campground, I saw tears in Jane's eyes. I wanted to say, "I told you so. Told you something like this would happen," but my mortuary training told me to put my arm around her shoulder and say, "It's okay. It'll be all right. You don't have to even talk to Bone if he calls again."

"It's not that. Not Boner. I made a fool of myself, Callie." She burst into sobs. Yes, Jane cries real tears. Her congenital eye condition prevents vision but has no effect on her tear ducts.

"What did you do?" I patted her shoulder.

"I told Dean how I feel about him."

"That's okay, Jane."

"No, it's not! He turned me down." Her sobs subsided. For probably the only time since I went to work for Middleton's, I didn't have a tissue with me. Jane wiped the tears from her face with her arm. "He said that he really likes me and that he's attracted to me, but he vowed to his wife he'd never cheat on her. Then he said that thing you always say about if they'll cheat with you, they'll cheat on you. He made me feel like a tramp."

"Jane, I can see the look on Dean's face when he's watching you. He really cares about you, but I told you from the beginning that he's married and though I've never seen his wife with him, I've never seen him flirting or 'with' another woman either."

"I know! I know! I'm such a fool, and now he thinks I'm cheap like Roxanne."

How could I argue with that? Best to try to divert her. "He doesn't even know about Roxanne, does he?"

"Not until that Boner starts spreading it all around." I patted her back some more. She squared her shoulders and stopped her sniffling. "I need some rest, Callie. I didn't sleep well after I touched Kenny's body last night, and I got up really early for coffee with Dean. I need a nap, and then I'll feel better and be myself again."

"Are you going to change jobs?" I asked as we resumed walking.

"No," she sighed. "And don't tell me anymore about how much fun bluegrass festivals are."

Just then, Jane grabbed my behind. She'd stumbled on a root I'd stepped over and not mentioned. If she'd been using her cane, she would have known it was there, but I didn't realize she'd stopped moving her cane and was relying on me for guidance. She tried to steady herself by reaching for me, and her hand landed on my derriere.

"What is *that?*" she screeched.

"My new underwear," I replied calmly and helped her rise from the almost fall.

"Are you pumping up your butt these days?"

"No, the cheeks of my panties are just padded a bit. The saleslady says it will give me 'lift' and 'definition.' Does it feel fake?"

She patted my behind. "No, not really. It was just a surprise. I haven't touched your booty often, only when I've bumped into it accidentally, but I wasn't expecting firm and fully packed."

"What did you expect?"

"Your usual bony butt. Callie, no matter how sad I feel, you always brighten my mood."

"Why, thank you. If I'd known a rounder booty would have made you happy, I'd have bought these panties long ago."

When we reached Broken Fence's band bus, the key wasn't in the hidden box the band members had shown us, but the door wasn't locked anyway. I called, "Hey, we're coming in," as Jane and I stepped into the cool air-conditioning.

"I'll be right out." I recognized Andy's voice. In a few moments, he came out of the bathroom door. Dressed for the stage, he wore black pants, a white shirt, blue vest, red tie, and of course the black stovepipe hat. "I've been in here tuning up and getting dressed for my next performance."

"Jane's tired. Wants to take a nap," I said.

"I'm gonna crash right here," she said and sat on the couch.

"That sofa's mighty comfortable," Andy said and picked up his guitar case. "Callie, are you staying here or going back to the show? I'm on next."

"Then by all means, I'm going back to the music." I managed not to flutter my eyelashes or talk with a Magnolia Mouth, but I was tempted.

On the path back, Andy and I talked about Happy Jack losing a bundle of money on the festival.

"I went down to the bridge earlier," Andy said. "There's a roadblock there to keep anyone from coming or going. Usually festival tickets are nonrefundable, but he'll have to do something for all the people who didn't get here in time to come on the island."

"What about the performers who *are* here? Is your pay based on attendance?"

"Nope, outright contract with set fee. Happy Jack felt confident this festival would be a big success. Now he's going to be pressed to pay those of us who're here, and we're playing more sets than the contracts call for since not all the bands made it in. It doesn't matter to me, but some of the bands are talking about asking him for more money for the increased performance time."

"How about the ones who were turned away at the bridge? Will he have to pay them, too?"

"I don't know, but I'd guess Happy Jack Wilburn's going to need a good lawyer to work out some of the problems."

The Pollyanna in me surfaced. "There's always a worse viewpoint, though. We're feeling sorry for grassers and Happy Jack. The real losers are Fred and Kenny."

"Yeah, and their families. I really sympathize with Fred's wife. You know, she gave up college scholarships to be with him and now, just when he's hitting the big time, he's gone and she has nothing."

So he'd talked more to Melena. I wondered when and where. Catty? Sometimes I am. *Meow, meow, meow.* "At least she doesn't have children," I said. "Kenny Strickland had a wife and a couple of kids. Besides, he'd quit his day job to go on the road with the band. Dean thinks Kenny was planning to wait until the band was doing well before getting private insurance."

"That's a problem with touring festivals for a living. No benefits. At least my mom and dad have a policy on me that's paid up and enough to cover a funeral, so I don't have that to worry about, but I don't have any hospital coverage."

His mom and dad? The Great Pretender was possibly even younger than I thought. Most grown men don't talk a lot about their parents.

"I'm confused by the lack of mourning I've seen." I really should have meowed this change of subject. Sheer cattiness on my part. "Melena doesn't seem very upset about her husband's death," I purred.

"Working in a funeral home, you oughta know people show grief in different ways." Andy's tone was matter-of-fact. He didn't seem to notice when Melena came on to him, but he didn't seem aware of my feline tendencies either. "I also can't figure out the connection between Fred and Kenny's deaths," he continued. "I think the same person killed them both. They'd crossed paths before, but from what I've heard, they had no close association, so why would they have the same enemy? Another strange thing is that Aaron Porter, the fiddler Second Time Around was replacing with Little Fiddlin' Fred, was already here, conveniently available to go back into his spot."

"I didn't know that, but I guess he was since he played with them this morning. I saw him last night, but I didn't recognize him without the black suit."

"Yeah, I talked to him earlier. Aaron said he just came to see how good Fred was. He thinks the band chose Fred to replace him because it would be unique to have a dwarf in the band. You know, a publicity thing, what with Fred playing a half-size fiddle and the way he danced around and cut up onstage."

"I never saw Little Fiddlin' Fred onstage. I've read about him in magazines and seen him on television, but I never saw him live."

"I've seen Fred perform," Andy said. "He was great, but between the two, I'd pass up a hundred times seeing Fred for one time seeing Randall Hylton. I just can't believe I never got to talk with him."

After that, there was no discussing the murders or Melena. Andy talked about Hylton until we reached the front row of the music arena. Bone was gone and had taken his chair with him. Andy sat in Jane's seat beside me and was quickly absorbed in the music while Melena sat on my other side talking to Aaron, not seeming to be paying attention to Andy and me or the band. In fact, she kept taking the jar from her bag and looking at the dead bugs in it.

Chapter Twelve

"There's a storm coming,
Feel the wind a'blowing."

Broken Fence always closes each set with a gospel tune. Arnie kicked off "Stand by Me, Jesus" with a rousing banjo intro, just the way I wished I could play. For a second, I regretted Jane wasn't there to hear it, but when I glanced at Andy sitting in her lawn chair beside me, I was glad Jane had gone back to the bus. I'd about decided Jane preferred her iPod music to the bluegrass I'd brought her here to hear. Andy and I had left her lying on the couch with her earpods plugged in.

Andy slipped me a wink. Some versions of the Bible interpret Proverbs 10:10 to say, "Beware a winking man," and I believe in the Bible, but I don't take every line literally. Besides, other biblical translations might be different.

The air was so humid it felt like a steam bath, and I hoped Andy thought the slight flush on my face was from the heat and humidity. Good grief, I'm a grown woman, not some blushing maiden. Meanwhile, Melena was still staring through the glass at the dead bugs in her jar. She put it into her denim tote and glanced over at Andy, but his attention was riveted to the stage. She stood, mumbled something to Aaron, and headed back toward the campground.

Dean's vocals rang high and loud . . .

> *"Dark clouds gathering over me.*
> *There's a storm coming.*
> *Rumbling thunder warns it will be,*
> *A hard wind, a cold wind . . ."*

From nowhere, without warning, the sky blackened.

> *"Oh, Jesus, stand by me—"*

Suddenly blinding sheets of gigantic raindrops poured from the clouds. Hard, driving wind pelted fat water bombs at the stage. I heard electrical pops and snaps before the first roar of thunder. Blue sparks arced in the amplification equipment as flashes of lightning pierced the sky. Everyone onstage scrambled down the steps.

Sopping wet, I jumped from my chair as Andy grabbed my arm.

"Come on!" he shouted.

Dean screeched, "Where's Jane?"

"She's in the bus," I yelled.

With Dean on one side and Andy on the other, I ran across the music area toward the food stands, heading for the path to the camping area beyond them. We'd almost reached the concession area when Dean yanked Andy and me to the side and shoved us facedown onto the muddy ground.

Anger replaced fear, and excitement pounded in my chest. Gratitude chased away the rage when I realized that a gust of wind had lifted the plywood Gastric Gullah stand and tossed it through the downpour, barely missing us.

Dean and Andy jumped up and pulled me toward the campground path. I stumbled. Dean grabbed me and carried me the rest of the way to the bus and right over the threshold like a sopping wet bride when Andy yanked the door open. Van and Arnie stood just inside with arms full of towels. Guess it's faster to get to shelter if a guy isn't slowed down by gentlemanly assistance to a woman.

"Where's Jane?" Dean's eyes darted around frantically.

"Probably the restroom," I said. No way she'd slept through all that thunder.

"I just came outta there," Arnie said and handed me another towel.

"Did you leave her at the stage?" Van's brow wrinkled.

"No, I brought her over here before the storm," I snapped. Buh-leeve me. I had no hard feelings toward Van or his question, but I felt like a drowned rat. An unhappy one. Well, not that I know exactly how a drowned rat feels, but I felt the way that sounds. My hair hung in limp strands, dripping on the floor into the puddles of muddy water pouring from our clothes. My face felt raw from the stinging rain.

Dean went to the restroom door and pounded. "Jane, are you in there?" he called, loud enough to be heard over the continuing rolls of thunder. Like Arnie wouldn't have seen her in the minuscule bathroom. Dean pushed the door open. No Jane. In the sleeping area, he tore the covers from the bunks. No Jane.

"She's not here." His tone reflected accusation as well as genuine concern. "Callie, are you sure you left her in the bus?"

"Right here in this room," I said. "I'm not in the habit of losing my best friend, nor of lying about where she is." I towel dried my hair roughly. Taking my distress out on my blonde curls I'd spent so much time straightening before coming to the festival. "Ask Andy. He was here."

"She was lying on the couch when Callie and I left." Andy picked Jane's iPod up from the couch. "Maybe someone stopped by. Jane went to their camper, and the storm came up too fast for her to get back. She'll probably be here as soon as this is over." He motioned toward the ceiling as though we could see through it to the dark skies and flashes of lightning outside.

Everyone changed into dry clothing, including me, even though Arnie, the smallest member of the band, was enough larger than me that I looked kind of like a hobo in his clothes. The storm subsided, moving away as fast as it had arrived.

"I couldn't see anything out there. How'd you see the Gastric Gullah coming?" Andy asked Dean.

"I wasn't sure what it was, but it looked solid and headed straight at us."

"Was it a funnel? Do you think it was a tornado?" I asked.

"No," Dean said, "I don't think so. Just high wind. It's a good thing everyone decided not to set up tables to sell CDs and T-shirts. He pulled the burlap curtain on the window over the kitchen sink aside. "The storm's cleared. Let's knock on some camper doors and find Jane."

The answer was the same everywhere we went. No one had seen Jane since I walked her back to the bus.

The storm had ravaged trees and thrown folks' outdoor camping equipment helter-skelter, but the edge of the heat had lifted, and the temperature dropped to a comfortable level for the first time in almost a week. The ground soaked up the water, making mud puddles dry out right before our eyes and leaving the surface barely damp after the heavy rains. Puffy white clouds floated in the bright blue sky.

Dean and Andy worked out a plan. Dean would check with law enforcement officers and Happy Jack Wilburn. Van and Arnie were to circle the campground again, double-checking campers. Andy volunteered to explore the beach beyond the campground and invited me to go with him.

Everyone agreed to meet back at Bob's Best Barbecue, but not for barbecue. The concession area was a mess with men working to restore order to tables, benches, and dining awnings. "Both Bob and Marie will reopen at 6:00 p.m." written in crayon on a paper plate taped to the barbecue truck announced the intentions of Bob's Best Barbecue and Marie's Grill. Gastric Gullah was nowhere to be seen.

Andy slipped his hand on mine, and walking hand in hand with him felt comfortable and natural. Good grief. My best friend was missing and I was thinking about how nice it was to be with a man who held hands. I tried to comfort myself that Jane had taken care of herself for years and would be found safe and sound.

"Callie," Andy said, "do you think that Jane—"

"Whass up?" we heard from behind us.

"Dalmation!" The kindergarten cussword escaped my lips. I recognized the greeting and the voice.

Andy and I stopped and turned back toward Bone.

"Where you two headed?" he asked.

"Jane's missing," Andy said. "Callie and I are going to check the beach area beyond the campground."

"Did you ask the other campers? Maybe she's visiting someone," Bone suggested.

"Been there. Done that." I slipped my hand out of Andy's. "Arnie and Van are checking the campers again, and Dean's gone to talk to the deputies and Happy Jack."

"I'll go along with you to the beach," Bone offered. "I've been here for a while helping Jack set up the campground, so I probably know this area better than you do." Bone laughed. "And if we don't find her, I'll pull out my dowsing tools."

"We shouldn't need a male witch with a forked branch to find water when we're surrounded by the ocean," Andy said.

"Apparently you suffer from the delusion that what I do is just sense water, especially underground, with a crooked stick," Bone said. "First, it isn't always a stick, though a Y-shaped branch can be carved to work well. I can dowse with a pendulum, two sticks, even two wire coat hangers. And we locate more than water. In the sixteenth century, dowsers searched for treasures and bodies."

"*Bodies!*" I exploded. "We aren't looking for a body. We're searching for Jane, alive and well."

"On the beach? After that storm?" Bone kicked a broken tree limb out of the way. "Besides, the tide's coming in. Won't be much beach to see then."

"Unless the wind blew her away, she may simply be lost and waiting for one of us to find her," Andy suggested.

"Not Jane," I said. "If Jane's lost, she'll be trying to find her way back."

"She's blind," Bone said.

"I *know* she's blind, but with her cane she can find her way around." I thought of Jane's shoplifting as a teenager. She got away with it for years, was furious when she got caught, though the judge let her off because of her "visual disability." Jane hadn't always made good choices, but she'd always been self-reliant.

The storm had scattered broken tree limbs among the palmettos. A white dogwood in full blossom lay with roots pulled from the earth, yet Spanish moss and wisteria still wept from some of the oak limbs. When we reached the beach, the pale beige sand was littered with broken tree limbs and some of the campers' belongings including a couple of aluminum lawn chairs bent beyond redemption and pieces of polystyrene large enough to be from coolers, not cups.

I scanned the beach and my heart leaped into my throat when I spotted something suspicious in a pile of debris. I froze, even more upset than I'd been the night before when I saw Kenny Strickland's body lying dead in my borrowed Winnebago.

Andy walked a few steps ahead of me. He obviously hadn't noticed what I saw, but he stepped back and touched my arm when he realized I'd stopped.

"What is it?"

"Over there." I pointed. A white stripe lay almost hidden in a pile of broken branches. "Is that Jane's cane?"

Bone hurried to the pile, kicked the debris aside, and lifted a white metal stick with a red tip, a mobility cane for the blind. He waved it in the air and then used it to scatter the heap in all directions until the sand was bare. I breathed a sigh of relief. No corpse. The cane was probably Jane's, and finding it here meant she almost certainly wasn't happily drinking Dr Pepper with a new friend, but until we found evidence otherwise, I chose to believe she was okay and would be found.

I reached out for the cane, and Bone handed it to me. Just holding it made me feel Jane was close. Andy, Bone, and I scoured the beach along the northern end of the island. We examined every clump of trash and every piece of driftwood. Like Jane could be hidden by a slender water-smoothed stick. Arriving at the bridge, we saw that the sheriff still had a roadblock. Actually two roadblocks, one on each end of the bridge.

"Should we explore the rest of the island?" I asked. "The undeveloped part?"

"Let's go to the food area first and see if the others are back," Andy suggested. "Maybe one of them has found Jane."

Chapter Thirteen

The first real book I ever read that wasn't about Curious George or some other critter was written by Mark Twain about a boy whose name was worse than Calamine—Huckleberry Finn. Huck's not so popular anymore because he says the *n* word, but I always skip over it.

The opening sentence in *Huckleberry Finn* is "You don't know about me without you have read a book by the name of *The Adventures of Tom Sawyer*." What's good enough for Mark Twain is good enough for me.

Without you have read a book called *A Tisket, a Tasket, a Fancy Stolen Casket*, you don't know how I feel about the number thirteen. I've been in buildings with elevators that go from the twelfth floor to the fourteenth. Buh-leeve me, if those rich folks who build fancy buildings think thirteen is unlucky, so do I.

Not only is thirteen unlucky, but I just don't like that number. I was thirteen when my brothers started calling me "Itty Bitty . . ." (a word I don't say). They laughed because my friends were wearing bras and Daddy refused to buy me one until I had something besides Kleenex to put in it.

For the above reasons, I, Calamine L. Parrish, refuse to write a chapter 13.

Chapter Fourteen

"Yo han' sutt'nly lazy 'en good-fuh-nutt'n. De stawm bruk uh stan' an' uh long cheer, en oonuh jabbuh same lukkuh monkrey. Jis gwi!"

The female voice echoed across the lot. Andy looked at me in total confusion.

Bone laughed and called out, "Rizzie!"

Where the missing Gastric Gullah plywood shack had been blown away from between Bob's Barbecue and Marie's Grill, a six-foot-long folding table stood.

My daddy is the crudest redneck anyone would want to meet. Well, actually, many folks would just as soon not meet him. At times, my brothers are as rude, crude, and socially unacceptable as our patriarch, and none of them hesitate to voice their preferences. Mike calls himself a "boob man"; Frank, a "butt man"; and Bill, a "leg man," who adds, "I like long-legged women with legs stretching from the ground to heaven."

The tall, dark-skinned woman arranging a gas cooker and ice chests on the table would have been perfect for all of them. Even in traditional Gullah garb, she obviously had

everything I longed for. Not longed for as in another
woman, 'cause I've never gone that way. Teased by Daddy
that the good Lord gave Parrish men brains and Parrish
women big boobs, but He gave Calamine (that's me) some
of each but not a whole lot of either, I'd improved my
bosom situation with a blow-up bra from Victoria's Secret.
But at five foot four, I don't have long legs, and until I
bought my new panties, the junk in my trunk was as flat as
my bosom is without my bra.

A bright scarf wrapped around the woman's head and
knotted in front hid her hair, but if it was like the rest of
her, it was glorious. Her chest filled out her white, scoop-
necked tee and J Lo had nothing on the shelf beneath her
floor-length, make that ground-length, wraparound skirt.
Legs? A split up the skirt showed the longest legs I've ever
seen on a woman. Her skin was dark, very dark, but not
ashy. A beautiful deep brown like Godiva dark chocolate
accentuated her white, white teeth and her jet black eyes,
which looked up at us when Bone called her name.

"Bone!" she exclaimed. "Gree bunce hab uh, fuh true.
De stawm done tek all us stan' en Tyrone ack lukkah . . ."
She waved her arm toward the short, thin African Ameri-
can youth who was unloading ice chests from the trunk of
a battered, rusty old Chevy truck.

"What's she talking?" Andy said.

"Gullah," I answered. "She told the boy that he's lazy,
his hands aren't good for anything, and that even though
the storm destroyed their stand and blew away their lawn
chairs, he's just jabbering like a monkey instead of helping
her. Then she told Bone that she has grief about the storm
and that Tyrone, the boy, isn't helping. 'Jis gwi!' means
'just go.' She's running the boy off because he's lazy."

"How do you understand all that?"

"I grew up in St. Mary. A lot of the Gullah folk who
used to live on islands moved into nearby towns. I have
Gullah friends, though most of them don't talk real Gullah
as well as she does anymore."

Bone turned toward us and said, "Rizzie Prophet, meet

Callie and Andy." He laughed. "And they're not tourists, so you can drop the Gullah."

Rizzie smiled all over her face. Wide toothy grin and bright, twinkling eyes.

"Never can tell," she said. "They might've wanted to buy some baskets." Turning toward the boy, she scolded, "You gotta learn to work harder. Take the truck back to the house and load it up again."

The boy hopped behind the wheel and gunned the engine as he headed away.

"How old is he?" Andy asked.

"Twelve," Rizzie answered.

"Is he old enough to drive?" I said.

"Been driving since he was old enough to see over the steering wheel when sitting on a pillow, since he was about nine." Rizzie grinned. "That's one reason the old ones are against this campground coming to Surcie. Afraid we'll wind up like Fripp, Hilton Head, and the other islands. Over-developed and over-lawed. Maum says even Daufuskie's changed since that man wrote the book about it years ago."

Dean, Van, and Arnie arrived as she spoke. They shook their heads back and forth. No news about Jane.

"I made an official report of Jane's disappearance," Dean said, "but the sheriff said an adult isn't considered missing for at least forty-eight hours. What kind of country bumpkin holds to that when two people have already been murdered here?" He frowned. "Said it wouldn't be surprising if Jane met some dude and crawled into his bunk with him. I felt like socking him. Bad-mouthing her like that." He coughed, then added, "I hope I haven't upset her in any way."

I interrupted. "Dean, Jane's no angel. She was kinda wild in her teenaged years, and Sheriff Harmon doesn't think much of her job. But I agree he's wrong. My instincts are bad about her being missing, real bad." I didn't add that she had been very upset about whatever happened between the two of them, about his turning down her offer of . . . whatever she'd offered him. She'd been upset, but I *knew* in my heart that Jane had not left the band bus of her own will.

"What *is* Jane's job?" Dean asked.

"What ya'll talking about anyway?" Rizzie quizzed.

Buh-leeve me. I'd rather answer Rizzie's question than Dean's, so I ignored him and turned to her. "My friend Jane went back to the band bus before the storm, but when we got there, she was gone."

"I can't see where that's much of a problem. She's grown, right?"

"Yes, but she's blind, and I don't think she would have tried to maneuver this campground by herself. Arnie and Van were checking with campers and performers while Dean here talked to the sheriff." I motioned to each man as I spoke his name.

"What were you doing?"

"Andy, Bone, and I walked around the beach on the campground end of the island. We found her cane on the beach."

I lifted the white stick into the air. I didn't want to let go of it. It was the only part of Jane I had at the moment. Her clothes and other belongings were in the Winnebago, but the cane was part of Jane, and I needed to be close to some of Jane.

Dean grimaced at the red tip of the cane. "I didn't know that," he said. "I need to go back and tell the sheriff she doesn't have her cane. Danged fool's got the island road-blocked, but he's not interested in a possible kidnapping. Not going to let anyone else onto the island or off the island. Happy Jack will lose his behind on this festival. There are only about forty or so grassers here, and two of the bands didn't get in last night, so they won't be playing. Jack wants the acts that are here to fill in and hopes he won't have to refund all the tickets."

"I'll go with you," Bone said. "I want to talk to Harmon and Happy Jack myself." They walked away, headed back toward the bridge.

Rizzie wrinkled her mouth into a scowl that spoke

disappointment as well as anger. "Only forty people and the sheriff's not letting anyone else in? Happy Jack promised me there'd be hundreds of folks here or I wouldn't have put all that money and time into building my stand. I'd hoped this would be a big success and earn me enough cash to start my food business. Now the stand's gone and I've thawed all this food from my freezer locker in Beaufort." She motioned toward the ice chests beneath the table. "Can't refreeze fish. I'll be back to selling baskets all summer."

"Selling baskets?" Andy asked. "Like chicken and hamburger baskets?"

Rizzie shot him the most exaggerated eye roll I've ever seen, and buh-leeve me, I've seen plenty.

"Sweetgrass baskets," I said. "Hundreds of years ago, West Africans on the sea islands along the South Carolina coast made baskets out of the sweetgrass that grows in the marshes. Nowadays, they sell for big money to tourists."

"Like Easter baskets?" Andy said.

"Beautiful, intricate decorative baskets. They're usable, but most people treat them like art, and they smell like sweetgrass for years," I answered.

"More like forever," Rizzie interrupted. "The baskets sell better if people know they're handmade by real Gullah people. That's why I speak and dress Gullah when I sell baskets and had planned to look and act all Gullah at my food stand." She glanced at her ice chests. "Not much use in setting this thing up. Forty fans plus musicians to feed between three venues won't make anybody any money." She sighed. "I might as well go get Tyrone to bring the truck back and pack up."

Yowza! The idea hit me like a bolt of lightning. I could picture the lightbulb shining bright over my head. "You live here on Surcie?" I asked.

"Yep, other end of the island."

"We walked along the beach, but I'd feel better if we did it again with someone who's more familiar with the island. Reckon you could help us?" I waited, but she said nothing.

Ex-cuuze me. I should've known not much is free in life, so I added, "I'll pay you for your time."

"Okay." Rizzie grinned at me.

"What's the first thing you think we should do?"

Rizzie looked up, pointed toward some southern clouds, and drawled, "Tree buds en hebben cawls us ober dere."

"Gullah?" Andy asked.

"Yep," I answered as my heart raced around in my chest then dropped into the pit of my stomach. "She said, 'Three birds in the sky are calling us.' I should have noticed them myself."

"Why?"

"They're buzzards. When they circle like that, they're looking for something dead on the ground." Death is my business, but the thought of what they might find made me break down and sob. Andy put his arm around my shoulders and pulled me into a hug. Like he could read my mind. The thought of *a* body didn't bring tears, but the vision of Jane as a corpse opened my floodgates.

Either Andy's comfort hug or my emotional outburst must have embarrassed Van and Arnie because they took off toward the camping area.

"Come on." Rizzie stepped around the table and motioned Andy and me to follow.

I had a hard time keeping up with their long legs. Rizzie stood only a few inches shorter than Andy's six feet, six inches, and I felt the more than twelve-inch difference between them and me at every step we took. I had to jog to keep up along the new scraped roads out of the camping area. Not easy for someone whose primary exercise is stretching the truth.

"Wait up," I called to Rizzie and Andy when I spotted Bone talking to Sheriff Harmon near the bridge.

"Any news?" I asked.

"Nope," Bone said.

"No real leads for either murder," the sheriff added.

"I meant any news about Jane," I snapped.

"Nope, it's like I told your tall friend . . ." Harmon paused a moment and stared at Rizzie and Andy. "Callie, are you shrinking or making taller friends these days?" He chuckled.

"I'm not shrinking, and that's not funny. I'm worried about Jane."

"Like I was saying, Jane could be shacked up anywhere on the island. She's too old for an Amber Alert. Guess you want me to issue a Jane Alert. Missing: blind female, good-looking, not always law-abiding."

"Wayne Harmon, I can't believe you said that." I glared at him. "Jane's slowed down a lot, and you sowed a few wild oats yourself in your early years."

"I've got two murders on an island with travelers who will leave the area as soon as I reopen this bridge. Show me some evidence that Jane didn't leave that bus of her own accord, and I'll get more interested. For now, I figure she's probably out having a good time."

"Her iPod was still on the couch in the band bus, and what about her mobility cane? Did Bone tell you we found it on the beach?" I held it up toward him. "Without this, Jane's not able to negotiate unfamiliar territory. She'd never leave the iPod or the cane on purpose."

Harmon smiled at me. Condescending. Like I was six years old. "Yes, Bone told me about that. I see you have it." He reached toward it, but I moved the cane behind my back. "Are there any identifying marks? Are you positive it's Jane's?"

"How many blind people have you seen on this island?" Most sarcastic tone I could rev up.

"Be patient, Callie," Harmon said. "If Jane doesn't show up soon, I'll assign someone to check into where she is. Let me have the cane."

I tried. I promise I tried to remain composed and give Wayne Harmon the respect he's due as sheriff of Jade County, but I'd grown up with him in the house with my brothers all the time, and I reacted as though he were one of them. I, Calamine L. Parrish, who no longer even *thinks* profanity worse than kindergarten cussing, flipped him a bird that wasn't circling over the other end of the island.

The "bad" finger. The moment I did it, I regretted my action, especially because Rizzie, Andy, and Wayne, too, laughed at me. With Jane missing, I was in no mood for humor, especially directed at *me*.

"You can have the cane when you accept Jane as a serious case. In the meantime, I'll find my friend myself," I retorted, tossed my hair out of my eyes, and headed toward the southern end of the island. Still holding the only part of Jane I had at the moment—the white cane.

"Look at her," I heard Wayne say to the others. "You can tell by the way she's walking. She's mad as the ninth piglet on an eight-nippled sow. Ever since she was a kid, she's pranced when she's furious."

"What can you expect?" Andy asked. "She's afraid the killer running loose on this island may have Jane."

Wayne lowered his voice, but I heard him anyway. "I've thought about that, and I do have deputies looking for Jane even though I think this is just another one of Jane's stunts. Watch Callie, will you? She doesn't always act wisely when she's prancing. I'll get the cane from her later."

Rizzie and Andy caught up with me just as I reached the end of the scraped road where it turned into a rutted path barely wide enough for a pickup. Plant life thickened immediately. Tall and short palmetto trees surrounded us. Below them, shrub-size, sharp-spined saw palmettos.

Rizzie stopped beside me. "You and the sheriff must be old friends."

"I've known him all my life, but I apologize for what I did back there. I just can't understand why he won't acknowledge that Jane could be the next victim." I trembled at the thought.

Andy put his arm around my shoulder again and said, "With the roadblock on the bridge, no one can leave. He should be able to identify the—"

Rizzie's laughter cut off Andy's words. "City boy, you really think this island is shut off by that lawman blocking the road? How do you think we got back and forth to the mainland before they built the bridge?"

"Hadn't really given it much thought." Andy withdrew his arm from around me and swatted at a mosquito.

"Boats. We've always traveled back and forth across the water. There's people living on this island right now who have a boat, but no car or truck."

"Guess Wayne figures whoever killed Fiddling Fred and Kenny came in with the festival," I said. Rizzie stepped around a sticky holly bush. Andy and I followed her.

"That dwarf was always pulling pranks on other musicians." Andy slapped at another flying insect. "Do you think one of his jokes made someone mad and in the heat of anger, they killed him?"

Buh-leeve me. If that had been Wayne Harmon or one of my brothers talking, I'd have exaggerated an eye roll at him or called him stupid, but I was thinking thoughts and feeling emotions about Andy that were completely unsisterly, so I tempered my words.

"Seems more likely that the murders were planned. Everybody saw Kenny take his bass out of the case. It was in full view during the whole set, so how did Little Fiddling Fred's body get in there? Like one of those locked room mysteries, some trick has to be involved."

"That's exactly what I meant." Andy winked at me again.

"Turn off here and follow me." Rizzie took a smaller path from the roadway and pushed aside a branch. She peered at the sky. "I know where those birds are. We'll be there soon."

My gaze followed hers. Only two buzzards now circled.

Chapter Fifteen

Dalmation! The branch Rizzie'd pushed away smacked me right in the face. By the time I finished sputtering and wiping my nose, Rizzie and Andy had stopped about a hundred feet ahead.

Lavender wisteria dripped from an oak tree behind them, and several dogwoods burst with white blossoms around the clearing. The storm hadn't done as much damage here. Beautiful.

No doubt where we were. Large conch shells with deep pink throats outlined areas covered with crushed oyster shells. Though they varied in size, all the bordered patches were rectangular, the shape of graves. Some had home-made wooden markers or big stones with names and dates painted on them. Only one had a granite headstone. Small, but obviously professionally made and engraved.

"What's all that stuff?" Andy pointed.

An assortment of items topped each site. A cornhusk doll and a tiny, carved wooden bowl sat on the smallest grave. A little girl. Ex-cuuze me. Getting my exercise jumping to conclusions again. It could have been a dwarf, but not likely because of the doll. Liquor bottles and home-made pipes crowded tools, pottery, and baskets on a lot of adult-size graves. On others, perfume bottles replaced the pipes.

Andy stepped ahead and leaned forward. As I shouted "No!" he picked up a Jim Beam bottle that lay among several ornate sweetgrass baskets filled with weathered packages of snuff and chewing tobacco.

"Put it back," Rizzie commanded.

Andy shot us a puzzled look, shook the bottle, and placed it exactly where it had been.

"You mustn't touch grave gifts," Rizzie scolded. "It's disrespectful."

"Sorry," said Andy, "but that bottle's almost full. Why hasn't anyone stolen it?" He waved his arm around, encompassing the entire cemetery. "Some of these things are valuable."

"They're guarded," Rizzie said, "guarded by those who lie here. To disrespect the dead is worse than dissing live folks. The Gullah would never desecrate our own graves, but who knows about other people? That's another problem with the campground and bridge. Eventually, the developers will want this end of the island. People will be over here rooting us out and destroying what we value."

"Is this voodoo?" Andy asked. "I've seen documentaries."

"No voodoo on this island, unless someone brought it in from the mainland since that bridge was built. Gifts for the dead are part of lots of cultures. Egyptians left treasures in the pyramids for their mummies. We've kept some customs our West African ancestors brought over here, including leaving favorite belongings with our loved ones. We've got root doctors, but it's not voodoo." She dismissed the subject and motioned toward the granite marker. "That's Grampa's. Maum had it brought to the island by boat—rowboat."

Grampa's final resting place was covered with gifts. Silently, I read that Methusalah Profit died twenty-five years before. Aloud, I spelled the last name engraved on the stone: "P-r-o-f-i-t."

"Bet you thought my name's P-r-o-p-h-e-t," Rizzie said. "Probably figured I was descended from John the Baptist." Andy looked surprised, but I spotted the tease in her obsidian eyes.

"No, Rizzie, I told you I grew up around here. I know about slaves having no last name before the emancipation, so they took the names of their owners or just picked a word they liked for a last name when slavery ended." I said it to Rizzie, but I was really talking to Andy.

"Sure did, and my family was more interested in earning money than telling the future, so it's P-r-o-f-i-t. Unfortunately, it hasn't proved prophetic yet." She looked up. Two buzzards circled close to us.

"Are the vultures because of the graveyard?" Andy asked.

"No, there's something near here that interests them. Buzzards like dead meat, not buried bones."

"I've got to find Jane," I said.

"We're almost there." Rizzie ducked beneath a draping wisteria vine. Andy and I followed her. In a few minutes, we stood at the edge of a salt marsh. Knee-high grasses, turning spring green from winter golden brown, waved faintly as a light breeze rippled across them.

"Over there!" Andy shouted and ran along the edge of the marsh. Before he reached the buzzard tearing at a crumpled form on the ground, the other giant birds swooped down and joined the buffet.

The sight tore me in two. Half of me wanted to move closer and see what they were eating. The other part of me wanted to scream and run away.

"Come on," Andy called as he approached the birds and they took flight.

Rizzie's long legs ran faster than mine, and she reached Andy first. The birds circled over us. Andy's arrival stopped their feeding, but they weren't ready to abandon the feast yet. They'd ripped open the body and exposed bloody innards, but there was no red hair. No gauzy purple fabric of Jane's dress. Their meal wasn't my friend.

"What is it?" I asked.

"Maybe a fawn," Andy said.

"You are sho nuff a city boy," Rizzie teased in an exaggerated drawl and laughed. "You don't see any fur around these pickings." She pointed to the edges of the torn carcass. "Feathers. It's a bird. Now look at the head."

"A pelican?" Andy asked.

"Very good." Rizzie smiled.

"What killed it?" Andy said.

"Doesn't matter," I interrupted. "We're looking for Jane."

As I followed Rizzie and Andy away from the marsh, I glanced over my shoulder. The buzzards resumed their gorge.

"I think," said Rizzie, "that we should circle along the edge of the island back toward the campground end. Look for signs of boats that may have taken your friend off the island. Along the way, there are a few abandoned shanties. We can check those and make sure she's not being held in one of them."

"Shanty" was the right word. When we reached the first one, we saw it was a one-room wooden shack that leaned perilously toward the left. Rizzie stepped into the opening, its door hanging from one hinge, and looked around. Andy and I crowded behind her. A few old dilapidated pieces of furniture lay scattered about, and there were holes in the ceiling with sky showing through them, but no Jane and no place for her to be hiding.

"Let's go," Rizzie said and led us back to the beach and along the water's edge until we reached a path that only she saw. She headed through underbrush, and we followed her to another shanty. The small porch, more like a little stoop, had rotted away and lay in pieces in front of the opening for the missing door. With their long legs, Andy and Rizzie stepped up into the building from the ground. I tried to climb, but Andy turned back and helped me into the doorway. No Jane.

Back to the beach. We took off our shoes and carried them as we walked barefooted at the edge of the waves, which were growing high with the incoming tide.

As we walked, I tried to talk about anything except my fears for Jane. Names interest me. I guess anyone named Calamine Lotion would be intrigued with how other people got their names. "Pulley Bone" Jones was obviously a nickname from the forked branch, like a turkey pulley bone, used in water dousing. I asked Rizzie, "Is your name West African?"

"Oh, no. Most of the people living on this end of the island now are here because they were born on Surcie and never wanted to leave, but before the bridge was built, young people moved to the mainland by boat. My father joined the Marines, met and married a Latina at Parris Island. I'm the result. When both of them were deployed to the Middle East, they brought me here for Maum to take care of me. My father died in the service, and my mother never came back."

"Your dad was killed in the war?" Andy asked.

"Yes, he's not buried here, though. My mother had him buried in a national cemetery even though Maum disagreed and didn't get to go to the funeral."

"And your name . . . ?" I said with a questioning look, then picked up a tiny conch shell and tossed it as far as I could into the ocean.

"Oh, that's right. You asked about my name. Rizzie is a nickname from Theresa. My real name is Maria Theresa Profit." She laughed. "So I'm mixed, but I got the Profit shade of skin so you don't see the Latina in me."

"If you grew up on the island, where'd you go to school?" Andy asked.

"We had a multigrade one-room school when I was little, but I went to high school on the mainland by boat. I completed my university studies in New York and then came back here because I like it." She narrowed her eyes at Andy. "And because Maum is getting too old to live alone and take care of Tyrone. He's not really kin, but Maum has had him since he was a baby. I make good money off the baskets and plan to open a Gullah restaurant, probably in St. Mary."

I opened my mouth to ask a question, but before a word escaped, I heard a familiar voice. "Little Sister! Is that you? Wait for us!"

The next thing I knew, a hundred and thirty pounds of Big Boy jumped on me, knocked me to my knees in the water, and kissed me all over my face. Big Boy was not who was calling me. The voice was my brother's; the kisses were from my Great Dane puppy, barely a year old, but growing bigger by the day.

My father and my oldest brother, John, jogged up to us. Actually, John ran and Daddy followed his own redneck beer belly at a much slower speed. My daddy looks like a mid-sixties-year-old Larry the Cable Guy off Comedy Central, and he acts even worse.

"Did the sheriff lift the roadblock?" I asked as I stood back up. Big Boy and I both jumped around trying to shake off the water.

"No, Little Sister," John replied. "We snuck in by boat over on this side of the island. Wayne ought to remember that we came here by boat and had parties on the campground end of the islands when we were teenagers before that area was developed. Guess he's either forgotten about boats or assumes whoever he's looking for came in with the festival fans in campers."

"I tried to call you," I said, "but cell phones are worthless on this island. There've been two murders and Jane's missing." Big Boy took off running back to the trees beyond the beach area.

"That's why we're here." John glanced back at Daddy, approaching us at his own speed—slow. "Odell called Dad's house after he picked up the bass player's body. I told him he should have called us after he picked up the first body. He knows how we feel about you and murders. He gave me the lecture that you're grown, but, Little Sister, you should have brought Jane and the Winnebago back as soon as that dwarf died." He looked toward Big Boy, who was standing behind a tree with his head sticking out on one side and his squatting back end showing on the other side. "You better call your dog," he said.

"He'll be back. He needs to potty. Where's his leash?"

"In my pocket." For the first time, I noticed the strap hanging down his pants leg. "Potty?" John continued. "I don't think you're ever going to outgrow those years teaching kindergarten. Why's he behind the tree?"

"He's gotten shy recently. He can't go if anyone's watching him."

"But we can see what he's doing."

"I said he's shy. Didn't say a word about smart. He thinks that tree is providing privacy."

"Don't let him wander off or we'll have to look for him as well as Jane. I still don't understand why you didn't come straight home when the fiddler was killed."

"The roadblock went up at the bridge immediately." I defended myself against all John's "should have's." I didn't bother to respond to his advice not to let Big Boy wander away. I wasn't the one who let him run loose without his leash in a strange place.

"You could have left before the sheriff even got here," John said. Now we had "could have's" as well as "should have's."

"Soon as you saw that body on the stage," John scolded, "you should have come home. Working at the mortuary, you surely know a corpse when you see one."

"I'm more worried about Jane than the murders," I said. Big Boy came running back toward us, but took off after a sand crab, barking and pawing at it.

"Did you bring a bag and the pooper scooper?" I asked John, who shook his head no.

"Don't worry about that here. Nobody scoops up after the deer, or other animals," Rizzie said to John. It was hard to read John's expression. Either embarrassment or confusion.

John frowned. "Odell said Wayne seems to think Jane just went off with someone, but since she found the body in my Winnebago, I think it's all connected. We came to help look for her."

"Thank you, and I'm sorry, but they've impounded your camper."

"Motor home," John corrected. "Can't you remember the difference?"

I continued, "Since you and Wayne are friends, maybe he'll release it soon." John was the least offensive of my brothers, and sometimes he'd listen to me. My other four older brothers always just talk right over me.

Daddy reached us and overheard the last part of the conversation.

"John," he said, "Calamine is obviously upset. Don't fuss at her like that in front of her friends." He gestured toward Andy and Rizzie. "She didn't plan to have a picker killed off in your fancy camper, and we came about Jane, not your new play toy." He motioned again. "Who are your friends here, Calamine?"

"This is Rizzie Profit. She lives on the island and is helping us look for Jane. Andy came from the midlands to perform. Daddy, you gotta hear him thumb-pick."

Daddy's face lit up and he grinned at Andy. "You're a thumb-picker? Any good at it?"

"I'm trying to be, sir." Respect oozed from his tone, and I wondered if this was the real Andy or the Great Pretender imitating someone he'd seen in a movie.

Daddy's face broke into a grin like he'd won the lottery. "Well, Mr. Andy Thumb-Picker, do you know why we had to come help look for Jane?"

"No, sir." I'm positive Andy expected a serious response, but I knew it would be another one of Daddy's chauvinistic jokes. It was.

"It'll be hard to track Jane because she's female, and women have smaller feet than men. Do you know why?"

"No, sir."

"Go on," I said to Andy. "Ask him why women have smaller feet than men. I've heard this for as long as I can remember."

"Okay," said Andy, "why are women's feet smaller?"

"It's one of those 'evolutionary' things. They have smaller feet so they can stand closer to the kitchen sink to wash dishes."

Daddy laughed. Andy and John smiled. Rizzie and I rolled our eyes.

Chapter Sixteen

Help? Did John say he and Daddy came to help? Their
assistance actually slowed us down. Daddy just can't
get around as well as he could years ago. John's problem
was that he kept being distracted by memories. He per-
sisted in telling us stories about when he was a teenager.
He and his friends had rowed over to Surcie Island to light
bonfires for weiner roasts and petting parties. As we
walked and he talked, Rizzie frowned at him. I doubted she
appreciated the island home she cherished being relegated
to a party place for adolescents.

Big Boy trotted along with me holding his leash in one
hand and Jane's cane in the other. I'd snapped his leash to
his collar, limiting his freedom, but I allowed him to explore the sandy beach as the incoming tide shortened the
distance from the waves to the trees and plant growth. Suddenly, he began barking ferociously.

A brown horse galloped toward us with a boy riding
bareback. He used a rope for reins.

"Tyrone," Rizzie called, but she could hardly be heard
over Big Boy's deep, loud *woof, woof*.

I jerked the leash as hard as I could to stop Big Boy when the horse reached us. My puppy was going crazy, jumping around, lunging toward the horse. None of Big Boy's usual puppy-sounding yapping. These were low, gutteral barks and growls. John grabbed the leash with me to help restrain the dog.

"Maum wants you to come home for a minute," Tyrone gasped.

"What's wrong?" Rizzie's eyes panicked. "She hasn't fallen or anything, has she?"

"No, she just wants to talk to you. Told me to ride Sugar to find you, then let you ride her home. Said for me to walk." He dismounted and handed the rope to Rizzie.

"I don't know why Maum needs me, but I gotta go," Rizzie said as she jumped onto the horse and turned back the way Tyrone had come. "I'll catch up with you later."

"Wait, let me pay you," I called.

"Pay me for baskets, pay me for food when I'm in business, but you don't pay me for helping look for a blind woman," Rizzie shouted.

"I gotta get back, too," Tyrone said and ran off behind her.

Big Boy settled down, and I said, "There went our guide."

"You don't need a guide. I know this island," John bragged.

We continued circling the island along the beach, but I thought we might find more clues if we were walking at low tide. When we returned to the campground end of the island, John suggested I show him where we'd found Jane's cane. That proved to be impossible because the waves of high tide covered the area.

"Do you know where you are?" John asked.

"On Surcie Island," Daddy answered without giving me a chance.

"Yes, but do you realize this is an inlet?" John asked. "At low tide, and I mean all the way at low tide, not just when the tide's going out, it's possible to walk across the inlet to Flower Island. There's a bridge from there to the mainland, so even with the Surcie bridge blocked, it would have been possible to remove Jane without a boat by crossing the inlet."

We looked across the water to the opposite shore.

"They're building condos on the other side of Flower Island," Daddy said. "Lots of traffic and new businesses going up over there."

"And maybe lots of places to hide a kidnap victim," Andy added.

Food for thought to me, but Daddy was having thoughts of food.

"Where can we get something to eat?" he asked.

"Two food stands between the music arena and the campground," Andy said.

"We might as well head over there," John said. "Can't see much at high tide."

Both Bob's Best Barbecue and Marie's Grill had reopened for business. The men decided on barbecue and were immediately handed baskets and drinks, but I stepped up to Marie's window and ordered a hamburger, which the server said she'd put on the grill immediately. I took Big Boy to John, Daddy, and Andy. Daddy tied the leash to the table leg. Back in line at Marie's, I heard a familiar voice.

"Whass up?"

I knew that phrase well enough to recognize Bone before turning around.

"Any luck?" he asked.

"No, but did you know that the spot where we found the cane is in an inlet and Jane could have been removed from the island there during low tide? Flower Island is on the other side of the inlet, and Daddy said there's a lot of construction going on over there."

"Yeah, I worked over there some," Bone answered.

"Water witching?" I asked.

"No, I do construction work as well as dousing. Was

helping build a crab restaurant, but the investors backed out of the deal." He lit a cigarette. "The ocean was almost at low tide not long before the storm. Jane could have been taken across or could have walked it herself."

"Not likely she could have gone by herself without her cane."

"Don't forget that storm."

I squeezed my eyes shut to stop tears from coming. If Jane had been walking across the inlet by herself during the storm, she might have been washed into the ocean. She might never be found.

"Hey, I didn't mean to make you cry," Bone said, then ordered two hot dogs. He leaned over me and asked, "Think there's any chance I could comfort you?"

"You're disgusting at times," I said and thought, *Most of the time.*

"In that case, double the onions," Bone said to the server. "Never can tell." He turned back to me. "Used to be a man who stood by the door at June Bug's club and asked every female to go home with him. 'Course, he said it a lot cruder than that. He swore he got lucky more often than he got slapped." He grinned. "Did you know June Bug's place burned last year? I heard his widowed wife set it on fire."

I made no comment, but I wondered if the guy by the door was one of the reasons Daddy and The Boys had forbidden me to go to June Bug's when I was younger. They hadn't wanted me there after I grew up, either, though I'd been there one time. By the way, I lump my five brothers together with the expression "The Boys." They're all older than I am, but aside from John, they'll probably be "boys" until they're all potbellied and gray-haired or bald.

Since my hamburger had to be cooked to order but Bone's hot dogs came from a rotisserie, he received his order before I did mine. "Want to sit with me?" he asked.

"No, I'm with them," I replied and motioned toward the

table with my father, my brother, my dog, and my hope-fully maybe someday boyfriend.

"Good, I'll join 'em," Bone said and headed toward the table.

By the time the server handed me my hamburger, the others had finished eating. "In olden days, dowsers located lots more than water," Bone was saying. "I'm partial to wa-ter and usually limit myself to dowsing for water. Water is clean. In my opinion, water is godly. Bread may be the staff of life, but water is the *stuff* of life, especially ocean water with the salt in it."

My brother John raised his eyebrows and looked at me. I knew he was thinking Bone was "another of Callie's weird friends," not knowing that Bone and I had just met and he certainly was *not* a friend of mine. At least Bone *wasn't* a friend of mine, until he added, "Yeah, I don't nor-mally dowse anything except water, but I'm considering using rods to try to locate Jane."

"I'd like to see that," Daddy said. John agreed that he and Daddy would follow Bone to his camper for the "witching" equipment.

"I might try to catch up with you later," I said as they walked away. Like Daddy, I wanted to see Bone dowse for Jane, but I didn't have any faith that he could do it, and I was sick and tired of Bone's obnoxious ways.

"I'll stay here with Callie," Andy said, making Big Boy happy by scratching behind his ears and making me very happy just because he wasn't leaving with the others.

"Tell me more about how you developed your act . . ." I began, but was immediately interrupted by the popping and snorting arrival of the Profits' beat-up Chevy truck pulling in between the two food stands and parking danger-ously close to the table that had replaced the plywood Gas-tric Gullah stand.

"Hey, Callie," Rizzie called as she climbed down from the driver's seat.

When I was a little girl and said "Hey," my brothers

always told me "Hay is for horses." A semantics professor at the university taught that "hey" for hello is a southern colloquialism while most northerners say "hi." In Southernese, that term refers to a state of moderate intoxication, by way of either alcohol or drugs. When I was young and said "Guess what?" my brothers answered "Chicken butt." I don't recall the professor ever mentioning that.

"I've brought my cookers," Rizzie said. "Maum wants me to cut the prices and sell as much as I can. Shouldn't refreeze fish." Andy helped Rizzie unload the truck.

"Maum wants to meet you, Callie, so ride back to the house with me, okay?"

"I can't," I answered. "I've got my dog with me."

"I'll dog-sit," Andy offered.

"Not necessary." Rizzie looked at him. "You and the dog can ride in the back, and Callie can sit up front with me."

"Isn't it against the law to ride in the open back of a pickup?" Andy asked.

"Not on this island, it's not," Rizzie told him.

My first reaction to this was horror and fright. My Big Boy had never ridden in the back of a truck. What if he tried to jump out? Ridiculous. I was letting my fear for Jane color all my thoughts and emotions. I rode in the open back of Daddy's pickups all the time growing up. Andy was an adult man, perfectly able to hold Big Boy's leash tight enough to keep the dog in the truck. Besides, if I suggested that Andy ride in the truck cab with Rizzie and I sit in the back with the dog, I'd probably insult Andy's masculinity.

It was just as well that Rizzie didn't say much during the ride because the truck made so much noise, I couldn't have heard her anyway. We left the campground, what Rizzie called the developed end of the island, and rode in the truck over the rutted roads we'd walked on earlier. She turned off onto a track I hadn't noticed before and parked in front of one of the better-looking houses I'd seen on the island. The front of the building was bricked while the sides were wooden. That's common in this area. Azaleas planted right below the porch were in full bloom, plastering the foundation in dark pink.

"Keep Big Boy in the truck," I called to Andy when I saw several hens and a rooster pecking around in the unfenced yard.

"Don't worry. He's already seen them," Andy replied and laughed.

I looked up, expecting to see the dog pulling at his leash to get himself a chicken. I'd intentionally never taken him anywhere near fowl of any kind. In rural areas, a chicken-eating or egg-sucking dog is sometimes put down if he can't be broken of bad habits.

Instead, Big Boy had his tail between his legs and was backing away from the side of the truck bed. Rizzie picked up a plump hen and held it toward Andy. Big Boy whimpered, cringed, and tried to hide behind Andy's legs. My big puppy, who weighed more than I did, was scared of a chicken, yet he'd felt brave enough to challenge a horse.

"He's quivering," Andy said.

"Put him in the front of the truck," Rizzie offered.

Andy tried, then I tried, but we couldn't coax Big Boy out of the back of the Chevy. He just cried and backed away.

"I'll sit here with him," Andy said.

Rizzie led me into the house, where her gray-haired grandmother sat in an old mission rocking chair in front of blazing wood in the fireplace. She clutched a quilt up to her chin. I could tell that though tiny and wrinkled now, in her younger years, she'd been a beautiful smaller version of Rizzie.

"Maum, this is Callie. You asked to see her," Rizzie said.

"Hello, Mrs. Profit," I said.

"Hello. I wanted to tell you that I've been praying for your blind friend to return," the elderly lady said. Her voice was tinier and even more frail than her body seemed.

"Thank you," I said.

"I apologize for it being so hot in here with the fire going, but old bones are cold bones. They need lots of heat."

"Yes, ma'am."

"I wanted to talk to you about something else, too. At first, I thought I should wait until your worries about your friend are over, but the more I thought about it, the more I wanted to see you today. As old and cold as my bones are, I don't want to wait too long."

"Yes, ma'am," I repeated. I had no idea where this was going.

"Rizzie," she said and motioned toward a chair, "bring that seat here for your friend."

I sat beside Rizzie's Maum and waited for what she wanted to tell me.

"Rizzie says that what you do is make people look nice after they die."

"Yes, ma'am." I fully expected Mrs. Profit to object to some aspect of the preparation methods, to forbid some procedure.

"What I want . . ." She paused. I waited.

"What I want," she repeated, "is for you to paint my fingernails when I die. I always wanted them red, but my husband didn't like red. I'd do it myself, but my eyes have grown so old that I don't see well enough."

"Maum, why didn't you ask me to do that for you?" Rizzie asked.

"You're working so hard to start your food business. I didn't want to bother you, but when you told me what Callie's job is, I knew she's not afraid of death and thought maybe she'd paint my nails red for me when I die."

"Mrs. Profit, I will be pleased to give you a manicure and polish your fingernails just as red as you like, but let's not wait until you're dead. I'll do it as soon as I can, so that you can enjoy them yourself."

"Bright red," she said.

"When the sheriff lets us leave the island, I'll put what I'll need into my purse, and when I come back to Surcie, I'll do your fingernails," I promised.

Mrs. Profit turned toward Rizzie. "I don't care what your grampa thought. I like red."

"What about your toenails?" I asked. "Want them red, too?"

"Sure do," the tiny voice said. Rizzie's grandmother smiled, and her face belied the years.

The lady was beautiful.

Chapter Seventeen

We were barely a half mile from Maum's house when Andy beat on the window of the truck cab, and Big Boy set up a long howl. I turned and looked out the back windshield. Andy was pointing over toward the driver's side.

Beyond the pitted road, Bone walked slowly over the marsh with his head thrown back and both arms jutting straight out in front of him.

"Rizzie," I said, "there's Bone. Let's see what he's doing and ask him about John and Daddy."

Rizzie hit the brakes, and the Chevy lurched to a stop. Andy and Big Boy piled out the back while Rizzie and I climbed down from the cab.

"Hey, Bone," I yelled, and he headed toward us, maintaining his slow, steady speed with his arms directly in front of him. As he neared, I saw that he held a smooth, forked branch at a direct ninety-degree angle from his body. The dowsing tool did look like a giant turkey pulley bone with Bone holding both sides and a long tail jutting away from him.

"Whass up?" Bone called when he neared us. "Any news on Jane?"

"Not that we know of," Rizzie answered him.

Big Boy jumped up on Bone and sniffed the branch.

"Down, Boy, down," I said, and miracles never cease, the dog actually sat. Like some of my former five-year-old students, Big Boy doesn't always follow my instructions.

"Thought you were going to water-witch for Jane," Rizzie said. "This grass isn't high enough to conceal a full-grown woman."

"I'm dowsing for anything related to Roxanne," Bone said.

"Roxanne? Who's Roxanne?" Andy asked.

"Oops, slip of the tongue," Bone mumbled. "I meant to say Jane."

Wanting to redirect the conversation, I said, "Where are Daddy and my brother? I thought they were with you."

"The sheriff's lifting the roadblock," Bone said, still walking slowly around us. "Your brother said they were going to take their boat back to the mainland and get your car to pick you up when the bridge opens."

"Sheriff Harmon's letting people leave? Has he arrested someone?"

"Don't know about the arrest, but he's releasing folks."

I turned toward Rizzie. "Let's get back to the campground," I said. "I want to find out what's going on."

Just as we climbed into the truck, Bone called, "Look here."

He'd stopped and stood perfectly still with his arms parallel to the earth. The long "tail" of the branch pointed to the ground. When he stepped away, the branch rose back horizontal in front of him. He moved back, and the stick again seemed to reach for the dirt.

"There's something here," Bone shouted with excitement. "Andy, dig around where the branch is pointing."

Andy handed me Big Boy's leash and stooped in front of Bone. He sifted through the earth with his fingers until he found something. A hot pink cubic zirconium earring, an earring just like the ones Jane was wearing when she disappeared.

Buh-leeve me. This was confusing. If Jane lost her cane on the beach near the inlet, how did her earring get on the dirt road on the other side of the island? Was it even my friend's earring? Jane didn't own any expensive jewelry. Most of her pieces came from discount stores or flea market sales. It was entirely possible that this earring wasn't even hers. Entirely possible she still wore both of her pink baubles.

"What do you want to do now?" Rizzie asked. "Follow Bone or go back to the campground? I've gotta get to the concession area and decide what to do with those coolers full of shark. I really wish everyone had to stay here at least through tonight, so I could sell some food."

"I'll go with you," I said. "I want to know about the one more day of the festival. Maybe the sheriff is letting people onto the island but not off."

Andy climbed onto the truck bed with Big Boy. Rizzie and I got back in front. Bone ran to my window.

"Here," he said, handing me the earring. "Give it to the sheriff and tell him I'll mark the place I found it."

Everyone seemed to be packing up when we reached the campground. Bob's Barbecue was gone, and the Marie's Grill folks were closing.

"Guess there's no point in trying to cook," Rizzie said. Andy offered to help her load the cooker and coolers onto the truck.

I didn't volunteer my services. I took Big Boy's leash and headed toward the bridge, hoping Sheriff Harmon would be there.

Two for the price of one. Well, I guess three for the price of one. Daddy and John were standing with Sheriff Harmon at the island side of the bridge.

"Did you arrest anyone?" I asked the sheriff.

"Not yet, but I have some leads. I think Happy Jack

Wilburn was going to stroke out if I kept Surcie Island closed off any longer, and I doubt it makes that much difference anyway."

"What kind of leads?" I said.

"Now, Callie, you know I can't tell you those facts," Sheriff Harmon answered.

"Then maybe I won't give you what we found that might be Jane's," I retorted.

"We've already played that game with Jane's stick," Harmon said. "Where did you put it?"

Ex-cuuze me. I'd forgotten the cane in the cab of Rizzie's truck.

"I'm not talking about that. I have something else now," I replied.

Daddy put his arm around my shoulder. "Calamine," he said, "stop fooling around and give Wayne any evidence you have. He's the sheriff and he's trying to find Jane as well as solve two murder cases. This isn't the time to act like a little girl."

"No," John added. "Stop playing games."

My feelings were hurt. It didn't seem fair for all three of them to gang up on me, but perhaps I was being foolish. I reached in my pocket, pulled out the earring, and handed it to Sheriff Harmon.

"Jane was wearing jewelry like this," I said.

"Do you know for sure this one's hers?" The sheriff took the earring and rolled it around in the palm of his hand.

"Not really."

"Where'd you find it?"

"Pulley Bone Jones found it on the road from Rizzie Profit's house on the other side of the island," I said.

"What about the stick?" the sheriff asked.

"I forgot and left it in Rizzie's truck. She's in the concession area loading up her cooking equipment."

"Okay, I'll go over there and get it. Let me know if you find anything else or think of something that might help." Harmon had on his cop voice. I knew I wouldn't get any info from him. I watched him walk toward the camp-ground.

"What about the festival?" I asked Daddy.

"It's over. Jack Wilburn's going to refund tickets or trade them for a bigger festival in the fall. Happy Jack isn't very happy at the moment."

"Neither is Fred Delgado nor Kenny Strickland," I quipped without thinking.

"Calamine!" Daddy scolded.

"Meanwhile, I left my laptop at the house with Mike and Frank," John said. "They're trying to create a 'Missing' flyer for Jane. Since you can leave now, the poster might look better if you take over that job."

"Where's Bill?" I asked. My five brothers, in order by age, are John, Bill, Mike, Jim, and Frank. Jim's in the Middle East on a U.S. Navy ship. John lives in Atlanta with his wife, Miriam, and their kids. He'd brought me the Winnebago for the festival and planned to spend the weekend with Daddy and the brothers, then drive the motor home back to Georgia. I worried that John would want to keep my Mustang until he got his camper back.

Mike and Frank were living with Daddy because they were both between marriages and girlfriends. Bill moved in and out of the house depending on how he and Molly were getting along. Sometimes he slept at home, sometimes at her place. The last I'd heard, he was back with Molly.

"No telling where Bill is," John said.

"He and Molly must be doing all right then," I commented.

"Who knows? He—" Daddy said gruffly.

"Callie," John interrupted, "where are your things? Let's get off the island before Wayne changes his mind."

"My clothes and belongings—or 'things,' as you call them—are still in your Winnebago. Sheriff Harmon wouldn't let Jane and me back in there after we found Kenny's body."

John waved toward my vintage Mustang parked by the road. "Pile in, then, and let's go."

Daddy and John took the front seats, and I sat in the back with Big Boy. I can't explain how good it felt to leave that island, though it's beautiful, nor how bad it felt not to have Jane by my side.

I insisted that we go by my apartment so I could shower and change clothes even though my place isn't on the way from Surcie Island to Daddy's house. I'd washed myself in Broken Fence's bus, but I was still wearing Arnie's shirt and shorts. The shower felt wonderful. I used lavender-scented body wash and rose-scented shampoo, then lathered on rich, thick honeysuckle skin lotion. I blew my hair dry and used heather-scented spray on it. By the time I walked out of the bathroom wearing khaki shorts and a floral-printed tee, I smelled like the bouquet on my shirt.

Expecting to see only Daddy and John, I was surprised to see Mike and Frank sitting on the couch. Frank jumped up and handed me a piece of paper.

"Check this out, Callie," he said. It was a flyer for Jane, giving information about her disappearance and the sheriff's phone number. Even had her photo on it.

"Where'd you get the picture?" I asked.

"Oh, I scanned one that I had," Frank answered with a self-conscious smile that confirmed my occasional suspicion that he had a crush on Jane.

"How'd you get here?" I asked my brothers.

"John called and told us to bring the computer stuff over. Said no telling how long it might take you to get yourself back together," Mike answered. "We think the quickest way to do this is to have copies made at FedEx Kinko's in Beaufort, then split up to post them everywhere. I brought tacks, tape, and a couple of hammers."

Daddy, John, Big Boy, and I rode in my car to Beaufort. I have a special harness-type seat belt for Big Boy. Mike and Frank followed in Mike's pickup. When the copies were ready, we divided them between the vehicles and assigned areas to post them. Daddy, John, and I headed toward the sea islands near Surcie while Mike and Frank would put signs up along the way from Beaufort to St. Mary and in town.

We put the ragtop down, and Big Boy looked like a spotted Scooby-Doo sitting tall in the back. I probably resembled Shaggy. We stopped every mile or so and nailed a poster to a telephone pole. We went into stores and asked permission to tape the flyers in their windows. I was watching out for places to post the notices, not paying much attention to where John drove.

I looked up as we bounced across a bridge. "Are we going to Flower Island?"

"Yes, let's plaster them everywhere. Maybe Jane did make it across the inlet during low tide, and one of the construction workers might have seen her," John said.

"Not much of a bridge," I commented.

"Oh, the rich folks who buy the condos will see to it that the bridge is replaced," Daddy said. "Lots of power in money."

The sun had set and the moon was high in the sky by the time we'd finished hanging flyers and asking people if they'd seen the girl in the picture. John offered to buy Daddy and me dinner, but I just wanted to go home. He called Frank and Mike on Mike's cell phone, and they eagerly accepted John's offer to feed them. I dropped Daddy and John off at Hooters to meet them.

When Big Boy and I got home, he was eager to be walked, but I was exhausted. I turned my back so he could do his business, then took him in, fed him, and flopped across my bed without even changing clothes. I thought I'd be too upset about Jane to sleep, but when the sound of Big Boy snoring right by my ear woke me, it was two o'clock in the morning. I hadn't even checked my answering machine when I got home. Hoping the flashing light I saw on it now signaled good news, I pushed the "Play" button.

"Callie," said Otis. "I hate to ask you this, but will you please come in tomorrow morning? I really need you."

I wondered how he knew I was off Surcie Island and back home, but in a town the size of St. Mary, news travels fast.

I wished it was good news more often.

Chapter Eighteen

Time is relevant. Five minutes waiting for something good is definitely longer than five minutes waiting for something unpleasant. As I pulled the Mustang into the mortuary's parking lot Sunday morning, it seemed I'd been gone for ages, though only two days had passed since Jane and I went to the festival. I understand that certain illegal substances can have the same effect, making time stretch beyond reality. No, I'm not talking from experience, and I'm not claiming to have read about it. Jane told me.

The thought of Jane brought a fresh flood of tears. Still no word from her or about her. Her kidnapping couldn't have been for ransom. Neither of us had any money, and her only relative was her father. The good Lord only knows where he is. He abandoned Jane and her mother when he learned his baby girl was blind. Both my heart and my head told me that Jane's disappearance was connected to the two murders on Surcie Island. But how?

When I wheeled around to my designated parking place in the back, I noticed a Gates Electric Company van parked beside a large delivery truck backed up to the loading dock. Otis stepped out of the building just as I closed my car door.

"Hey, Callie," he called. "Any news about Jane?"

"Not a word," I said.

"I appreciate your coming in for Mrs. Martin. Hated to call you, but I really need you for this. She's ready for you in your workroom." Otis motioned for the driver to back the truck closer to the loading dock.

"Any special instructions?" I asked. Sometimes folks specify things, like what color nail polish they want me to use. Though I'm like a girl Friday at Middleton's, my official responsibility is to create beautiful memories of our clients' loved ones, and Otis calling me showed he recognized how well I do my work.

"No," Otis called back. He held up his hand for the truck to halt, then added, "She's the worst case of jaundice I've ever seen. There's a picture on the counter for you to see how the family wants her hair."

The truck driver opened the rear of the truck and began strapping a large casket-sized rectangular crate onto an industrial dolly.

"This way," Otis told him when he finished. The driver pushed the dolly behind Otis straight to the prep room. I was right behind them.

I thought Mrs. Martin's family must have ordered a custom coffin, especially since it was being delivered on Sunday morning. Otherwise, Otis would have led the deliveryman to the casket display area, but that didn't make sense. Even if it were for Mrs. Martin, my workroom is where a body is usually casketed.

While I was gone, someone had removed one of the two embalming tables from the prep room. Then I got it. The crate didn't hold a casket. Otis and Odell were replacing one of the tables. Clyde Gates, the electrician, stood in the corner. He looked at me and winked. What's with all this winking?

"Do we have a new prep table?" I asked Otis.

Busy helping the truck driver place the crate where the missing table had been, Otis ignored me.

"Not quite," Clyde said.

"We don't ever embalm two at a time anyway," Otis said when he and the driver had the box off the dolly. They began opening it.

"Then what is it?"

Otis swept his hand across his hair implants, which always make me think of sprouts. He looked down and meticulously picked a piece of lint from his expensive black suit.

"Something I've wanted for a long time," he said. "I don't have room for it in my apartment, and I decided it made more sense to put it here."

If it waddles like a duck, looks like a duck, and quacks like a duck, it's probably a duck. This crate wasn't walking or talking, but it sure looked casket-sized and casket-shaped. I just couldn't picture Otis wanting even the most elegant or unique coffin at his apartment. What would he do with it? Put a piece of glass on top and use it as an oversized coffee table?

When the box was uncrated, it looked like a slightly flattened casket covered in heavy opaque plastic with a nine-by-twelve-inch beige-colored envelope taped to it. Clyde pulled off the envelope, opened it, and removed a stack of papers. "Yeah," he said as he read. "I see exactly what we need. Won't be hard to hook it up. I'll bring in the supplies and get started." He grinned as he left. "Sure you don't mind paying overtime for this, Otis?"

"Not at all. I'm eager to try it out. I promised you overtime when I called you as soon as I knew it would be here today."

Otis signed the delivery papers and removed the plastic. I realized what they'd uncrated about the time Odell entered the room.

"What's that?" he boomed.

Odell and Otis are identical twins who decided years ago that Otis would always wear black suits and Odell would wear navy blue so that people could tell them apart. It's no longer necessary since Otis got hair implants and

Odell shaved his head. Odell is also addicted to barbecue—
any kind. Chicken, beef, or pork. Pulled or chopped. Red
sauce, mustard sauce, or vinegar and pepper. The difference in his and his vegetarian twin's diets has resulted in
forty pounds of bulk, but they stick to their designated
colors.

I, by the way, am not allowed to wear navy blue or
slacks or skirts on the job. I wear black dresses with stock-
ings and plain black leather pumps, which is what the
twins' mother wore when she worked at the funeral home.

"Is this some new piece of embalming equipment? You
didn't ask me about buying anything," Odell said as he
lifted the lid. "Do you put the body inside? What does
it do?"

I tried, I promise I tried, but I couldn't help teasing. "It
changes the color of the skin," I said to Odell. Clyde, at the
door, guffawed.

Odell scratched his bald head. "I saw Mrs. Martin on
Callie's table, and she's mighty yellow, but I don't think
you oughta go making big purchases without discussing
them with me, Otis."

Clyde and I howled with laughter.

"After all," Odell continued, "we've dealt with more severe discoloration before, and I'm sure Callie can cover
Mrs. Martin's yellow with airbrushing if makeup won't do
the job."

Otis's words were so low that I barely heard them. "It's
a tanning bed."

"A *what?*" Odell bellowed. "What the . . ." Odell said a
word I didn't use even before I took up kindergarten
cussing. "Why the [another bad word] would we want to
tan a corpse?"

"It's not for bodies. It's for me," Otis murmured.

"Then why is it *here?*" Odell's voice lowered a few
decibels.

"I don't have room for it in my apartment, and I decided
it would be better here anyway. It'll be good for business
because I won't have to take off to go to Bronze Bods. I can

just fit tanning into my workday." A hopeful expression crossed his face. "You and Callie might even want to use it."

Buh-leeve me. I knew it was time to get out of there. "I'm going to set Mrs. Martin's hair," I said and left before anyone had time to reply.

In my workroom, I put on my smock and gloves, then lifted the sheet that covered Mrs. Martin up to her chin. As usual, Otis had put panties and a bra on the lady. I view our work like a medical task and wouldn't be offended by a nude body, but Otis and Odell are very respectful of corpses and of me. When embalming is completed, bodies are washed and dressed in underwear before being moved to my space for cosmetizing.

Nope, that's not a mistake. It's the word for what I do. Like I said, I earned my South Carolina cosmetology license in high school vocational ed, and that qualifies me to do hair, makeup, manicures, and pedicures in mortuaries.

The longer I'm in this business, the more aware I become of the special language of funeral homes. I call it Funeralese. In that special mortuary language, I'm a cosmetitian who cosmetizes. Dead people aren't corpses, cadavers, nor bodies. They're called by their proper names, and they are prepped, not embalmed. Don't misunderstand; they actually *are* embalmed. We just don't call it that.

Anyway, back to Mrs. Martin. Definitely yellow. Not a subdued Dijon shade. She was bright. Almost like French's mustard that goes on hot dogs. Not gourmet hot dogs either. Cheap ones with red frankfurters. Jane loves those hot dogs, especially with extra onions.

My stomach clenched, and I trembled. Where was Jane? Was she alive? Was she being mistreated? I reached up to wipe away tears with my gloved hand but the latex just smeared the wetness on my face. I grabbed a handful of tissues from the supply table, sat on a stool, and fought to keep myself together. Where was Jane? What was happening to her? The thoughts repeated themselves. I'm always reading mysteries, and my mind couldn't deal with all the horrible things I'd read about kidnappers doing to their prey.

When I finally regained control, I sprayed a diluted setting gel on Mrs. Martin's hair and curled it with big brush rollers. Some cosmetitians would have airbrushed a flesh tone only on her hands, face, and neck, but I covered every speck of skin that wasn't beneath her bra and panties. In the photo, she'd appeared pale. When I was done, she had a light, creamy complexion without a hint of yellow.

Like a robot. I felt like a robot going through the motions, but working on "automatic." Manicure with clear polish. Makeup. Hair comb-out. All the while, I was thinking of Jane. When I finished, I returned to the prep room. Clyde and Otis were checking out the controls on the tanning bed. Odell was leaving, grumbling about Clyde being paid overtime to work on a Sunday.

"Hey, Otis," I said, "where are the clothes for Mrs. Martin?"

"Don't have them yet. Family will bring them." Otis glanced at his watch. "I thought they'd be here by now."

A soft, instrumental version of "Blessed Assurance" announced that someone had come in. Spiritual music plays over the sound system anytime the front door opens at Middleton's.

Otis said, "That's probably the Martins now." He headed for the hall.

I hurried to take off my smock and gloves so I could ask if they wanted color on Mrs. Martin's nails. The prep room bell rang, letting me know Otis wanted me up front. A light on the panel showed that he'd rung for me from one of the consultation rooms.

When I reached them, Otis was sitting not with the Martin family, but with Melena Delgado. She wore a short denim skirt, stretchy white shirt that bared her shoulders, and white flats. She rose and asked, "Any news about your friend?"

I choked a little as I tried to answer, and Otis said, "No word at all about Jane."

"I'm so sorry. I know you're upset. Don't know how you're working. Not knowing and all."

Dalmation! How dare she insinuate that I shouldn't be working? Or that maybe I was less upset than I should be? Wasn't she the widow who was flirting with Andy *on the day her husband died*? Wasn't she the widow who reached to catch a bridal bouquet the very next day?

The Middletons stress always being courteous at work no matter what is said or done. I could feel my jaw clench, and I shook a little with anger. Otis motioned me to sit in one of the overstuffed chairs and defended me in his smoothest undertaker voice.

"Miss Parrish came in for a short while because we really needed her today for a special assignment, but I also believe that it's better for her to keep busy than to sit home and worry."

Melena backed off immediately. "Oh, of course! I didn't mean to imply any criticism. I'm just surprised to see her here."

"Then why did you ask for her?" That's the most confrontational thing I've ever heard Otis say to a customer.

Melena had the good grace to look embarrassed. "I guess I just wanted you to be aware that Callie and I know each other. Since she's who told me about Middleton's." She glanced at me. "I'm sorry if I upset you, Callie. We just have to hope that if something happens to Jane, it will be like my poor Fred, and she won't suffer."

From what I'd heard, there was hardly any way Fred didn't feel anything when that tuning fork was rammed into his brain, but if she wanted to believe it was a painless death, I wasn't about to argue about it. Neither was Otis.

"That's okay," Otis said in a soothing tone. "Now, what can we do to help you?"

"As I said when I came in, I'm Melena Delgado, and my husband was the fiddler who died at the bluegrass festival Friday. Someone from here carried his body to Charleston for the autopsy." She paused.

"That was Mr. Middleton's brother," I said and nodded toward Otis.

"Well, I've talked to Fred's family up north, and they've

agreed to have the service here in South Carolina. I'm from Adam's Creek, and my family has a crypt there, so I thought I'd have you handle the services and everything when they release Fred to me."

"Of course. We'll be pleased to serve you," Otis said as he pulled a set of planning papers from a drawer.

"Do you know how long it will take for the autopsy? What I mean is, how soon should I expect Fred's body back from Charleston?"

"No way to tell. We certainly will pick him up as soon as he's released. If you plan now, we could have the service the following day."

"Oh, no." Melena's eyes widened in shock. "I need time to get the word out, so his music friends can all come. Fred was very well known."

"No problem." Otis looked down at the planning papers. "Is your crypt in the mausoleum at Eternity Perpetual Care in Adam's Creek?" he asked.

"No, it's not a crypt like that. It's a family crypt over in the old Baptist churchyard."

"Was Fred a Catholic?" I asked and immediately regretted my politically incorrect assumption that the last name "Delgado" meant the man was Catholic.

"We haven't been much of any religion since we spent so much time on the road after we got married, but I was raised Baptist, and there's room for Fred there, so I don't see any need to buy a burial plot." Melena sniffed. I handed her one of our aloe-imbedded tissues. She wiped at her nose, then held the tissue up to her eye as though to wipe away a tear. Just like before, there were no tears in her eyes, but I handed her another tissue anyway. Can't have the bereaved wiping away fake tears with a boogery tissue.

"Just a Closer Walk with Thee" played softly through the hidden speaker in the consultation room, and Otis nodded at me. I wanted to stay and listen to Melena's plans, but that music meant someone had opened the front door. That nod meant for me to go see who it was.

"Oonuh hongry?" greeted me.

"Kind of," I answered Rizzie.

Today she wore Skechers, jeans, and a T-shirt that had "Great Gullah Girl" printed on it. Only about half an inch of hair all over Rizzie's head kept her from being as bald as Odell, but the short hair emphasized her fine bones and ebony eyes.

"Had to come to town to buy the red polish for Maum. I saw all the flyers about your friend posted everywhere. When I passed by this place, I remembered you work here and turned around to come back and see if you've heard anything and if I could take you to lunch."

"No, still no word," I said. "I'll bring the red polish. You don't have to buy it."

"If Maum told me to buy it, I buy it. Sorry Jane's not back yet." "Sorry" is a word I hear often in my business, but Rizzie said it like she meant it. "Can you go to lunch with me?"

"I'd love to, but I don't know if I can. I'll have to check with my boss, and I can't interrupt him right now. He's in a planning consultation with Little Fiddlin' Fred's wife."

"You mean widow," Rizzie corrected.

"Yes, I mean widow. She's going to bury him in Adam's Creek."

"Yeah, Bone's from around here, and she's his sister, you know."

"I knew that."

"Why don't you show me around while your boss is busy?"

"Not much to show. Middleton's is about like any other funeral home."

"Not like Gullah."

"Gullah funeral home? Guess I never thought about that."

"Not a whole lot different these days, though some Gullah still want the body brought to the house for the wake, and we still bury our dead in island cemeteries like the one you saw. Don't need all that perpetual care stuff they try to sell in town. The way we see it is that if anyone's surviving in a family, they'll keep the graves clean, and when there's no one left to care for them, there won't be anybody to mind if they get grown over." She laughed. Full, rich, and throaty.

I showed her through Slumber Rooms A, B, and C, our chapel, the consulting room that wasn't in use, my office, and the kitchen area.

"But I want to see the private rooms, where you embalm the bodies."

"First, I don't embalm anyone. I'm not licensed to do more than hair, makeup, and clothing. Second, I could lose my job for taking any unauthorized person into the prep rooms."

"Then I suppose it's out of the question for me to watch an embalming?"

"Afraid so. Privacy laws. Why would you want to see it anyway? I deal with death all the time, but I still don't like to watch embalming. Why would you want to?"

"Back in the old days, when someone died, the family built a coffin and washed and dressed the body. Neighbors gathered and did what needed to be done. They dug the grave, had the funeral, and left the gifts there like you saw. That's how Maum wants to be buried when she dies. She's never been off Surcie Island, and she doesn't want to be brought off when she dies. She wants to be buried in the old way, but I'd like to picture her body staying like it is, so I want her embalmed. I thought maybe if I watched one, I could do it myself."

"Rizzie, embalming isn't a do-it-yourself project you can learn by watching or taking a home improvement class at Lowe's. When the time comes, you let me know, and I can probably get Otis or Odell to go to the island and take care of your grandmother. I'd be lying to you if I told you that embalming will mean she's going to stay the same forever, though."

"Can I just see your room where you put on the makeup?" she asked.

"No. Maybe I'll show it to you some other time when there's no one in there."

"Have you got Little Fiddlin' Fred in your workroom?"

"No, he's still at the medical center in Charleston."

Just then, Melena and Otis came from the consultation room. "I really appreciate your help," Melena said to Otis. She stared at Rizzie before her face lit up into an expression of recognition. "I saw you at the campground, too, but I don't think I got your name." She extended her hand to Rizzie.

"Yes, I was at the bluegrass flop," Rizzie said. "I'm Rizzie Profit, and I know you're Melena Delgado." She released Melena's hand. "I'm sorry for your loss."

The widow wiped her eyes with a tissue she'd been holding. I wondered if she'd wiped her nose on this one, too.

"It's going to be hard going on without Fred, but we have to just grin and bear it."

I didn't know if Melena realized what she'd said or if the surprised expressions on everyone else's faces made her aware of it.

"I didn't mean that the way it sounded," she stammered. "It's just an expression. I don't mean anyone should grin about Fred's death."

"We understand, Mrs. Delgado." Every time I think I've heard Otis talk in the smoothest, most soothing tone possible, he kicks it up a notch. His voice would have calmed a wild bull. "Call us if you think of anything else or change your mind and want a wreath and folding chairs delivered anywhere."

"I'll be in touch as soon as the sheriff says Fred can come back."

"We'll notify you if we hear before you do. It's our responsibility to pick up your husband from the medical center. We would have had to contact you when we received word to go for him."

Melena looked confused.

Otis explained, "We would have needed to ask you if Mr. Delgado was to be sent somewhere out of town or to another local caregiver."

"Caregiver?" Confusion turned total on Melena's face.

"He means service provider, another funeral home," I said.

Melena nodded understanding and left.

Otis closed the door behind her and softly said, "Grin and bear it?" He looked at Rizzie, realized she'd heard, and apologized.

"Don't worry about it," Rizzie replied. "It was a strange comment for her to make, but she's probably under a lot of stress."

"Yes, we see people react in many ways." Otis nodded.

"I stopped by to check on Callie and invite her to lunch. She said she didn't know when it would be convenient."

"Oh, sure." Otis smiled. "You go on to lunch, Callie. I brought a sandwich from home, and Odell should be back soon."

"What about Mrs. Martin?" I asked.

"I peeked at her while Mrs. Delgado went to the ladies' room. You did a great job. It looked like you're finished except for dressing, and you can't do that until the family brings the clothing."

Rizzie and I had almost reached her beat-up Chevy truck when Otis ran out calling, "Callie! Wait, Callie!"

My heart leaped into my throat. Had somebody called about Jane?

"Have you put up flyers in Adam's Creek? Someone needs to take a look at Mrs. Delgado's family crypt. Make sure there's space for another entombment and see if we need a brick mason. Why don't you drive over after lunch? You can put up posters and check the cemetery. I'll dress Mrs. Martin when the clothes come. Otis and I can handle her visitation tonight. And Callie"—he paused—"I'll pay you for the whole day."

I almost reminded him that he was paying Clyde Gates overtime for Sunday work, but I kept my mouth shut.

Chapter Nineteen

Ten minutes later, Rizzie and I headed down Highway 17 in my Mustang. She wasn't in a hurry to get back to Surcie Island and suggested lunch in Adam's Creek since I had to go there anyway. I had boxes of flyers, nails, tacks, a hammer, and tape in my car, so I offered to drive.

The weather was perfect South Carolina spring—not hot like the week before, but not cool enough for a jacket either. We put the top down before leaving the funeral home and left her truck parked at Middleton's.

Rizzie Profit seemed like a very nice person, but Jane usually rode in the passenger seat. She liked to ride with the ragtop down. She'd tie her long red hair back with a scrunchie, but it still flew all around and flapped against her face and rose-colored glasses. Rizzie was nice, but I wished she were Jane. Not that I wanted Rizzie to be in any danger—I didn't want the two of them to trade places—I just wanted Jane beside me. I didn't want anyone kidnapped. That's what it had to be. No matter that the news commentators were calling her just "missing," Jane didn't leave that band bus of her own will. She might have left her cell phone on the table because it didn't work on Surcie Island, but no way would she have left her iPod on the couch or gone off without her cane.

Riding in an open-top convertible isn't conducive to conversation. I was glad; I didn't feel like talking. After *Six Feet Under*, my favorite television shows are *Cold Case Files* and *Forensic Files*. I knew from those programs and from reading true crime books that when people go missing, they might not be found for months or even years. The most awful thought was that some persons are *never* located. How could their families survive without ever knowing?

The first suspect was usually the spouse or lover. That didn't apply to Jane. She had no spouse and unless her and Dean's friendship had gone further than I thought, no recent lovers either. Even if she and Dean had connected, which I really doubted considering what Jane had said when I took her to the band bus, I couldn't believe he would hurt her. Good grief. Sure, he'd already hurt her feelings, but he wouldn't hurt her physically. He was too nice.

Then again, what do neighbors and coworkers always tell reporters when some guy is arrested for having a dozen corpses in his basement? "Oh, he was such a nice fellow. Always polite and helpful." I tried to remember if Dean had been away from the stage area during the time Jane would have left the bus. I knew he'd been visible performing part of the time, but I couldn't be positive about every minute.

Something brushed my arm. I swatted at it before realizing Rizzie was trying to get my attention. I slowed down and apologized.

"It's okay," she yelled. "I knew you were lost in thought, but you just passed the Baptist church. It's on this side of town, before Adam's Creek really begins." I pulled over and did a U-ee to reverse directions. Sure enough, the church was down about a mile on our right.

I parked at the edge of the parking lot, which was about

half full. We could hear "Just as I Am" being sung, and I knew the service would be over soon. We walked past the old building. Painted white, it had a small steeple topped with a weather vane. A sign stated the church was built in the early 1900s. Grave markers surrounded the back and both sides. Not flat bronze memorials, these were granite or marble stones. Tiny carved angels and crosses, some of them no more than ten inches high, marked children's burial spots, and one statue that looked amazingly like the Washington Monument stood fifteen feet tall.

"What are we looking for?" Rizzie asked.

"The crypt or mausoleum where Melena wants to bury her husband," I said and swatted a little insect away from my face.

"What's the difference?"

"Most folks don't distinguish any difference these days. Modern perpetual care cemeteries have large mausoleums where caskets are put aboveground in niches. After the casket is placed, the cover's sealed. Some old churches have crypts beneath the floor so that people walk over the graves."

Rizzie glanced back at the white wooden building.

"Not churches like this. I'm talking about ancient places in Europe." I flung my arm out, pointing to the whole cemetery. "One of these little buildings will probably be what we've come to see."

The crypts in this churchyard differed from mausoleums as well as from each other. The first place we stopped was a red brick structure about the size of two caskets sitting on the ground side by side. The front end had been bricked shut on one side but remained open on the other. A plaque on the sealed side showed that Mr. Thomas Jenkins died about ten years ago. Mrs. Jenkins, if there was one, was either still alive or had chosen not to lie by his side.

The most impressive structure was a large, probably ten-by-twenty-foot marble miniature Greek temple. "Mitchell" was the name engraved over the door.

"How do we know when we find the right one?" Rizzie asked.

"I'm looking for one with 'Jones' on it. Pulley Bone Jones is Melena's brother, so I think the family name is Jones."

Rizzie and I wandered off in different directions. We moved slowly, reading the family histories engraved on some memorials. Many plots were bordered with bricks or stones. Some graves were neatly kept while others grew scraggly weeds. Wisteria grew up several of the larger monuments, draping lavender flowers down to the ground. Miniature azaleas planted on some sites were opening in spring blossoms of pink, violet, and white, and one grave was covered with daffodils, a soft blanket of yellow flowers.

"I've found it!" Rizzie called from the very back of the churchyard. She stood in front of a concrete block structure about twelve feet square and eight feet tall. When I reached her, she pointed to a painted sign over the door with the name "Jones" in old English style.

Otis wanted to know whether the door was bricked or mortared in. If so, we'd need a brick mason to open the crypt. If the caskets were aboveground, this vault probably wouldn't hold more than four caskets, two on each side. How many were already in there? What was the chance the vault stood over underground graves, which would require diggers as well as a mason if Melena wanted Fred's casket buried?

"Not quite so fancy as some of the others," Rizzie commented as she absentmindedly pulled a vine from a crack in the wall.

"Newer, too. I doubt the Jones family could afford marble or granite, now or whenever this was built."

The blocks stopped with just one row on either side of the door. The opening was wide, plenty of room to pass in a modern casket, and it wasn't cemented shut. A large metal, looked like steel to me, door was hinged on one side and held closed on the other by four hasps with heavy padlocks.

The locks looked new. "Gonna need keys or a hacksaw to find out exactly what's inside," I said.

Rizzie touched the door, rapped her knuckles on it. "What ya doing," I asked, "trying to wake the dead?"

A nervous giggle escaped her lips.

"I don't know why I did that. I was thinking about the crypt in the legend about a girl who was buried alive. She had diphtheria or some horrendous disease and they thought she was dead, but it was just a coma. Years later, they opened the crypt and found her skeleton at the door with the finger bones splintered and ragged from trying to escape."

"Oh, yes," I interrupted and lowered my voice to a witchy ghost-story tone. "And after that, the door wouldn't stay closed. No—matter—what—they–did!" I wiggled my eyebrows at Rizzie.

"Yeah, that one. I wondered if that's why there are so many locks. I mean, I doubt there are grave gifts in there to worry about being stolen. Who are they locking out?"

"This isn't the vault in that legend. That's in a church cemetery on Edisto Island. It was a marble building with a thick, solid marble door, and it was lots older than this. I believe the girl was buried in about 1850."

"Have you ever seen it?"

"My brother Jim stopped and showed it to me one time when we went to Edisto while he was home on leave. The marble door was lying on the ground broken into three pieces."

"Could you see the coffins inside?"

"No, they were buried underground beneath the cement floor."

"Then how did the girl get out of her casket?"

"Jim said that the caskets were originally stacked in there on biers, but the family buried them after they found the girl's skeleton."

Rizzie shivered slightly in the warm sunlight. "Are we done here?" she asked. "This is a little spooky."

"You're not scared, are you? The Surcie Island graveyard

didn't seem to make you feel skittish." I turned and walked toward the car. Rizzie took baby steps with those long legs of hers so she stayed right by my side.

"I know, but I've been in and out of there my whole life," she said. "This is different. I'm not psychic or a medium or anything, but it was almost like I could hear sounds coming from in there."

"Not likely. I assure you that either there's no such thing as ghosts or if they do exist, they don't hang around their physical remains or I'd have seen one at sometime working at the funeral home." Buh-leeve me. That's what I said, but my arms broke out in goose bumps.

When we reached the car, I pulled a roll of tape and a flyer from the box on the backseat, went back, and taped Jane's picture on the front door of the church. If a member of the congregation had opened the door while I was on the porch, I would probably have tee-teed my panties.

The drive into Adam's Creek was slowed by stopping at every little store to ask permission to post a flyer. No one refused. Most people had heard about the "missing blind girl."

Several people said they'd been praying for Jane. I thanked them sincerely. I'm not in church every Sunday, but I *do* believe, and I'd been praying a lot myself since yesterday.

"Do you have any special place you want to eat?" Rizzie asked.

"Not really. What about you?"

"Ever been to the Burgerarium?" she asked.

"No, never even heard of it, probably couldn't pronounce it if I had. Where is it?"

"Right up here on your left."

I saw the sign, pulled in, and parked. Hoped the food would be Gullah. My bad. The name said it all. It was a burger joint.

Sitting at a plastic booth, we both ordered sweet iced tea. "You're gonna love this." Rizzie grinned. "The cook pats out each hamburger and grills it after you order. No prepackaged patties. My two favorites are the pimiento burger and the chili burger, so I combine them. One bite and you'll be hooked." When the server brought the teas, we ordered two custom pimiento-chili burgers.

"It'll take a few minutes," Rizzie said. She leaned across the table and whispered, "You know why I really want to learn to embalm?"

"I've already told you Otis or Odell can come to the island whenever the time comes, but why would you want to embalm?"

"When I was little, I heard that story about the girl being buried alive and ever since then, I've worried about that happening to Maum. The place back there gave me the creeps."

Neither of us would say it, but I knew what Rizzie was thinking. Embalming prevented anyone in a coma from suffering the fate of the buried alive in those scary Edgar Allan Poe stories.

"There were things about death and burials that psyched me out before I started working for Otis and Odell, but now I've got used to the job, it never bothers me at all," I lied.

"Did you know I've never been to a funeral except on Surcie? Even when I was away at college, no one I knew died, but I know I want Maum embalmed."

"No problem. I told you we can handle it."

"And I'm so glad there are no small children in the family. Tyrone is the youngest and he's too old for passing."

I took a sip of tea. "Passing? What do you mean?"

"When someone dies and that person has a close child or grandchild, the little boy or girl has to be handed back and forth over the coffin to keep the dead from haunting them. I was passed over my grampa. It terrified me. I was afraid they'd drop me in on top of the dead body."

I'd heard about this Gullah custom, but I didn't know it was called passing. Rizzie's eyes filled with tears, and I changed the subject. Besides, even though talking about death didn't usually bother me, the conversation mixed into my fears for Jane and made me feel squeamish, too.

The waitress, whose name was Shirley according to the tag pinned to her very ample chest, arrived with the two fattest burgers I've ever seen. The buns were big, and the layers stuck out of them. The meat was thick, about three-quarters of an inch, sitting on a bed of chili that dripped out over the bottoms of the buns. Melting pimiento cheese separated the meat from lettuce, tomato, and thick slices of onion.

My brothers always accused me of having a big mouth. I proved them right when I took a bite. "This is the best burger I've ever eaten," I said and wiped my mouth with a paper towel from the roll on the center of the table.

"Can't beat 'em," Rizzie said. The food was too good to ignore, and we talked very little as we ate, paid, and returned to the car. After another hour of nailing and taping flyers about Jane on telephone poles and in windows, we headed back to St. Mary.

When I dropped Rizzie off by her truck at the mortuary, she asked, "Do you work tomorrow?"

"Only if they really need me."

"Want to search the island again?"

I hesitated, not knowing what might happen between now and then, hoping Jane would be home by tonight.

Rizzie said, "I'll call you tomorrow morning at low tide from the inlet." She held up her cell phone. "This thing is worthless on the island except at the inlet." We exchanged numbers. The old Chevy popped and snorted as Rizzie drove away.

Chapter Twenty

Never in a million years would Jane have believed what I did after Rizzie left the parking lot. I pondered stepping inside and talking to Otis or Odell. I considered going home and playing with Big Boy. I thought about going to McDonald's drive-through for ice cream, but I was too full of that giant hamburger. The sheriff had promised to call on my cell phone as soon as he knew anything. There was no reason to go to his office.

I, Calamine Lotion Parrish, who goes to her dad's house only when required by family obligation or to borrow something, wanted to go home. Not home to my duplex apartment. Home where I'd spent my childhood. Home where I hoped I'd find Daddy and some of my brothers.

Headed toward the home place, my mind was full of Jane. Memories of Jane. Fears for Jane. Everywhere I looked, I saw her face. Not only in my mind. With my eyes. We'd plastered the town with flyers, and driving along, I saw how thoroughly we'd accomplished our goal to be sure

everyone knew my friend was missing and to call the sheriff with any leads or sightings.

I've often called my daddy's house the most depressing
building in the county. In the state. Possibly in the nation.
It's covered with dark gray shingles because they were on
sale real cheap. The black roof and trim add to the Munster
effect. Every time I drive up the long driveway, the colors
depress me, but today gray and black became comfort colors. I needed home.

Ex-cuuze me. If I hadn't quit swearing when I stopped
cussing, I'd have sworn nothing could have been funny so
long as Jane was missing, but that would have been a lie. At
least, when I pulled up and saw what I saw at my Daddy's
house.

I smiled. I burst out laughing. I roared so hard that I had
to brake the car to a stop so I wouldn't run off the driveway
into the ditch.

Spanish moss and blooming wisteria waved from the
old live oaks arching across the drive. Scraps of white
cloth draped the shrub bushes planted along the front of
the house. My brother Bill rushed frantically around the
plants, pulling off the pieces of white. When I realized
what he was collecting, I guffawed so hard I did wet my
pants, but just a drop or so.

The white cloths weren't towels. Clothes. My brother
was grabbing underwear off the bushes. When he looked
up and saw me, he ran even faster and stumbled. Under-
shirts and jockey shorts flew from his arms, fell from the
air, and landed all around him.

"What's going on? Is the clothes dryer broken?" I managed to call through my giggles.

"Help me!" he shouted. "Hush and help me get all this
up before Pa and John get back."

Plucking my brother's unmentionables off the plants reminded me of my younger years when we'd had no clothes
dryer and had to hang everything on clotheslines out back on
wash days. When I started wearing bras, I was embarrassed

to have them seen outside. I tied a string from my window curtain to the closet doorknob and hung my underwear on that to dry. I posted a big "Do Not Enter" sign on my bedroom door.

In the house, Bill said, "Bring 'em in here," and headed toward his room. We dumped everything on his bed, and he pulled the door closed behind us when we went back to the living room.

"Thanks," he said. "Do you want a Coke?"

"No, I'll take a beer." This was a long-standing routine. I always asked for a beer at my dad's house, and my family always turned me down. Puh-leeze. I'm over thirty, been married and divorced, but the men in my family still think of me as a little girl, too young and innocent to drink. At least they give me soda. It could be a glass of milk.

I sank into Daddy's old couch and accepted the can of Coke Bill brought to me from the kitchen. His can was Busch. The favorite brand of beer at the Parrish home place was whatever was on sale when one of them shopped.

"Did you hang your clothes out there to dry?" I asked Bill, only half teasing.

"No, Molly did that." He paused, then added, "Thanks for helping me get them in before Pa and John saw 'em. They went to the sheriff's office to meet some woman who called here looking for you. Said she'd lost your cell number and the sheriff wouldn't give it to her."

"What woman?"

"I don't know. Wanted to talk about Jane. Said her husband died."

"Delgado?" I asked.

"That's it!"

"Her husband was the fiddler who was killed at the bluegrass festival."

"Yeah, Pa and John told me about that. Anyway, she was at Harmon's office looking for you, so they went to meet her."

"And how'd your underwear get in the front yard?"

"You know I've been staying at Molly's house most of the time, so a lot of my clothes ended up over there. She brought 'em back while I was at the Piggly Wiggly and left them on the shrubbery." He waved toward a large bouquet of mixed spring flowers stuck into a pitcher on the dining room table.

"Who are those for?" I asked.

"They were for Molly, but I doubt they'll make any difference, so I may give them to Lucy instead."

"And who's Lucy?"

"New girl I met at the Quick Stop. I pumped her gas for her. We got to talking, and I've been showing her around St. Mary. She just moved here."

"Thought you were serious about Molly."

"I am."

"Then why are you running around with this Lucy and how did Molly find out about it?"

He bristled, squared his shoulders, and answered in an argumentative whine. "I ain't running around with Lucy. Nothing between us. Just been showing her around town."

"Don't you speak to your sister in that tone." The voice was gruffer than Bill's. Daddy stood in the door with John right behind him. "What's the matter? Did Molly catch you with that new skirt you been chasing?"

"No, somebody told her they'd seen me with Lucy, and she won't listen to a word I say." Bill gave me a pleading glance that I read to mean, *Please don't tell them about my underwear.*

John laughed. "A town this size can be seen in one day. You should have known Molly would hear about you driving all over with that blonde."

"You've seen her?" I asked.

"He had her over here for dinner Friday night while you were at the festival," John answered.

"Get me a beer so we can set down and talk to Calamine," Daddy said. He sat in his recliner while Bill and John got him an Ice House.

"This woman who was married to that midget . . ." Daddy began.

I interrupted him. "Fred Delgado wasn't a midget. The term is 'little person,' and if you're not going to call him that, at least refer to him as a dwarf, not a midget. His arms and legs were short, but his body was full-size. He was probably an achondroplasic dwarf."

"Talking to you is like talking to a dictionary," Daddy grumbled. "How'd you know that anyway?"

"I had a little person student when I taught kindergarten. I read up about it then." I paused before adding, "Now, what does Melena Delgado have to do with you?"

"She was looking for you. Said she'd lost your cell number and called here thinking you lived here. Asked me if I'm your husband. I had to laugh at that, but I told her about your divorce and taking back your maiden name."

"Thanks for putting my business on the street," I muttered.

"Everybody in town knows all about it. If I didn't tell her, somebody else would." He slugged down the rest of the beer, crushed the can in his hand, and tossed it to Bill, who took it to the kitchen. "Anyway, John and I went and met with her and Wayne Harmon at his office. She wants to hold a vigil for Jane."

I burst into tears. He said "vigil." I heard "memorial service."

John, the oldest and most demonstrative of my five brothers, pulled me close and wrapped me in a hug as I sobbed against his chest.

"Jane's not dead," I cried, "not dead."

"Nobody said she's dead," John comforted. "Vigils are for the living, too. They're to show support for finding the missing person. Besides, after Mrs. Delgado left, Wayne said that sometimes a vigil provides clues about who might be a person of interest in a kidnapping case."

I leaned back from John and looked up into his eyes. "Do you mean the sheriff finally agrees that Jane didn't just run off with someone?"

"Seems like it. He's got crews combing Surcie Island looking for Jane. He even mentioned the Peterson case and how the husband's behavior at the vigil confirmed suspicions of him."

"Will it be tonight?"

"No, first Wayne wants to get your okay on it. With Jane having no relatives, he counts you like her next of kin. Told the woman she'd need to talk to you. I've got a cell number for Mrs. Delgado so you can call her."

I reached for my cell. John put his hand on mine to stop the action.

"Wait a minute. We need to talk about this before you call her. Otherwise, she'll be telling you what to do. In your state of mind, you'll let her make the decisions. The sheriff suggests that it be somewhere easy for him to do surveillance. You'll need to get some publicity, line up speakers. Then there's candles. Usually the people at a vigil hold candles. You may even want a printed program to pass out. Someone has to make the arrangements for all that."

"Oh," was all I could say while I wondered if Otis and Odell would give me a salary advance.

John knows me well. "Don't worry about the money, Callie. I'll pay for it, but I want you to arrange the vigil before you call Mrs. Delgado. If she has good suggestions, you can adapt your plan, Little Sister, but know what you want and discuss it with Wayne before you call the woman."

He nudged me onto the couch.

Bill pulled a lined yellow legal pad from the bottom shelf of the television stand and brought it and a pen over to the couch where I sat. He jotted headings down the side of the paper: when, where, who, supplies, publicity.

Though Daddy, Bill, and I all contributed ideas, most of our decisions came from John's suggestions. We decided to have the vigil Tuesday night. That would give us two days to publicize the event.

A lot of discussion went into location, but we finally agreed on the bridge to Surcie Island if the sheriff would agree to block it off.

"Who" would be everyone we could round up to attend.

"It's supposed to be a spiritual kind of thing," John said. "Could you get the preacher who does most of the services at Middleton's to come say a prayer for Jane's safe return?"

"No way am I going to have Reverend Cauble there," I answered. "Every time he does a funeral, he tries to save everyone in the audience, and he doesn't mind calling everybody sinners. I don't want him there talking bad about Jane. I can probably get Lisa Owen from Beaufort to sing, though."

"Isn't she a bar singer?" Bill asked.

"She sings in nightclubs, but she sings a lot at funerals, too. Besides, she's got kind of a Patsy Cline sound that Jane loves. The problem's going to be finding a preacher."

Daddy chuckled. "Calamine, if you'd get yourself back in church, you could call Pastor Dan Christianson."

Puh-leeze. The last thing I needed right then was a lecture from Daddy about my not going to church every Sunday. I didn't say anything.

"Pastor Christianson would remember Jane from when she went to youth group with you. Want me to ask him about praying at the vigil?"

"Would you?" I asked in disbelief. I had assumed Daddy would make me call the preacher I hadn't seen in several months of Sundays.

"I'll call him right now."

Daddy picked up the portable telephone and walked toward the kitchen.

Bill, John, and I discussed publicity. Bill listed radio and television stations in Beaufort, Hilton Head, and Charleston. St. Mary's newspaper as well as the *State, Beaufort Gazette,* and *Charleston Courier.* More flyers. Then John suggested trying to get some national media attention, checking with *Nancy Grace* and other programs like *America's Most Wanted.*

After Daddy brought the phone back and said Pastor Christianson had agreed to speak, I called Lisa and asked her to sing. She said, "Sure, Callie. I'll be there and I'll

bring accompaniment and a sound system for the music
and speakers. Just choose the songs you want."

While Lisa and I talked music, I heard Daddy telling
John that Pastor Christianson had told him about a religious supply store in Beaufort where we could buy candles
with saucerlike holders to catch wax drippings so they
wouldn't burn people's hands.

John suggested we ride over to the sheriff's office and
go over the tentative plans with Harmon before discussing
them with Melena Delgado. He called Wayne, who said,
"Now's fine. Come on over."

As sad and upset as I'd felt, planning the vigil fired me
with enthusiasm. Maybe it would help bring Jane home.

Bill and I had to ride backseat because John wanted to
drive my Mustang, and Daddy got up front with him. Redneck, redneck, redneck. Jeff Foxworthy should add, "You
might be a redneck if you put the owner of the car in the
backseat, just because she's your sister!"

Chapter Twenty-one

Pepsi or ginger ale. Even Daddy hadn't requested a beer after the sheriff asked if we wanted something to drink when we reached his office. John went over our plans with Wayne, stopping occasionally to refer to Bill's notes.

"Only one thing wrong," the sheriff said. "I don't want to close off the bridge for this."

"Why not?" I snapped. "You didn't mind closing it and keeping all of us in that campground."

"Be nice, Calamine," Daddy whispered.

"The problem," Sheriff Harmon said, "is having all those folks on the bridge. You know just as well as I do that some of them will do a little drinking before they come. I don't want anyone falling over the railing and drowning."

"Hadn't considered that," I said. "We thought it would be an easy place to confine the group for your people to observe them."

"How about St. Mary Community Park?" Sheriff Harmon suggested.

"Can we get permission?" Daddy asked.

"No problem. I'll take care of it."

The issue of permission hadn't crossed my mind. "Do we have to get a permit?" I asked.

"Nope." Sheriff Harmon grinned. "It's not a parade, Callie."

"Better be careful," Bill cautioned, "she's not in the best of moods."

Harmon apologized before adding, "Will you contact Mrs. Delgado or do you want me to? She's already called back twice to see if I've talked to you."

"Why's she so interested?" I asked. "Seems like she'd be more concerned about what's going on with the investigation into who killed her husband than in Jane."

Sheriff Harmon gave me a puzzled look. "I thought the same thing, Callie," he said. "Maybe she thinks finding Jane will help solve Delgado's murder, figures if we find out who took Jane, we'll find who murdered the two musicians."

I called Melena Delgado's cell number from the sheriff's office. John had been right. She was disappointed that we'd planned without her.

"Mrs. Parrish, I wish you'd called me earlier. I wanted to help plan the vigil."

"Oh, Mrs. Delgado, you helped by suggesting it. Thank you so much. I'm going into Beaufort and have flyers printed tonight. Perhaps you'd like to help post them tomorrow." Mortuary training has helped me be more diplomatic than I used to be.

"Mrs. Parrish, I want to do more than just help put up posters."

"Well, it's pretty well planned now. By the way, it's *Ms.* Parrish, not Mrs."

"Excuse me. I didn't know. I thought it was Mrs. since your father told me you'd been married."

She didn't drag out 'ex-cuuze' like I do.

"I switched to 'Ms.' after my divorce," I said. Actually, I use "Miss" whenever I meet a good-looking potential date, but there was no point in telling her that.

"Call me if I can do anything," Melena said.

"I will," I answered. After only the briefest pause, too
short for her to say anything else, I added, " 'Bye now," and
disconnected.

I thought I'd have to take Daddy, John, and Bill home,
but Wayne offered to drop them off so that I could go
straight to Middleton's computer and design the vigil flyer
since we hadn't thought to bring John's laptop with us.
That's an advantage to living in a little town like St. Mary.
I doubt seriously that the sheriff in a large city would give
folks a ride while investigating two murders and a kidnapping.

Sitting in my office at the funeral home, I felt brainless. I
had no idea what to put on the flyer. The first one had been
simple. Missing, name, photo, and contact number for the
sheriff. I finally put a big "V I G I L" across the top in large
block letters, "for missing person" in smaller letters, Jane's
name bigger again, photo, description, then the date, time,
and location for the gathering.

The page on the screen looked okay to me, so I printed
out a copy to take to FedEx Kinko's. Like the "Missing
Person" flyer, it was cheaper and quicker to have them
copied than do them on the mortuary computer printer,
though if I'd asked, Otis and Odell would probably have
okayed using their supplies.

While on the computer, I decided to check the condolences for Mrs. Martin. At the end of each obituary on our
website, there's a place for e-mails. We print them out and
add hard copies to the memory books given to loved ones.

Immediately upon the page appearing on the screen, my
name in the middle of the messages caught my eye. Among
the "so sorry, we'll be thinking of you" e-mails was my
name in giant, bold red letters: "CALLIE PARRISH." In
smaller letters, but still in red: "Jane feels no pain."

I keened a mindless wail that sounded nothing like me.

Otis and Odell ran into my office asking what was wrong,
but all I could do was bellow that anguished wordless cry. I

managed to point to the red letters on the computer monitor screen.

"That's good, Callie," Otis soothed.

"No!" I shouted at my boss. I couldn't stop myself. "Can't you see? It means she's dead. Jane's dead."

"Not necessarily," mumbled Odell. "It might be a prank or it might mean that she's somewhere safe and sound. Jane herself might have sent it."

Otis and I gave Odell *What kind of fool are you?* looks.

"Jane can't e-mail unless she has her special equipment at her apartment, and she's not there."

"How do you know?"

"Jane wouldn't be playing games. She'd tell me where she is and that she's all right."

Odell picked up the phone and called the sheriff's department. The dispatcher connected him to Sheriff Harmon, who said he'd head right over and ended with, "Don't delete. Whatever you do, don't delete that message," so loud we could hear him even though Odell held the receiver mashed against his ear.

I calmed down enough to look at the screen more carefully. There wasn't an electronic signature or any information to suggest the identity of the sender. I hit "Reply," but even when I right-clicked on the address line, I found nothing.

The sheriff arrived and scolded me, vowing he'd said, "Don't touch it."

Odell scolded right back. "Don't fuss at her. You said not to delete the message. She didn't delete." The sheriff called for a computer specialist and forbid any of us to touch the computer again until after the law enforcement official finished with it. I didn't tell Otis or Odell, but I immediately thought that by the end of the evening, our hard drive would be hauled off like John's Winnebago.

Harmon picked up the flyer from the printer tray, handed it to me, and said, "This looks great. We don't need you here right now. You can go get your copies made."

Odell followed me to the back door. "Callie," he said,

"the medical center is releasing that fiddler's body. His wife's coming in again tomorrow at ten. I know you'll be busy setting up this vigil thing, but I'd really like you to be here for the planning session. Mrs. Delgado seems to think knowing you is important. Maybe she thinks being your friend will get her a discount. I don't know, but I want you here if possible."

"She's not my friend, but I'll come if you want me to."

I thought about Melena and Rizzie on the drive to Beaufort. Both acquaintances seemed to want to be better friends than I did. My best friend was missing, and I wasn't looking for a replacement.

At the print shop, I signed on to the Internet on a rental computer, composed a press release about the vigil, and e-mailed it to newspapers, radio stations, and local television news departments. I seriously doubted the mortuary computer would be available for a while, though Odell swore Middleton's couldn't get along without it and had mentioned buying a new one if ours was removed. I'd wanted to buy a personal computer for ages, but every time I saved enough money, an unexpected bill came up. I'd spent my last computer savings to have the vet crop Big Boy's ears so he'd look like the purebred Great Dane he is.

The clerk suggested enlarging the flyers from eight and a half by eleven inches to eleven by seventeen poster size. The larger sheets were much more noticeable and legible. He also gave me a discount, wished me luck, and taped a vigil notice beside the "Missing Person" notice already posted on the window.

The ride home was slow, but when I pulled into my drive, I felt good that most of the roads in Beaufort and on the drive home were plastered with flyers about the vigil for Jane.

I heard Big Boy yapping and barking before I got the door unlocked. He jumped at me, putting his front paws on my shoulders and lapping his tongue over my face. "Yes, Boy," I soothed. "I'm home. Let's go out." I grabbed his leash from the doorknob and clipped it onto his collar.

Once in the yard, Big Boy ran around yapping and wrapped the leash around my legs. I let go of the leash, and he bounded up to the little oak tree at the edge of the yard. For the millionth, well, maybe just thousandth time, I hoped he'd hike his leg to the tree, but no, my Big Boy still tinkles like a girl dog. He squatted, looked at me, then stood again. He squirmed just like a kindergarten child doing the tee-tee dance.

"Okay, I know I should have named you Shy Boy."

I turned my back to the dog and soon heard the *swish* of my overgrown puppy relieving his bladder like a fancy female poodle.

The thought of food made my stomach tie itself in knots, but I filled Big Boy's bowl with Kibbles 'n Bits, then rinsed and refilled his water dish. By the time he'd finished eating, I was out of the shower and in one of my comfort nighties, a floor-length flannel washed so many times that it was soft as a cotton ball. Big Boy and I crawled into my bed, snuggled into a spoon position with his back to me, and I lay there listening to him snore. I couldn't sleep.

The shrill ringing of the telephone startled me.

"Callie?" Bill asked as though he didn't recognize my voice. "Did I wake you?"

"No, it's okay," I answered.

"I hate to have to tell you this. I know you're worried about Jane, but please don't let Big Boy outside without his leash."

"I never let him out without going with him. Why?"

"Molly and I just had a big argument, and she says she wants back everything she ever gave me, including your dog, but you don't have to let her have him."

"I'll be careful."

"Okay, and Callie?"

"Uh-huh."

"Call me if you need me." He cleared his throat. "Good night."

Dalmation! As if I didn't have enough problems, Molly wanted to repossess my dog. "Jane feels no pain." Who sent it to me? Whoever e-mailed it knew that I was Jane's closest friend and apparently knew about my responsibilities at Middleton's.

What did it mean?

Chapter Twenty-two

"A gold-plated casket like that James Brown had," Melena Delgado said. "That's what I want, and it has to be adult-size. Fred might not have been tall, but he was a full-grown man."

Otis silently made notes while Melena described the funeral she wanted for her husband. Her brother, Pulley Bone Jones, sat beside her opposite Otis and me at the conference table, but he wasn't saying anything.

I'd neglected to set my alarm the night before and stayed awake until the wee hours of the morning worried about Jane and Big Boy. End result: I overslept and wheeled into Middleton's only minutes before Melena and Bone arrived.

The widow took a sip of coffee from the Dunkin' Donuts cup she'd brought with her. "I want special flowers, too," she continued. "A great big casket spray shaped like a fiddle, with a ribbon across it that says 'Little Fiddlin' Fred' in gold glitter." Another sip of coffee. "And special clothes, but I'll supply the outfit I want him to wear."

Whew! I thought. Since dressing the deceased is part of

my job, I was glad she'd supply clothing. I had little idea where or how to buy a suit for a dwarf. I'd seen Fred Delgado play on television, and I remembered he seemed broad-shouldered though his arms and legs were short. He'd also been a far flashier dresser than most grassers, many of whom wear jeans or, if they dress up, sedate suits with bolo ties, expensive boots, and hats.

Otis shifted positions in his chair. "There shouldn't be any problem with the floral arrangement, but I'm going to have to check on the gold-plated casket. I don't think I've ever seen one of those in our supply catalogs."

"Can't you check with the funeral home that was in charge of James Brown's services to see where they got it?" Bone asked.

"Yes, we can do that. I don't remember the name of the mortuary, but Callie can find it on the Internet."

Puh-leeze. I had a vigil to organize, wanted to search for Jane, and now I'd be driving around to get on someone's computer since ours wasn't available until the sheriff's investigator finished with it.

Bone looked over at me and wrinkled his eyes. I wasn't sure if he was making a face at me or flirting.

Melena put her Dunkin' Donuts to her mouth, frowned, and placed it on the marble-topped table. She glanced over at me. "Don't suppose you've got any coffee here?" she asked.

Otis and Odell stress to me constantly that I'm always to be polite to the bereaved. This woman had been widowed less than a week ago and she'd volunteered to help plan a vigil for my missing friend. I had no reason to dislike her, but I did. She knew there was coffee in the building. The smell of the high-dollar brand used at Middleton's wafted through the air.

"I made coffee just before you arrived," Otis said. "I'll get some for everyone." He left the room.

What kind of deal was this? Making and serving coffee is part of my job. Otis is one of my bosses. The only reason he'd started the pot was because I was late. Why was he serving it? Being nice to me because of Jane? Maybe, but more likely he'd interpreted Melena asking me as an insinuation that refreshments were a woman's work. Odell is like a grizzly bear, but Otis sometimes displays sensitivity. This was one of those times.

While Otis was gone, Melena took a small notebook from her purse and began making notes. Bone leaned across to me. "You look very different, Callie," he said.

My job requires that I dress a certain way, the very opposite of the shorts and tees I'd worn at the campground. When they hired me, Otis and Odell specified that I wear black. Nothing else. So far, neither of them has complained that I frequently change my hair color, but regardless of the shade, I wear it the same way to work: swept back into a sedate bun at the nape of my neck. Dignified. I may not act that way, but I try to look dignified at work.

Before I could respond, Bone added, "I think I like the 'Bluegrass Rules' top and shorts better."

Ex-cuuze me. What business was it of his and who gave him the right to criticize my appearance? I thought about telling him so and asking him who cared what he thought, but Otis arrived carrying the large silver coffee service with Wedgwood china cups. We drink out of mugs in our offices. Odell and I would welcome disposable cups up front, but Otis likes propriety.

He poured a serving and handed the first cup and saucer to Melena. She snapped the lid off her large Dunkin' Donuts container and poured the steaming coffee into it. She held it over to Otis and said, "You might as well fill 'er up. I can never get enough coffee. It's not decaf, is it? I don't like unleaded."

"We only make decaffeinated coffee when it's requested," Otis replied in his smooth undertaker voice. He poured cups for the rest of us before saying to Melena, "I believe you said yesterday that you have a crypt in Adam's Creek where you want Mr. Delgado to be laid to rest. Is that correct?"

Melena took a long drink before she responded, "Yes, we'll be putting Fred in the Jones family crypt."

"We'll need keys or for one of you to let us in to see what needs to be done there," I said. "The crypt is locked with four padlocks."

"How do you know that?" Bone asked.

"I took a look at it yesterday when I was in Adam's Creek."

"I didn't know you'd be going over there without permission," Melena snapped.

"The church cemetery is open to the public, and I wanted to put vigil posters up in Adam's Creek anyway," I answered.

"Callie said there are some vines and weeds around the structure," Otis said. "I'm sure you'll want that cleaned before the service, and we'll need to see inside also to determine specific needs."

"I'll go with one of you and let you in tomorrow morning," Bone volunteered, "or I can drop the keys off for you."

Otis looked down at the papers on the table. "Will you need us to arrange for a pastor and music for the service?" he said.

"No," Melena said, "I'll take care of that."

"Are there any other special requests?"

"Yes, I want the casket moved to the church in a carriage pulled by horses."

"White horses like James Brown?" Otis asked, still writing.

"No, black horses like in those films I've seen of the assassinated president. What was his name? Kennedy."

"Where will the service be?"

"At the church, but I want the carriage to carry Fred from here to Adam's Creek."

"That's a long way."

"It's so classy, though." She popped the top off her cup and held it out to Otis for another refill. "Can he lie in state here?"

"In state?" I knew I shouldn't have said it before the words were out of my mouth. Otis raised an eyebrow at me.

"You may certainly have the visitation here," he said. "Mr. Delgado will be arriving this afternoon and should be ready tomorrow morning. Do you know when you want the visitation and service?"

"I have to give his friends and fans time to travel here, and the vigil is tomorrow night, so I think the visitation day after tomorrow and the service the following day."

"And you'll be bringing Mr. Delgado's clothing to us later today?"

"Yes, after lunch."

Otis smiled and looked up at Melena and Bone. "You realize I won't be able to give you the price until we find the casket and we know what will need to be done at the vault."

Melena's eyes flashed, and she sat back. "What do you mean give us a price?" Her expression and tone were equally offended.

"Services must be paid for before the funeral. We accept cash, credit card, or assignment of a valid life insurance policy." I'd heard Otis say this so many times that it was like listening to a recording.

"But back at the campground, Callie here said that Middleton's would be glad to take care of it," Melena protested. "I didn't know I'd have to pay anything."

Everyone turned and looked at me. "I meant we'd be glad to serve you, but I never indicated there'd be no charge," I sputtered. "Why would you think our services would be free?"

"Fred was a star," Melena whined. "I thought you'd do it for the publicity."

"No, ma'am. We can't do that." I was glad Otis didn't go any further. Little Fiddlin' Fred was pretty well known in bluegrass circles, but Otis isn't a bluegrass fan. I feared he'd say, "I never heard of him 'til we picked up his body." No, Otis wouldn't do that. First, he's too polite. Second, he never says "body." He always refers to the deceased by name.

"How much do you think it might be?" Bone asked.

"Can't tell until the casket is selected, and I'll have to arrange the carriage and see what that will cost." He arranged the papers into a neat stack. "How much has to be done at the crypt will be another factor. Will we need to excavate or will the casket be placed aboveground?"

"There are some family members buried beneath the vault," Bone said. "But there's one coffin already aboveground and a shelf above it." He turned toward his sister. "Melena, it will be cheaper to put the casket on top of the one that's there than to dig another grave beneath the building."

"That's fine, just fine." Melena stood, picked up her cup, and headed toward the door.

Bone grabbed Melena's purse and hurried behind her, still talking. "We'll be back with Fred's costume this afternoon. Can you check on the casket and carriage as soon as possible?"

"Certainly," Otis said.

Melena turned back toward me. Her tone was icy. "Oh, Callie, I'll be too busy with Fred's arrangements to help you with your vigil."

Otis and I both walked them to the front door. "My Soul Will Fly Free" played over the sound system as they left.

"Costume?" Otis asked me when they were gone.

"He dressed fancy to perform. I'm sure they'll bury him in stage clothes." I coughed, then added, "I didn't indicate our services would be free."

"I know that. Don't worry about it. Go take care of your vigil arrangements."

"What about that gold-plated casket?"

"Odell loves rock and roll, rhythm and blues, and soul music. Everything but classical. He'll probably remember the name of James Brown's mortuary. It was named in the newspapers. I just don't remember which one. Keep your cell phone on. I'll call you later."

One of my brothers was a big James Brown fan. I

couldn't bring myself to sing "I Feel Good" as I left. It was just too inappropriate. But I did a reasonably good job of "Please, Please, Please," even if I did drag it into "Puh-leeze, Puh-leeze, Puh-leeze."

Chapter Twenty-three

My mind bounced around like a jumping bean as I drove toward Beaufort to pick up candles for the vigil. I didn't know how much they'd cost or how many to buy. I hoped my Visa charge account had enough credit available to pay for them. John had offered to pick up the bill, but I'd forgotten to get a check from him.

Halfway to Beaufort, I realized I hadn't turn my cell phone on. I had it off during the planning session with Bone and Melena. The minute I restored power to the cell, it chirped.

"Callie Parrish," I answered.

"Hi, this is Rizzie Profit. Is there any word about your friend?"

"Nothing."

"Do you want to come look for her on the island some more? The sheriff has several crews searching, but you and I can still try to find her."

"I'd like to, but I'll probably be tied up most of the day. I'm getting ready for a vigil for Jane tomorrow night, and

Middleton's is handling Little Fiddlin' Fred's services, so they'll be calling me in after he gets here from Charleston."

"Heard about the vigil on the radio and saw a public service announcement about it on television."

I grinned to myself. My time on FedEx Kinko's rental computer had been worthwhile.

"You'll be embalming the fiddler?" Rizzie asked.

"No, remember I don't embalm. My work begins after the embalming. I do hair, makeup, and clothes."

"Can I watch?"

"I couldn't let you do that. It would violate Mr. Delgado's privacy."

"Oh." She sounded really disappointed. What was with her? Did she have some morbid fetish? "You said when Maum passes, you'd get one of your bosses to come to the island to take care of her. Would you come, too, and help me get her dressed and pretty?"

"Yes, I'll do that, but is your grandmother ill? Why are you obsessing about her dying?"

"She's not sick. She's just old, and I worry about her."

"I promise you that when the time comes, I'll get you the help you need." I thought about Melena Delgado. "Rizzie?"

"Yes."

"When you need us, you'll have to pay the Middletons for their work, but I'll do my job off the clock, free for you, okay?"

"I'm not looking for charity." Huffy tone. Insulted.

"Didn't mean it that way. I just don't want to mislead anyone."

"I'm not giving you free sweetgrass baskets, and when my restaurant opens I expect you to pay for your food."

"Deal."

"I'm going out to search some more." She giggled softly and added, "I'll keep an eye on the sheriff's people, too."

She disconnected the phone. I flipped my own cell

closed and shivered. I feared her finding Jane. I didn't think Jane was still on the island alive, and I didn't want Rizzie or anyone else to find her dead.

At the religious supply store, I was pleasantly surprised to see Gwen Foster, an old high school friend, working there.

"Callie!" she said when I walked in, "I haven't seen you in ages. How are you doing?"

"Not so well. My friend Jane—"

Gwen didn't give me time to finish the statement. "Yes," she interrupted, "I saw the news about the murders at the festival and about Jane Baker on television. I'm not a blue-grass fan, so I didn't know the men, but I remember you and Jane from school. It's such a shock when something like that happens to someone we know. Do you think she was really kidnapped or could she have wandered off and gotten lost on the island because of her blindness?" Gwen paused for breath.

"I think she was kidnapped, and I believe it's related to the two murders. I've come to buy candles for the vigil to-morrow night."

"Sure. I'll give you a discount, the same one we give to churches. What kind do you want?"

"What do you mean?" Good grief. Was she asking if I wanted a Baptist or Methodist or Jewish discount?

"What kind of candles? We've got several sizes, and do you want the slip-on wax catchers?"

"I thought they were made onto the candles. Why don't you recommend what you think is best?"

"Let me show you." She went to the back and came out with several cartons of different-size candles. She also had a box of white cardboard circles with an X cut into the cen-ter of each one. "See. You just slip these onto the candles. Leave enough room at the bottom to hold the candle." She demonstrated.

"You could just buy candles and make the wax guards yourself," she suggested. Like I couldn't afford to buy them for my best friend's vigil. Well, actually I couldn't, but I counted on John reimbursing me. "Cut circles or squares out of cardboard or heavy paper and punch a hole in the middle," she added.

"No," I said, "I'll buy the guards. Wonder how many I should buy?"

"Purchase more than you need. You can return any you don't use and get your money back."

As Gwen processed the charge slip for 250 candles and guards, she told me about her children. Three of them. Showed me a picture and pointed to each one. "This is Miranda. She's my oldest, then Danielle, and the baby is my boy. His name's Kadge."

I didn't quite ooh and ahh, but I came close. They were cute kids. What Southerners call cottontops, with blond hair the color I retouched mine every three weeks.

Gwen handed me a pen, and I signed the charge slip. She reached for my bagged purchase, looked over my shoulder toward the glass window, and asked, "Is that your blue Mustang?"

I really thought she was going to say something like, "Cool car," but instead she said, "Better go check it. Somebody just put something under the back bumper."

"What do you mean?"

"I saw someone bending over the back. When he stood up, he pulled his hand from beneath your car."

Shih tzu! What would a person be sticking under my car? Should I go out and look or should I call the sheriff? No, not the sheriff; Beaufort's patrolled by a city police department.

"Are you okay, Callie?" Gwen asked.

"I don't know. I can't imagine what someone would be putting under my car."

"Do you think it could be a bomb?"

"A bomb? Why would anyone do that?"

"I don't know. Do you still read mysteries? Someone's always blowing up Stephanie Plum's cars in those books."

"I'm not Stephanie Plum, and I'm not a bounty hunter."

"Yeah, but something bad happened to your friend Jane

and now somebody might be after you. I don't think you should go out there. We need to call someone." She reached under the counter.

"Are you sure the person touched my car? He could have been picking up something dropped on the ground," I suggested.

Gwen's eyes bugged before she even had a chance to answer me.

"Down! Get down and spread 'em!" The voice was loud and harsh. "Face down!"

I turned around and saw two policemen with guns drawn. Pointing at me. I spun back toward Gwen to see who else was there just as two more officers ran in and a big hand grabbed my shoulder. Another voice barked, "Down! Now!"

"Who? Me?" My voice shook, but not half as much as my body.

"Yeah, you!"

I sank to my knees, then slid flat onto the floor and spread my arms.

"Put both hands behind your head!"

I did.

"Why are you doing this?" Gwen wailed.

I tried to look up at her, but the big hand pushed my face back onto the floor.

"You set your burglary alarm off. Was this woman attempting to rob you?" Big Hand asked.

"No, I pushed the button to get you to come check the car out front. Somebody may have put a bomb under it."

"A bomb? Why would you think someone did that?"

"That blue Mustang belongs to Callie Parrish," Gwen said. "Her best friend is that blind girl who's been kidnapped."

"Missing," said another policeman. "We don't know if she was abducted yet. For now, it's a missing person case."

"Callie believes Jane was kidnapped, and she's known her since they were born."

Jane and I didn't meet until her mom brought her home

from the school for the blind when we started high school, but I didn't bother to correct Gwen. She told the policemen how she'd seen a person appear to put something under my car.

I just lay there, looking around as much as possible without lifting my head. I could see dust bunnies under the edge of the counter, and I imagined how my black dress would look when I stood. Ridiculous for them to keep talking and not let me up, but I couldn't see if the cops had holstered their guns, and I had no intention of checking it out.

"Where is this Parrish woman?"

"Right there on the floor," Gwen said.

No apologies from anyone as they helped me up. Guess they figured they were only doing their jobs. The one I thought of as Big Hand called headquarters and stepped outside to talk. After a few moments, he returned.

"You two ladies need to move as far back as possible in the store. A specialist is coming over to take a look."

Buh-leeve me. Nobody had to tell me twice to move away from a potential bomb. Gwen and I went to the back. I took my bag of candles and guards with me. They were already charged on my Visa. I didn't want them to melt if the bomb were real and started a fire.

More officers outside directed people away and taped off the street with yellow tape. Yellow's one of my favorite colors, so bright and cheerful, but over the weekend I'd seen enough yellow tape to last a lifetime.

An armored-looking van pulled onto the street and parked down the block. Someone wearing an outfit like a space suit in old movies climbed out carrying a little machine on wheels. Reminded me of a canister vacuum cleaner. He placed it close to my car before moving behind the van. As the machine rolled toward the Mustang, little antenna-looking sticks came up. Then it scooted under my car.

I held my breath, waiting for the big bang. Nothing exploded.

After what seemed like forever, the space suit man came from around the van, holding a control device. He bent by my back bumper and put his hand beneath the car, then punched the remote control, and the robot rolled out from beneath the vehicle.

Other officers began removing the yellow tape, and Mr. Space Suit Man came into the store. "Which one of you owns the Mustang?" he asked Gwen and me.

"It's mine," I stammered. "You didn't find anything, did you?"

"Sure did. Is there any reason for you to have a GPS tracking device on your car?"

"Not that I know of." I trembled.

"It's probably what the saleslady saw the man put on your Mustang. Let's fill out some paperwork, and we'll see if we can find out why."

Much later, I left the religious supply store with promises to the Beaufort police to let them know if I thought of anything that could account for the GPS tracker on my car and promises to Gwen to call her sometime so we could get together and I could see her beautiful children in person. She seemed genuinely disappointed that I didn't have any little ones. Said I was missing out on the best part of life.

I felt that I wasn't just missing out on the best parts. My whole existence was in the pits. My best friend had been kidnapped. My brother's ex-girlfriend was threatening to take my dog. A customer had tried to make my boss think I'd offered the mortuary's services for free, and if Otis shared that with Odell, he'd throw a hissy fit. The sheriff still had my older brother John's motor home impounded, which probably put me right at the top of his caca list at the moment, though so far, he'd been kind about it. I was in charge of organizing a vigil, and I'd never even been to one. And now, someone was trying to track me. Tracking brought thoughts of the year before when the OnStar system had led to my rescue from a killer.

Dalmation! What now? I said when my cell phone chirped.

"Callie? Callie Parrish?" The man's voice was deep and familiar, but not immediately recognizable.

"Yes, this is she." I gave my schoolteacher response.

"Dean Holdback here. Is there any word about Jane?"

"Nothing."

"Oh." His voice faltered for a moment. "I saw on television that you're holding a vigil tomorrow night, but I was hoping she'd be found before then." Dean paused again and lowered his voice. "Callie, Jane and I had an awkward moment before you took her to the bus. Not an argument, and I thought I'd handled everything okay. She's really great, and I have to admit I'd find it mighty easy to want a relationship with her if I weren't married. I'm worried sick about her. Do you think she would run away if she got upset?"

"No, Dean, I don't believe she ran away. Somebody took her out of the bus."

"I'd almost rather think she ran away than that she was kidnapped." I heard him blow his nose. Was he crying? When he spoke again, his voice was stronger, almost businesslike. "I just wanted to let you know that Andy Campbell and I are coming down from Columbia. Is there anything we can do for you?"

"You can do exactly what you just said, come show your support for Jane." My heart was doing cartwheels, so it was difficult to think, much less talk. Then I thought of something. "Dean?"

"Yes."

"Could you bring your guitars and sing a few songs? I've got Lisa Owen, a singer from Beaufort, but more music and less talk would be good."

"Be glad to."

"And Dean?"

"Yes."

"None of those bluegrass love songs where people die or get killed. I want hopeful music."

"To be honest, Jane, I can't think of an exactly 'hopeful' song. Want to make requests?"

Puh-leeze. He'd just told me Andy was coming back and now he wanted me to think of song titles? "No, just happy songs. You can even do 'Rocky Top.' Jane likes that."

Dean moaned. I'd heard him complain that all anyone who's not a grasser wants to hear from a bluegrass band is "Rocky Top." Personally, I love "Rocky Top" myself, but then I'm not a bluegrass purist.

When we'd said our good-byes and I'd flipped my phone closed, I felt better than I had all day. Things could be worse. Jane hadn't been found, but I still believed she was alive. The Beaufort cops could have frisked me as well as having me lie on the floor. Dean's call had lifted my spirits. He was a friend. I'd be glad to see him, and the big plus was that he was bringing Andy.

Maybe the world wasn't so bad after all. Not good, but not totally horrible either.

Good grief! My best friend was missing and I was actually looking forward to seeing a man who was coming to a vigil for her. Disgusting!

Then I thought of Jane. If she knew what I was thinking, she'd say, "Go for it," or "You go, girl," or even "Sic 'em, Callie!"

I smiled.

Then I cried some more.

Chapter Twenty-four

scape. My favorite method of getting away has always been books.

While I'd like to say that I spent the rest of the day productively, I didn't. When Sheriff Harmon heard about what happened with my car from the Beaufort police, he called Daddy and The Boys. They stormed into my apartment insisting I go home with them.

"I don't want to go anywhere," I argued. "I've got to get this vigil organized."

"No, you don't," John said. "We're going to do it for you. All you have to do is show up tomorrow night. We'll take care of everything."

"I knew you were off today, John, but aren't the rest of you supposed to be at work?" I asked.

"We took off to help you," Bill said. I wondered if I would have seen them at all if nothing unusual had happened in Beaufort. Except for John, my brothers don't have to look very far to find a reason to take off from their jobs.

Mike ordered a couple of large pizzas from Domino's while Frank went to the Piggly Wiggly for beer, Cokes, and

a box of Moon Pies. After they'd all made pigs of themselves with the pizza and beer, they fed pizza to Big Boy
and would have given him beer if I'd let them. Like, their
sister is too young for beer, but her dog could have it. John
gathered the beer that was left out of the fridge to take with
them. He also grabbed the one Corona I'd had in there
when they arrived. I made him put the Corona back.

Bill checked the door three times to be sure it was
locked, and they finally left me alone like I wanted.

Knock, knock.

"Who is it?" I called through the door.

"It's me, Frank. Pa said to tell you to phone us if you
need anything or change your mind about coming over to
the house."

"I will," I called through the door. I knew if I unlocked
it, they'd all come right back in.

Agatha Christie is always good for distraction. Big Boy
and I lay across the bed with *Murder on the Orient Express,*
but I couldn't get past the idea that I should be doing something for Jane.

The phone rang. It was Rizzie telling me she'd found no
sign of Jane and that the sheriff's people were still looking.

The phone rang. It was Otis telling me that Little Fiddlin' Fred's body was being held in Charleston another day
or so, but that he and Odell would work with Melena and
Bone on her plans. "Stay home and rest," he said.

The phone rang. It was Daddy calling to be sure I was
all right.

The phone rang. It was Daddy again. "Calamine," he
said, "I've been thinking. We need to start a reward for information about Jane. I'm going to sell my prewar Gibson
banjo and donate the money to start a fund."

"You don't have to do that," I said, but I was really
grateful. I thought it possible that banjo was the most valuable thing Daddy owned.

"Who else is there to do it?" he replied. "John's going to
post it on that eBay auction place for me."

"But Daddy—"

"Don't argue with your daddy." He hung up.

Maybe there was something more we could do. I called information and got the number for the National Association for Missing Persons. A very nice lady went over ways to get publicity and assured me that the vigil and a reward were both good proactive moves to make. I felt better and reboarded the Orient Express with Mrs. Christie.

After the train ride, I read one of those food mysteries. That wasn't an especially good choice because Jane is such a good cook, it made me think about her. I also started feeling guilty again that I wasn't out searching.

Coke and leftover pizza followed by a Moon Pie for dessert ended my rotten day, but no book or food could comfort me or help me escape my worries.

Chapter Twenty-five

My legs felt sticky with sweat, making me wish I'd worn panty hose or slacks. I sat on a metal folding chair on the makeshift stage of an eighteen-wheeler flatbed. John had arranged to have a trucker friend pull it into the St. Mary Community Park before the sheriff blocked off the entry road to the assembly area. It was set up with portable steps. Might even have been the same steps Happy Jack had put at the front of the stage at the festival.

At first, I'd dressed in work clothes for the vigil, but all black was too mortuary, too funeral, and I was having a hard enough time not thinking of this as a memorial service anyway, so I changed. Shorts seemed too casual, and I'd settled on a blue sundress with leather sandals. The heat and having to sit with my legs neatly tucked together weren't helping the drops of perspiration creeping down my thighs. The gnats flying around our heads didn't do much to make me any more comfortable.

"Vigil." I'd looked up the word in my dictionary. It means "the act of keeping awake, alert." I'd hoped to find details, a pattern or outline of how to conduct a proper vigil for a missing person, but it hadn't turned out to be necessary. Daddy and The Boys had taken over all of the details after my experience at the religious supply store, but could I really expect my redneck family to plan something this important properly? I hoped so.

The lady from the National Association of Missing Persons had called back to check on us. She affirmed we were taking the right steps. Seeking publicity through all forms of media, posting notices, and holding a vigil were all recommended ways to keep a missing person in the public's eye, and would, according to the woman, help find Jane.

She also said that more than fifty thousand adults are classified as "missing" in the United States. Some of those fifty thousand are, no doubt, people who left home saying they were going to pick up a loaf of bread or a six-pack of beer and never returned because they'd run off to start a new life. Some had been abducted, molested, killed, and would eventually be found as skeletons. Horrible, but not as bad to me as never finding your loved one, never knowing if the person was dead or maybe somewhere enduring torture and pain for years. These were my greatest fears: that Jane would never be found and that she would suffer.

Daddy and John sat onstage with me along with Pastor Christianson, Lisa Owen, several people from the Jade County Commission for the Blind, and two teachers from St. Mary High School.

Frank and Mike circulated as people arrived, passing out candles with wax guards and lighting them even though the sun hadn't set. I'd been afraid no one would show up, but the crowd grew steadily. I scanned the people, searching for a glimpse of Dean and Andy. I didn't see them . . . yet. I had no doubt that Dean was a man of his word and would be there soon.

Bone and Melena strolled around, being stopped occasionally by people who were probably expressing their sympathy for Melena's loss. My brother Bill walked across the park and stopped at the end of the flatbed. He had his arm around a blonde-haired woman I'd never seen before.

"Who's that?" I asked John, elbowing him and nodding toward Bill and the blonde. "Is that Lucy?"

"Yes," he whispered. "That's who Bill's been showing around town and had out to the house for dinner last weekend." He chuckled. "Years ago, Confederate Railroad put out a song called 'Trashy Women.' I think Lucy could have modeled for the album cover."

"I remember that song. In fact, Bill used to play the CD a lot."

"He sure did." John smiled.

The woman was shrink-wrapped in an overflowing halter top and short shorts—hot pants, cooter cutters, whatever anyone calls pants so tight and high that nothing is left to the imagination. Her sandals were six-inch platforms. Maybe that's why she kept leaning or falling into Bill. Rubbing up against him. True to the words of the song, she looked a lot like a "cocktail waitress in a Dolly Parton wig." I vowed to darken my blonde hair ASAP.

I might even decrease the inflation in my bra. Puhleeze, that was a ridiculous thought. My air bosom wasn't anywhere near the size of Lucy's flesh one. Not one, her flesh pair. I wouldn't fit into any of my clothes with that much chest. Come to think of it, Lucy's chest didn't fit into her clothes either.

John stood and walked to the microphone. "Good evening, ladies and gentlemen, I'm John Parrish. Thank you for coming tonight to show your concern for Jane Baker. I'm sure we are all here for the same reason: to express our support and desire for Jane to be safely returned to her home and loved ones. Pastor Dan Christianson will now lead us in devotions."

I can't repeat what Pastor Christianson said because I wasn't listening. I was scanning the crowd searching for Andy. Well, Dean, too. People just kept coming. Some of them I knew, but there were a lot of strangers. Photographers snapped pictures, and a video camera with "NBC" stenciled on the side was aimed at the stage.

The crowd stood respectfully watching Pastor Christianson. Except my brother Bill. He was whispering in Loose Lucy's ear, and she was laughing. I wanted to go down there and smack both of them.

John and Daddy had insisted I sit up on the "stage." They wanted me to speak about Jane, but I couldn't. I just couldn't. I knew I'd break down and sob if I tried to talk because I burst into tears every time I thought of her, which was almost every minute.

The teachers spoke of Jane's being the first blind student mainstreamed through St. Mary High. The folks from the Commission for the Blind each said a few words about Jane. They didn't mention the bad habits of her youth nor the time the commission had made such a big to-do about her giving blind people a bad name when she was caught shoplifting. I smiled when I remembered Jane's reaction to their reproach. "What are they gonna do? Cancel my membership in the world's blind people?"

When Lisa Owen was introduced, she walked up to that microphone like she owned it. Like she owned the whole world, for that matter. She had a guitar in her hand and was wearing a red-sequined spaghetti-strap dress with ruffles around her knees. Dressed like she did to perform at clubs in Beaufort. I was glad she hadn't worn the dowdy brown dress she wears when she sings for funerals at Middleton's.

"I'm Lisa Owen," she said, "and I've been invited to sing for you tonight. When I thought about what songs to do, my mind went to hymns because we're all praying that God will see fit to send Jane Baker home safely, but first, I'm going to do a song for Jane. Every time she's ever been anywhere that I sang, she's asked for a Patsy Cline, so, Jane, this is for you."

The medley of Cline numbers lasted almost fifteen minutes and included some tear-jerking pieces like "Crazy" and "I Fall to Pieces," but instead of making me cry, they made me remember happy times with Jane. The applause was enthusiastic.

"Now," Lisa said, "I'm going to sing my favorite hymn.

Join me if you like." I expected "Amazing Grace," but I was wrong.

With only a guitar accompaniment, Lisa sang "How Great Thou Art" with as much power as I'd ever heard it done. Everyone out there sang with her except Bill and Lucy, who just happened to be sharing a kiss at that moment. Now, I didn't want to go down there and smack him. I wanted Daddy to go down there. Daddy can smack a lot harder than I can. That would serve Bill right. Then again, it would also be disrespectful to Jane.

Since there was no roof over the park, I couldn't say the applause brought down the house, but it was thunderous and long. While people were still clapping and yelling, a bus pulled up the drive. A bus with a magnetic "Broken Fence" sign on the side. Dean must have convinced the deputy at the park entrance to let the bus through by telling him the band was part of the vigil program. I expected to see Andy and Dean step out, and they did, both carrying guitar cases. What I didn't expect was all the other musicians with instruments who piled out of the bus like clowns who keep coming and coming out of a phony little Volkswagen at the circus.

John had planned to invite anyone who wanted to speak to come up after Lisa sang. I leaned over to tell him to wait, that these guys would perform, too, but he'd already stood and gone to the microphone.

"If anyone would like to speak now, please come forward," John said. The first person was Melena Delgado. She'd only known Jane a few days and, according to Otis, her husband was now lying in his coffin over at the mortuary, so what did she need to say? I should have expected what came out of her mouth.

"I'm Melena Delgado, and most of you don't know me. I grew up at Adam's Creek as Melanie Jones, and I've been gone for many years, but I had the good fortune to meet Jane Baker last weekend at the bluegrass festival on Surcie Island. She seemed to be a really nice person and, like all of you, I hope she's home soon." She waved her hand, shooing away a mosquito or moth. I couldn't tell exactly what it was. Then she said what she'd come up there to say.

"I wanted to speak to you for another reason," Melena continued. "I've been gone from Adam's Creek so long because I was traveling with my husband. He was one of the most talented musicians in the world, and he was tragically struck down last weekend. The funeral services for my husband, Little Fiddlin' Fred Delgado, will be tomorrow afternoon at three o'clock at the Adam's Creek Baptist Church. Fred's body will be moved to the church at one o'clock for visitation for two hours before the service so that people from out of town can attend the wake and the funeral the same day. There will be a lot of Fred's friends and fans there. You are all invited to attend."

Silence. Bone met Melena at the steps and assisted her down. More silence. What could people do? Applause wasn't an acceptable response to an invitation to a funeral. As Bone and Melena walked through, people spoke softly to her. I assumed they were expressing condolences, maybe even telling her they planned to attend Fred's services.

Otis and Odell each came up and said a few nice words about Jane, about how they'd grown to love her since her friend, Callie Parrish, had come to work for them. They both gestured back at me when they said my name. John leaned close to me.

"Callie," he whispered, "you need to speak. Jane has no family and you're her closest friend. You need to stand up for her." He nodded toward the musicians standing outside the bus. "Then introduce your friends. I think they've come to perform for Jane."

Fright makes me heave. It always has. When I was a little girl, it was a good thing. My brothers learned early not to scare me. It wasn't worth Daddy making them clean up what I threw up. In school, standing in front of a group of people was terrifying. My oral reports always ended halfway through with my mad dash for the girls' restroom. In college, I'd learned that I had no trouble talking to little people. Not little people like Fred Delgado. Little like five-year-olds, so I'd taught kindergarten before working at Middleton's, but speaking to a class of preschoolers was nothing like standing in front of this crowd that numbered in the hundreds.

I shook my head no. John leaned over again, but before he said a word, Daddy bent toward me from the other side and said, "Do it for Jane, or I'll get up and make a speech."

Now, I know my father is a redneck, and he named me Calamine Lotion Parrish when he was drunk, trying to think of a girl's name and something pink, but he is a loving person and would probably have said some great things about Jane. On the other hand, he can't talk very long without telling some chauvinistic joke, so I stood and walked slowly up to the microphone. I looked out, and the crowd grew to thousands in my mind. My stomach roiled and gurgled. I spotted Sheriff Harmon nodding and smiling at me. He was a friend of all five of my brothers and knew me growing up. He probably expected me to hurl any minute.

I cleared my throat and managed to squeak out, "I'm Calamine Parrish." Don't know why I said that. Hardly anyone except Daddy ever calls me anything but Callie. "This is hard for me," I said. "I'm not comfortable speaking to crowds, but talking to you tonight isn't half as hard as missing my best friend, Jane." I told them about how Jane can cook and take care of herself though she's completely sightless. I told them how she'd come from the school for the blind in ninth grade and been like a sister to me since then. I did not tell them about Jane's wilder days when she shoplifted and tried drugs. I didn't tell them she earns her living talking sex on a 900 number either.

The video camera was trained right on me, but my stomach had quieted. "If you know anything, anything at all, about the disappearance of my friend Jane, please call the Jade County Sheriff's Department or any other law enforcement office. Bring her home."

I sat down before I remembered what John had said about the bluegrassers, so he stood and announced that now we'd have more music. To my everlasting appreciation, John then suggested that we clear the stage and turn it over to the "pickers." I'm not too fond of that term. Makes me think of five-year-old noses, but Dean, Andy, and the other musicians helped remove the chairs from the stage and congregated behind the mic. Lisa left the stage with the rest of us, but Dean called her back up to sing with them.

Jane would have loved the music. No songs about death. No songs about killing. Lots of fast-moving music that inspired some people to dance on the grass. Not slow-dancing either—clogging and even some shagging. By the way, the shag is the state dance of South Carolina and has nothing to do with the other meaning of the word, and I'm not talking about carpet.

My intention was to have a word with Bill, but people kept stopping me to talk. Rizzie ran over. She hugged me and told me that, so far as she knew, no one had found anything related to Jane.

Melena and Bone wanted to talk. Bone flirted. Melena bragged about how great the vigil was and how glad she was that she'd suggested it. She still thought a horse-drawn carriage would be wonderful to carry Fred from the mortuary to the church even though the casket wasn't gold-lined, but she didn't want to go to too much extra expense because she knew Fred would want her to use part of the insurance money to finish her college education. She captured several insects in her jar while we spoke. I finally got away from her and headed toward Bill and Lucy.

Sheriff Harmon cornered me before I got there, saving Bill a tongue-lashing and maybe more for his inappropriate behavior. I really did feel like smacking him. The sheriff asked me to step away from the stage area so we could talk.

"Callie, you did good with this. And the posters and publicity are right, too. I should have gone along with you on Jane being taken out of that bus from the first minute we knew she was missing." He smiled. "What's this I hear about you and the Beaufort police?"

I told him all about my encounter from my point of

view. I asked, "What's going on with the murders? I've been so torn up about Jane that I haven't kept up with the news on Little Fiddlin' Fred and Kenny Strickland."

"You know perfectly well that I'm not supposed to tell you about cases, but I will tell you we've got reports back, and it seems they were both victims of the same killer. We don't have significant fingerprints on anything, though."

"Why do you think it's the same killer if there aren't any fingerprints?"

"MOM."

"Oh." I knew that MOM wasn't some new strand of DNA. It stands for motive, opportunity, and means. Usually when an investigation answers these three, the crime is solved. "All three?" I asked.

"No, but the means are related. Both men were killed with weapons made of stuff musicians use, but more important, both victims were sedated before death."

"Chloroformed?"

"Not chloroform, but a type of ether. It would have subdued them before the actual murders. They would both have been unconscious at the time of their deaths."

"That would explain why Fred was still enough for someone to ram a tuning fork up his nose and how Kenny could have been strangled from the front without a lot of defensive marks on him."

"Yes, and Callie, there probably is some connection between those two and Jane . . ."

"Don't say it. Don't say that to me!" I yelled. "I don't want to hear it. I just want you to find her."

"I'm trying, and so is everyone else."

Curiosity calmed my hysteria for a moment. "Why? Why do you think now that Jane was taken when before you insisted she'd run off? And what's the connection between her disappearance and the murders?"

"I can't tell you."

"You started it, so you tell me." My words were angry until I realized this was Wayne Harmon, the same Wayne who'd given me gum when he hung out with my brothers when I was his friends' bratty little sister. I changed my tactics. Let my eyes fill with tears, which wasn't hard to do because it seemed I was crying constantly anyway. Then I put my hand on his sleeve and said, in my most little girl, though not Magnolia Mouth, voice, "Please."

"Okay, but you keep it quiet. I sent Jane's cane to the lab. It has the same chemical on it that was used to sedate the victims. It's not visible, but the analysts found traces in a pattern consistent with an ether compound used on sponges having been poured or spilled on the cane." He frowned. "I'm sorry, Callie."

I don't know what might have happened then if a song hadn't ended and we hadn't heard a scream. Would I have fainted or yelled or just sobbed? I'll never know. Sheriff Harmon ran toward the sound, and I was right behind him.

The noise came from the front corner of the stage where I'd last seen my brother Bill with Miss Trashy Woman Lucy.

The blonde bimbo was teetering away from Bill, hands covering her mouth and part of her horrified expression, but not blocking her screams, as she tried to right herself on those ridiculous shoes.

Bill's face was also partially covered, but not by his hands. He held his arms up over his head, blocking his face with his elbows. He was jumping around trying to turn and run. Daddy stood beside him, and every time Bill tried to step away, Daddy pushed him right back toward the petite redhead who was whacking him with a plastic grocery sack.

I'd wanted to smack my brother. His girlfriend, Molly, or should I say *ex-girlfriend*, wasn't just swatting him, she was beating the you-know-what out of him. Just as the sheriff got to them and reached out to take the plastic bag, it broke and showered Bill with its contents. I recognized many of the items as little dog figurines he'd bought for Molly when things were good between them. I saw a few jewelry boxes fall at Bill's feet, too.

Molly had been screeching, "I hate you! I hate you!" but

when the sheriff pulled her back and restrained her by wrapping his arms around her, she burst into sobs.

Bill still tried to get away, but Daddy held him right where he was.

"What's going on?" Sheriff Harmon asked.

"She just ran up and started hitting us," Lucy said. No, actually, she whined.

"Should I take all of you back to my office to discuss this?" Harmon said.

"I want her arrested," Bill said. Daddy released him and Bill swiped his hand across the blood under his nose. "I want her in jail."

"No, he don't," Daddy said.

"I do, too."

Daddy pulled Bill over to the side and whispered in his ear for a few minutes.

"Okay, Pa, okay," Bill muttered to Daddy, then turned to Harmon and Molly. "Let's all go home. Wayne, I don't want to press any charges against Molly. I just want to go to the house and get cleaned up."

"Are you sure?"

"I'm positive. Just forget it."

"Do you want me to . . . " Lucy started, but Bill shook his head no at her.

As Daddy led Bill away, I heard him say, "Boy, how many times have I told you a man can't stock two shelves? And even if he can, it ain't worth the bother."

"I'll get one of my men to take you home," Sheriff Harmon said to Molly.

"No, I've got my car in the parking lot. I'm sorry. I just saw Bill with that woman on television, and I went crazy."

"On television?" I asked.

"Yeah, the vigil's on TV—live coverage. I hadn't planned to come, but I got so mad I just couldn't stay home. I brought the things Bill gave me to return to him, but when I got here, I wasn't able to stop myself."

"Go on home, Molly," the sheriff said. "I'll walk you to your car. Life will seem better tomorrow."

I looked around me, expecting everyone to be gathered with us, but most of the people were still watching the musicians and seeming to ignore what had happened. Dean announced that it was midnight and the vigil was over. He invited everyone to sing "Amazing Grace" with them.

When the song ended, people began leaving the area, still carrying their lighted candles, most of which had burned down to barely stubs above the wax catchers. I realized that I never got one, never lit a candle for Jane. Nevertheless, the vigil had been a success. Even been shown on television. That's what the woman from the missing persons' group had said. Involve as many people as possible and keep Jane's name and picture in front of the public.

"Want to go somewhere for a cup of coffee?" a familiar voice said in my ear.

"It's after midnight," I answered Andy. "In this town, they roll the streets up before eleven."

He leaned in closer to me. "Do you have any coffee at your place?"

I grinned. "Yes, I do."

"Got your car?"

"Yes, I do."

"Let me tell Dean I'm riding with you," he said and walked over to Dean.

The thought never crossed my mind that if he rode to my apartment with me for coffee, he wouldn't have a way back to wherever all the musicians were staying.

C'est la vie.

Chapter Twenty-six

*H*ot! Buh-leeve me. My first kiss with Andy was a volcanic eruption. He didn't waste any time waiting until we were at my apartment, either. When we walked up to the Mustang in the parking lot, he set his guitar case down, opened the driver's door, turned, and reached for me. The embrace was tight, and the kiss, the right thing to do. It even seemed fine when it deepened. Then I thought about us grubbing in public as cars passed leaving the vigil. We were behaving exactly like Bill and Lucy. I pulled back from Andy's arms.

"I'm sorry," he said softly. "I've wanted to do that since I met you." He put his guitar in the backseat, walked around the car, and climbed into the passenger side. I sat and pulled the driver's door closed for myself.

"No, don't be sorry." I backed the car out of its parking space. "I wanted that kiss as much as you did, but not out here where everyone's driving by."

"You're right." He grinned. "I just couldn't help myself." He touched my shoulder. His hand set off fire that swept through my body and settled below. "You're holding up well, Callie. I've been worried about you."

"It's not easy. I cry a lot, but I'm trying to stay busy putting up flyers and getting the word out about Jane." I didn't see any point in telling him about the Beaufort police incident.

"I'm proud of you." He turned on the radio and fiddled with the buttons until he found WXYW.

Neither of us spoke the rest of the way, just listened to the music. Right before we arrived at my apartment, we heard a public service announcement about Jane. "Did you arrange that?" Andy asked.

"I sent releases everywhere: newspapers, radio, television, and even the World Wide Web."

"Nice," Andy said when I pulled the Mustang into my driveway in front of the brick house where I live.

I wasn't sure if he meant the announcement or my building, but I responded as though he referred to my place. "It's not all mine," I said. "It's a duplex, but nobody lives next door."

While I fumbled with the key, Andy leaned over and smelled the red geraniums in the terra-cotta pots on either side of the front door. He'd see more of those if he went to the mortuary while he was in St. Mary. The Middletons have lots of planters on the wraparound veranda at the funeral home, and they pay St. Mary Florals to keep seasonal plants potted in them. I had a similar one that was broken during an attempted burglary. When I replaced it, the containers were buy one, get one free, so I put a planter on each side of the door. I can't afford to have the florist maintain mine, so when the flowers are changed seasonally at work, I go to Wally World in Beaufort and buy the same kind. Right then, we had red geraniums in the pots.

"Really nice," Andy said when I opened the door. Excuuze me. I live here. I know that avacado green shag carpet from the '60s is not *really nice*. The only thing really nice in my apartment was shut up in the bathroom, so I went directly and let Big Boy out. I was glad that Molly hadn't repeated her threat to take him back when I saw her at the vigil, but then, she was otherwise occupied at the time.

As always, Big Boy got excited that I was home. He's learned not to wet on the papers I put down for him, so he's usually in a big hurry to go outside. He's also in a rush to see his "mama." I know I vowed not to get all silly about this dog, but I'd found myself calling him with, "Hey, Big Boy, come to Mama."

That started after he had his ears cropped, which the vet called a procedure, but which, so far as I'm concerned, was surgery. I rubbed the dog's head and told him, "Down," when he put his front paws on my shoulders and licked my cheeks. Big Boy is an enthusiastic kisser. This thought put my mind back on Andy.

I took Big Boy's leash from the doorknob, clipped it onto his collar, and handed it to Andy.

"Would you mind taking him out for a minute while I put on the coffee?" I asked.

Andy accepted the leash, but said, "Do you really want coffee?"

"I thought you wanted coffee."

"I just want to spend time with you. Forget the coffee, and we'll take Big Boy for a walk together."

Too long. It had been far too long since I'd gone for a moonlight walk holding hands with a man. Not that I don't date. There's this doctor I see sometimes. He's nice, but I only hold his hands when I'm trying to stop them from unzipping my jeans. Jane tells me that my holding out will drive him away, but it hasn't yet. Sometimes, I think it's what keeps him coming back. I'm not *playing* hard-to-get. I just can't see myself in an open relationship, which is what the doc wants.

Big Boy stepped behind a bush and squatted as he always does. "He still tee-tees like a shy little girl," I commented.

"Are you a shy little girl?" Andy's voice was a seductive tease.

"Well, I don't hide behind bushes to go to the bathroom, but I don't hike my leg either."

Andy chuckled.

We must have walked a mile from the house, just talking. Andy told me that he and the other musicians were camping at Happy Jack's on Surcie Island and would stay in the Low Country for Fred Delgado's services tomorrow, then head upstate for Kenny Strickland's funeral. He said that he'd gone with the members of Broken Fence to see Mrs. Strickland. Kenny was from a large, supportive family, so the band had come down for the vigil.

"Has there been any reason suggested for either murder?" I asked.

"Not that I know of," Andy said.

I told him what I'd been doing to get Jane's story into the spotlight. We stopped while Big Boy investigated a mole tunnel. Andy's second kiss was even better than the first. We walked another block or so before I said, "We'd better turn around."

Back at the front door to my apartment, Big Boy rushed past us. "Where's he headed?" Andy asked.

"He's tired. He'll jump on the bed hoping I don't make him get down."

Andy snaked his arm around my waist. "Do you think there's room for all three of us in there?"

Ex-cuuze me. I had no intention of bedding down with a man while my dog was in the same room, much less the same bed. Andy must have sensed my reaction. "It's too hot for coffee," he said, "do you have anything cold to drink?"

"Probably beer or soda," I said and led him into the kitchen. "What's your pleasure?"

Andy grinned. I realized what I'd said. Kinda like the old "Coffee? Tea? Or me?" But to his credit, he didn't answer, just stepped in front of me and opened the refrigerator door. He stood on the other side of it peering in at the meager offerings. I don't keep a well-stocked pantry or fridge under the best circumstances. With all that had happened, I knew there wasn't much.

"Well," he said, "you've got a Coke and one Corona. Which do you want? Don't count on any lime with the Corona. The one in here looks like it shriveled up and died six months ago."

"Doesn't matter to me. I'll take whatever you don't want."

Andy laughed. "I want the beer, but maybe you should have it. You seem very tense. Perhaps it will help you relax."

"If you think one beer is going to get me drunk and turn me into a loose woman, you're mistaken." I said it jokingly, but I meant every word.

"Give me a glass, and I'll pour half of it for you. I would *never* attempt to use alcohol to have my way with a woman." At first, I thought I'd insulted him, but the sparkle in Andy's eyes showed me he was teasing.

I handed a glass over the refrigerator door. Andy poured it about half full, then gave it back to me, still over the door.

"Let's go sit in the living room," I said.

"I can't," Andy said and took a pull of beer from the bottle.

"Why?"

"I don't want you to see what you do to me."

Good grief! Like a gal who's been married as well as grew up with five brothers, all of whom went through puberty, had never seen a woody tent before. "I'm going to the restroom," I said. "You come on out of the fridge and bring your beer to the couch. I'll be back in a minute."

I did that to give him time to cool down. I promise that's what I meant, but while in the bathroom, I realized that my words could have been misinterpreted, making him think I was in there preparing to respond to his condition.

Why now? Why when I was so upset about Jane? It had been a long time for me. The chemistry was great with Andy, and I knew that Jane wouldn't think bad of me if I gave in while she was missing—but I would. The physical desire was there, but I felt too emotionally tired, too worn out. Besides, I'd never bought into the sex-as-sport point of view and although I felt like I'd known Andy forever, it had really been only a few days.

I ran the water a long time, scrubbing my hands like a doctor preparing for surgery.

"Get your hands clean?" Andy said when I joined him on the couch.

"Yes," I said softly.

"Taking time to think?"

"Uh-huh."

"It's okay," he said. "As much as I want to make love to you, I understand this isn't the best time for romance." He picked up the remote and turned on the television. He flipped through the channels, hitting nothing but infomercials until he was up in the high hundreds and found soft music. "Do you dance?"

"Sometimes."

"Want to dance now?"

"Okay." We stood, and with his arms wrapped around me, we slowly swayed back and forth to the music. I thought of Jane. She hates dancing. Tears filled my eyes, and he wiped them away, whispering, "It's okay, Callie, it's okay." After a while, he backed me to the sofa, sat down, and held me while I cried.

I awoke to the tinny *brrrrring* of the phone with the sun beaming through the blinds onto the couch where I'd slept in Andy's arms. I let it ring. Andy brushed his lips across my neck.

"I'm sorry if I led you on," I said. "I'm not a tease."

"Callie here. Talk," my answering machine told the caller.

"Hey, Callie," I heard Otis say. "Did you oversleep? Mrs. Delgado has delivered clothes for her husband. What time will you be here? We've got to move him at noon. At least, that's the plan for now. That woman changes her mind every five minutes."

I picked up the receiver and told my boss I'd be at the mortuary shortly. Andy politely moved back while I talked.

I really liked that. Donnie, my ex-husband, used to delight in touching me and licking my ears when I was on a business call. He thought that was cute or sexy or something, but buh-leeve me, it was just aggravation.

"Do you want me to take you to the campground?" I asked Andy when I hung up.

"No, I'll call Dean on his cell to pick me up from the funeral home, but first, can I have that coffee you promised me last night?"

"Would you make it? I have to dress for work."

By the time I showered and came out wearing a black dress with my hair sleeked back into a bun, Andy had poured two cups. He'd also found a few slices of bread and made toast. Elvis toast, fried in butter in a black cast-iron skillet. Well, at my house, fried in margarine, but still very fattening and very delicious.

When Andy walked me out to the Mustang, he kissed me again at the door. If Otis and Odell weren't waiting for me, I might have turned around and led Andy back into my apartment. "Are you thinking what I'm thinking?" he asked.

"Probably, but I have to go to work."

"Probably?" His eyebrows and lips puckered into a little boy pout.

"Definitely," I assured him.

After we parked in my space behind the mortuary, Andy kissed me again. He whispered something.

"I couldn't hear you."

"Another time, another place," he said and winked.

Trite.

But probably true.

Chapter Twenty-seven

"**O**tis, where are his clothes?" I called as I walked from my workroom to the prep room. I didn't yell, because we don't speak loudly or shout in the funeral home even when there are no other living persons on the premises.

In this case, Andy sat up front in one of the overstuffed chairs in the entry area. Buh-leeve me, from the feelings he stirred up in me, Andy was definitely a live one. He'd had no luck calling Dean's cell while Dean was on the island, but just as I decided I'd have to take him to Surcie Island and be even later to work, Dean had called Andy and told him the grassers were off the island and headed toward St. Mary. Now, Andy was waiting for Dean while I was supposed to be grooming and dressing Little Fiddlin' Fred.

The problem was that the casket sat on a bier by the wall and Mr. Delgado lay on the gurney, neatly covered to his chin, but there were no clothes hanging on the rack. I'd peeked under the sheet to see if Otis had dressed him, though that would have been very strange since I hadn't yet applied makeup or done Mr. Delgado's hair and nails. Sure enough, Mr. Delgado was wearing only the white boxer shorts supplied by Middleton's Mortuary.

Most of the time, the door to the prep room stays locked. Both Otis and Odell have keys, but anyone else has to be admitted by one of them.

"Wait a minute, Callie, I'm com . . . ," Otis answered me as I nudged against the normally locked door. This morning, of all mornings, the door wasn't tightly closed. I pushed it open just far enough to see Otis climbing out of his tanning bed. There would be no tan lines on my boss. He was as commando as a man can be. I was speechless, rooted to the spot with my mouth hanging open and my eyes bugging.

"Eeee!" Otis screamed as I yanked the door shut.

I've heard many words for the male package, from the kindergartener's "pee pee" to some hard-core words from my ex, Donnie, that my brothers probably have also spoken, but never in front of me. The funniest expression for boy privates I've ever heard is "twig and berries."

Those were the words that popped into my mind during that microsecond when the door was open and I saw a full frontal view of my tanned-all-over boss. Perfect description for his appendages—twig and berries. The only thing worse than seeing Otis nude would be to see Odell. Come to think of it, they're twins. Seen one, seen 'em both.

Eeyuuuh! The sound effects were mine this time, but not aloud. Only in my mind, which quickly switched to recovery mode. I didn't believe Otis and I could ever get beyond the incident if we acknowledged it. Best to pretend it didn't happen.

"Otis? Are you all right? Did you fall?" I asked in my kindergarten teacher voice as though I hadn't seen a thing.

"I'm okay. Be there in a minute," he mumbled.

"I just need to know where Fred Delgado's clothes are," I said through the door.

"I put them in your office," he answered.

"Okay, I'm getting started now. I'll be in my workroom," I assured him.

Sure enough, an opaque Lundin's Formal Wear garment bag hung on a hanger from the doorknob to my office.

Usually Otis or Odell leaves clothing on a special rack in my workroom. Otis must have been in a hurry to get to his tanning bed when Mrs. Delgado came by.

Back in my area, I pulled on a waterproof smock and gloves before I opened the plastic and removed the suit to hang it up. I'd expected stage duds, and the suit was fancy, but not country or bluegrass. What Melena had brought for her husband's burial was a formal black tuxedo with a pleated white shirt, black cummerbund, and bow tie. Shoes are kinda optional, but in the bottom of the bag was a shoebox with new black silk socks stuffed into formal black patent leathers.

I removed the sheet. Mr. Delgado looked tinier on the gurney than he had when I'd seen him on television. I confess I'd been dreading working on Little Fiddlin' Fred. I absolutely hate when we have children's funerals. Death is sad, as most good-byes are, but when it's a child, it tears me up. I'd worried that anyone so small as Fred would have the same effect on me. His arms and legs were short, but, like I said, Mr. Delgado's torso was muscled and he had broad shoulders. Hopefully I wouldn't have the reactions that I have when I work on small children.

A knock on my door. I don't lock it, but I was surprised to think Andy would search me out. I'd told him that only mortuary employees are allowed in work areas, but he probably wanted to tell me Dean had arrived and they were leaving. I opened the door to Otis, standing there with a red face. Either he was embarrassed or he'd overstayed in the tanning bed.

"I wanted to tell you," he said, "to be very gentle with Mr. Delgado's head."

Duh, I thought. "Respect" is the key word for how Middleton's treats all deceased. I'm never rough, but even a cosmetician who wasn't as conscientious as I am would have enough sense to use extra care with autopsied individuals.

"Due to the manner of Mr. Delgado's death," Otis continued, "I had to do some rebuilding of his nose."

"Thanks for letting me know. A friend of mine is in the

entry hall waiting to be picked up. Could you check and see if he's still there?"

The color of my boss's face had faded from crimson to its usual tanned hue, and I decided that Otis had been worried about the fact that I'd seen him. Since I acted as though I hadn't, I hoped our working relationship would continue unchanged.

"Sure," he said.

In a few minutes, I heard laughter from the entry area and the sound of footsteps in the hall.

"Hey, Callie," Otis called, "Andy and I are going to have coffee in my office. We'll be listening for the front door. Call me when you're ready to dress Mr. Delgado, and I'll come help."

Mechanical body lifts in my workroom enable me to dress and casket even large adults by myself, but Otis always assists if he's around. Neither of my bosses has ever been discourteous to me in any way, but Otis is usually more thoughtful than his brother, Odell. Of course, Odell's thoughts are usually on food, especially barbecue.

Sometimes I airbrush makeup, but having been cautioned about the nose, I chose to apply everything delicately by hand. When necessary, I clip hairs from ears and noses, but Mr. Delgado was already well groomed. No wild hairs curling off his eyebrows, either.

Women receive manicures and nail polish, clear or color of survivors' request. Men's hands frequently take much longer for me, even though I buff the nails instead of polishing them, because a lot of men's hands have never received much attention. Fred's nails had obviously not been neglected. I wondered if that had been one of the ways Melena took care of him.

As I pulled new socks onto Fred's feet, I remembered my promise to give Rizzie's Maum a manicure and pedicure. I planned to take my whole nail kit to the island and let the lady choose which shade of red she liked.

Laughter kept spilling through the walls from Otis's office. I was glad to hear it—most of the time, Otis is very serious. Just as I decided to dress Little Fiddlin' Fred by myself and leave Otis and Andy to their visit, the notes of "What a Friend We Have in Jesus" sounded. Someone had opened the front door of the funeral home. I hoped Dean had come for Andy and that the arrival wasn't Melena wanting to see her husband before I finished my work. At Middleton's, we don't like making customers wait.

Dalmation! I heard Melena's voice, followed by Andy's.

"Are you done?" Otis asked through my door.

"Almost. Just need to dress him."

"I'll help," Otis said and came in. "Your friend Andy is very entertaining. I left him with Mrs. Delgado until we're ready to move Mr. Delgado into Slumber Room A." He helped me with the tux, and I was surprised he didn't comment on how fast we got Little Fiddlin' Fred clothed and in his casket. Buh-leeve me, the last thing I wanted was for Melena to have a lot of flirting time with Andy while we prepped her husband for the public.

"Did you see the memorial table?" Otis asked as we slowly pushed the bier into the hall and to the side door of Slumber Room A.

"No," I said, though I wasn't paying much attention to Otis. I was trying to hear what Melena and Andy were saying at the front entry.

"Mrs. Delgado set it up when she brought his clothes in," Otis said. I wondered if this were a mild reprimand for my being late. Usually the bereaved leave what they want, and I put together the memorial table display. I'd been nagging Otis and Odell about doing video memorials, but so far they weren't ready to spend the money.

"She insisted on fixing it herself even when I assured her that you always make beautiful arrangements," Otis continued as we entered Slumber Room A. We situated the bier and casket so that Mr. Delgado's left was to the wall. The room was filled with flowers, including the fiddle-shaped casket spray and several more wreaths with musical themes. We put the floral fiddle on the bottom half of the casket and arranged the others around the room. The guest register stand was already by the main door.

Andy and Melena entered, with Andy holding her arm as though he were escorting her to the prom. Melena had on a pale yellow peasant blouse, pulled off the shoulders as most of her blouses seemed to be, a denim skirt, and yellow sandals. Otis stepped to her other side and the two men escorted Melena to the casket.

We're always careful when survivors see their loved ones in the casket for the first time, and if Andy hadn't been there, I would have stood with Melena and Otis, but I figured two men could handle Melena if she reacted by fainting, screaming, or, even worse, trying to climb into the coffin. I didn't want to leave the room, because I wanted to hear what she and Andy said, so I turned to the memorial table.

Otis told the truth when he said I'm good at arranging displays. That probably evolved from creating learning centers and bulletin boards while I taught. I would like to say that Melena should have let me do my job, but I couldn't have done any better than she had.

Several large silver-framed photographs of Little Fiddlin' Fred provided background. Centered on the table, his fiddle rested on an unusual stand that put it at about a forty-five-degree angle to the surface. Surrounding the instrument, Melena had fanned bluegrass magazines opened to articles about her husband. Among them, she'd placed fiddling awards Fred had earned through the years.

"Why is the bottom half closed?" Melena asked.

"This is what you selected," Otis responded in his undertaker voice. "It's not meant to be fully open like a couch casket."

"What do you mean a couch?" Melena said.

"Caskets that have one lid from head to foot," Otis continued. "This is the one you settled on, which is called a half-lid."

"Oh, this is much better," Andy said. Mentally I thanked him for getting into the conversation. Melena had wanted a full-size adult casket, and we'd positioned Mr. Delgado so

that his upper torso filled the top half. Centering his body
on a full couch would have emphasized his height and
made him look even smaller than he really was.

"Okay, I didn't realize that." She turned away and said, "I
left some things in the hall." She stepped out and right back
in only a minute later with a fiddle bow in one hand and a
small silver-framed photo in the other.

"Can you put these in his hands?" Melena asked Otis.

"Certainly," he said, though we prefer to have anything
the body is to hold before we do the prep. I knew that Otis
would make it work even if he had to close the doors to the
room and superglue the items into Fred's grasp. "Is there
anything else you want changed?" he asked.

"No, just let him hold the bow and my picture, and if
anyone comes here before the service, it's fine for them to
see him." She looked at Andy and motioned toward the
register stand. "Did you sign yet?"

"I will now."

"It Is No Secret What God Can Do" rang softly from
the speakers.

Dean Holdback entered and gave Melena a little hug.
He looked at me and mouthed, *Any word?* I shook my head
no. Dean stepped up to the casket and looked down.
"Never saw Fred decked out so fancy," Dean said.

"I wanted him to look nice," Melena said. "You know,
Fred was very talented. He could have been a violinist if
he'd wanted."

So that explained the tuxedo.

Dean signed the register, then offered to buy Melena a
late breakfast. "Oh," she said, "brunch would be fun, but I
have to be back here in time for the procession."

I gave Otis a *What procession?* look.

He nodded so slightly that no one would have noticed
but me. I could read his expression. It meant, *I'll tell you
later.*

"I'm meeting the others at a place called the Snack
Shack," Dean said. "I understand it's not far from here, so
we'll have you back whatever time you say." He glanced at

me. "You're working aren't you?"

It felt like I waited a full two or three minutes for Otis to tell me it would be all right for me to go with my friends. He said nothing, and they left without me.

As soon as the front door music stopped, I asked Otis, "What procession? I thought the body was being set in the church at one o'clock for visitation, followed by services at three."

"Mrs. Delgado's brother called me this morning. Said they never found horses and a carriage any less expensive than I quoted, so Mrs. Delgado asked the group her husband was supposed to perform with to let him be moved in their band bus."

"What?" I sputtered.

"Not so strange. We've had firefighters who were taken from the chapel to the cemetery on fire trucks." Otis was realigning the floral arrangements so the spaces between them were equal.

"How are they going to get a casket on the bus?" I asked.

"They're not. Jack Wilburn is supplying a trailer that the bus will tow with the casket. Mrs. Delgado and close friends will follow in a procession."

"She doesn't plan to walk that far, does she?"

"No. Jack Wilburn arranged with Cowboy over at the Truck Corral in Beaufort to lend them a car for Mrs. Delgado. The others will drive themselves. We're not supplying but one vehicle. No funeral coach and no family limousines. I haven't decided if this is to economize or for show."

"Have you ever seen Cowboy's car?"

"Not that I remember."

"He drives a bright red Solstice convertible."

"Well, you know my policy. The customer is always right so long as the bill is paid." He looked a little embarrassed. "Odell is preparing the crypt in Adam's Creek. Mr. Jones didn't bring the keys until this morning, and Odell left thinking the service was in the church and everyone would leave before the casket was moved. They've decided they want a short graveside prayer in the cemetery, and I need you to drive the van over there with a load of chairs and an awning."

There went my hopes of spending more time with Andy before lunch.

Chapter Twenty-eight

It seemed Jane watched me all the way as I drove the van
from St. Mary to Adam's Creek. Every mile or so her
face looked out at me from one of the flyers we'd posted
along the road. It didn't matter that the eyes in that picture
were sightless. I felt she could see me—see that I was
slightly guilty. I'd thought about Jane off and on since I
woke that morning, but my mind had been distracted first
by Andy, then by Melena and the funeral arrangements.

I dabbed my eyes with a tissue, pulled the van in as far as
possible on the road in the churchyard, and parked. We
don't drive across graves. That's a matter of respect, but
there's also the consideration that no vaults were used
around the oldest caskets in these graveyards. Not only are
some of the graves sunken, but there is a strong possibility
that the weight of a vehicle would put a wheel in a new hole.

Jake, one of Middleton's part-time workers, began unloading and carrying the folding chairs toward the concrete
block crypt. I walked over. The metal door stood open. I
stepped in.

Odell wore tan overalls instead of a suit.

"Hey," he growled, "did you bring chairs and a tent?"

"Yes, Jake's unloading them now."

"Can't see why Otis lets people change plans at the last minute," Odell grumbled. "Should have stayed just the way it was planned. Visitation and service in the church. Everybody goes home, and we move the casket in here. Now she wants everyone to come from the church to the vault for prayer when the casket is placed."

The building seemed larger from inside. The walls were unfinished concrete blocks and mortar. The floor was concrete, and the ceiling looked like plaster or stucco. Cracks formed patterns across both. Otis was using a broom to knock down spiderwebs and deserted dirt dauber nests. I watched him, avoiding looking at the cobweb-covered plain pine casket that sat on one side of the room.

Odell handed me the broom and pointed to a dustpan and trash can. "I'm going to help get the tent up. How about sweeping up the floor and wiping that off for me?" He motioned toward the wooden box.

My job description is extensive, but this was a new assignment. I am *not* spooky, but that old coffin festooned with spiderwebs wasn't quite like the bright shiny metal or deeply polished wooden ones at work. I've never been part of a disinterment, and I was a little worried that the rotting wood would collapse and I'd be face-to-face with a long-dead, not well-embalmed corpse. A real horror, not one from the movies.

When I gently swept the broom across the top of the casket, disintegrated blossoms and ribbon fell to the floor. I'd never thought about leaving flowers in a crypt to wither, die, and remain there perhaps forever. I shuddered a little at the thought and then told myself, *Don't be ridiculous. The people are dead, so what difference does it make if flowers die, too?*

I'd almost finished getting all the trash into the can when Odell came in.

"We're about done here, Callie. I'll ride back with you. Jake is gonna grab lunch here in town and meet me back here after the service."

"There's nothing to dig, is there?" I asked.

"No. Mr. Delgado's casket will be set in here. I'd thought we might need to replace the rotten shelf over the existing grave, but Mr. Jones told me to put Mr. Delgado on the other side and leave a center walkway."

I picked up the trash container and walked toward the door.

"You missed a spot," Odell said and pointed to the opposite corner from the casket. I carried the broom and dustpan over and stooped to brush a little pile of broken glass onto the pan.

Plastic. Not glass. The trash consisted of several pieces of broken plastic. Pink. The same shade as Jane's rose-colored sunglasses.

Women of the Old South were known to speak what I call Magnolia Mouth Southernese and to have "the vapors." When I was a child, I thought "the vapors" must be some horrible disease, like ringworm or scabies. As an adolescent, I wondered if "the vapors" was another term for "monthly visitor." Only when I became an adult, did I realize that the expression referred to feeling faint and perhaps passing out.

Modern gal that I am, I had the vapors like a lady of the Old South.

I awoke in Odell's arms, which was frightening in itself.

"What happened, Callie?" he asked. He was wiping my face with a wet cloth while Jake stared at me as though I'd transformed into some big-eyed extraterrestrial being. For an instant, I wondered what the cloth was and where he'd gotten the water in the middle of a church graveyard. Then I saw Jake shove a Styrofoam ice chest filled with Pepsi-Colas toward Odell for him to rewet the cloth in the melted ice.

"What happened?" Odell repeated.

I pointed to the corner.

"Did you see a snake or sumpthing?" Jake asked. Like a reptile would make a country girl faint.

"Jane," I managed to say. "Jane. I think Jane's sunglasses are all broken up in the corner over there."

I sat up by myself while Odell gathered the plastic and held it out to me in his open palm. "Sure does look like the lenses from her glasses," he agreed. "Everything's ready here. Let's call Sheriff Harmon and head back to St. Mary."

He folded the pink pieces into the wet cloth he'd used to wipe my forehead, and I realized that it was a handkerchief. He shoved it into his pocket. I hoped Odell hadn't been suffering from his allergies.

I waited in the van while Odell closed and locked all of the padlocks, but when he called the sheriff, Harmon said for us to wait there and warned us not to empty the trash can. Where did he think we'd dump it? Middleton's doesn't scatter garbage around graveyards.

Jake handed each of us a Pepsi from his cooler and said he'd bring us back sandwiches. I explained how to get to the Burgerarium. Odell gave him money and said he'd rather have a barbecue sandwich than a hamburger. Matter of fact, he wanted *two* and a side of home fries.

The day was pleasant, neither too hot nor too cool, so Odell and I sat in the folding chairs under the Middleton's Mortuary awning. He pulled the handkerchief from his pocket and looked closely at the plastic pieces.

"You realize," he said, "that Jane is not the only person who might have had shades this color."

"When was that body buried in there?" I asked.

"The records show that he's been there since the mid fifties."

"I don't think that plastic has been on the floor almost fifty years," I said.

"No," Odell replied, "I don't think so either. It's not even dirty." He nodded toward the church. "Did you go in there?"

"Not yet. Why?"

"When the Baptist preacher unlocked the building for Jake and me to set the guest register up, we saw that they've decorated the church."

"Put flowers in there?"

"Not just flowers. We brought some arrangements over with us this morning, but Mrs. Delgado has ferns and candelabra arranged all around. She's got stands of candles like people use for weddings. Wouldn't pay for a separate visitation, but she decorated."

"At the vigil, Melena said she was having visitation and funeral the same day for the convenience of musicians traveling here for the services," I said. Odell didn't reply. "Did you know that the body is being brought on a trailer being pulled by a band bus?" I asked.

"Don't say 'body.' Call the man by his name," Odell corrected me.

Ex-cuuze me. It wasn't like I'd been talking to the bereaved when I made that slip in my Funeralese.

Before Odell had time to launch into a lecture about not using the words "body," "corpse," or, heaven forbid, "cadaver," a Jade County Sheriff's Department cruiser pulled up.

Sheriff Harmon looked at the contents of Odell's handkerchief and transferred the pieces to a brown paper bag which he taped shut. I will never understand how officers determine what evidence goes into plastic ziplocks and what goes into paper sacks.

Odell unlocked all the padlocks on the metal door. Sheriff Harmon leaned over and examined the hasps and locks.

"These look new," he said. "Wonder if they're meant to keep something in or out?"

"Nothing in here to steal," Odell answered. "There's only one cheap casket and it's been here over fifty years." He pulled the metal door open wide.

The sheriff didn't step in. He leaned through the opening and looked around.

"I'm calling forensics in to check it out," he said. "I'll tape it off."

"That woman will have a fit if you put yellow tape here," Odell objected. "What if we take down the awning and pack up the chairs?" he suggested. "We'll tell her the inside of the crypt needs some repairs before we can entomb Mr. Delgado."

"What if her brother insists on seeing the damage?" I said. "He brought you the keys but he's probably got copies. He could just go in and look."

Odell shot me a look that clearly said I should learn to be quiet. "When Jake gets back with lunch, I'll leave him here to guard it," he said.

"Not good," Sheriff Harmon disagreed. "If those glasses are Jane's, the Jones and Delgado families are connected to her disappearance. I'll stay here until forensics arrives. Where's that trash can you told me about?"

I expected the sheriff to go through the debris, but he didn't. Just slipped the entire can into a large paper bag and closed it with tape.

Odell gave one of his sandwiches to Harmon. After we finished eating, the three men took down Middleton's canvas awning, folded it, and packed it in the van. They were stacking metal chairs when the forensics team pulled up. I wondered why we didn't wait until the techs finished before packing. If they finished quickly, we could still have had a brief ceremony at the crypt.

Odell called Otis on his cell phone and told him we were headed back to St. Mary and would arrive barely in time for Odell to drive the limousine with the ushers behind the "cortege." That's how Odell said it. "Cortege" in quotes. Duh. I realized that Odell had objected to Melena's plans for a graveside service at the crypt all along.

Jake stayed at the church with the van. Odell drove like a bat out of a four-letter-word back to St. Mary in the SUV he and Jake had brought to Adam's Creek. I sat beside him and attempted to keep my balance while brushing the dust off my black dress. Odell kept a supply of clothing at the mortuary and would dress for the funeral there. I didn't have extra clothes at work and wouldn't have time to go home to change.

"Fool woman. Wanting all this folderol, changing plans constantly, and Doofus letting her do it. Sometimes a man just has to say no. All this business with the horses and band bus is probably just to keep from paying the funeral coach and family car fees. Procession? This will turn out more like a circus parade. I'm going to have a word or two with that doofus brother of mine."

Silence. Followed by *"Hyumph,"* which means Odell is really ticked off.

He turned toward me.

"Where's that place Jake bought lunch? That was good barbecue. I could use another one."

"It's in the opposite direction," I answered, wondering why we were speeding if he had time to stop for more food.

When we reached Middleton's, Odell didn't turn into the parking lot. He pulled under the covered carport drive and said, "You go on in. Tell Doofus I'll be right back. I'm going over to Shoney's."

I stepped out. Before closing my door, I heard him *"hyumph*ing" again.

Chapter Twenty-nine

"**Where's** Odell? Why isn't he with you?"

No hello. No how are you. Otis was full of questions. He was removing florist cards from the potted plants, wreaths, and floral sprays that overflowed Slumber Room A.

"He'll be back shortly," I said. "He's gone to Shoney's."

"Just look at all these flowers." Otis waved his arm. "I believe these are the most we've ever had for one funeral, and Odell's already taken some to the church this morning." He put the cards into a white box labeled "Delgado," placed the box on a side table, then leaned over and repositioned two pots of hothouse azaleas so they were precisely aligned.

"Why'd Odell say Mrs. Delgado can't have a prayer in front of the mausoleum?" He looked up at me.

"The sheriff is having the crypt checked by forensics."

"Why?"

"We found pink plastic that we think came from Jane's sunglasses in there," I said.

"According to Mr. Jones, the building has been locked

up for years." Otis wiped a smudge of pale yellow pollen off the sleeve of his black suit.

"I don't know, but the sheriff says all those locks look new and there's a possibility that Jane has been in there, or at least, her shades were."

"Oh." He paused. "Well, Odell needs to get back here and change clothes before the family arrives."

"I don't need you telling the hired help what I should do." Odell growled from the doorway.

For Odell to call me "the hired help" instead of my name showed he was really ticked off.

"What did you have for lunch so fast?" I asked, hoping to distract Odell. He ignored me, continued talking to Otis.

"Where's this band bus that's leading the way to Adam's Creek?" he asked his twin brother.

"They're supposed to be on their way now."

"And who's going to drive it?"

"Their band driver, I guess."

"Why didn't you tell them a funeral home employee has to drive any vehicle transporting the deceased?" Odell snarled.

"Is that the law?" Otis asked. "A fireman drove the fire truck when the Franklin family used it to take Mr. Franklin to the cemetery."

"I don't know if it's law or not, but it would be a good policy. Does the trailer they plan to use have sides on it? What's to prevent the casket from sliding off and falling on the road? I think we'd be liable if that happened. Am I going to have to start sitting in with you on all your planning sessions?"

"To do that, you'd have to stay here instead of going out to eat all day," Otis snapped. "At the rate you're growing, when you die, we'll need to custom-order a deluxe fat casket."

"If you don't stop making ridiculous decisions, I might have my body sent to Beaufort and let someone there handle my arrangements."

This was the ultimate insult. When either brother wants

to offend the other one, he threatens to let some funeral home other than Middleton's "handle" his funeral.

"Whatever," Otis muttered. He turned away from Odell and pointed toward the box. "Callie, be sure to pull name tags from any more flowers that are delivered and add them to the box. Print out hard copies of condolence messages that have come in on the new computer, too. The man who delivered it while you were gone has everything loaded and ready."

Odell and I left Otis arranging plants and flowers. Odell went into his office. I went to mine and pulled up our website. A lot of messages had been added to the Delgado condolences page. I was printing them when I saw my name again. This time it wasn't in red.

TELL CALLIE THAT JANE IS IN NO PAIN.

I yelled for Odell. He came running in wearing dress pants and socks. His unknotted tie hung down the front of his unbuttoned white shirt. Otis was right behind him.

"Why?" I sobbed. "Why is someone doing this to me? Does it mean that Jane is dead? Or could it actually mean that she's being treated well?"

Mortuary workers spend a lot of time comforting distraught people. Otis and Odell both did what they'd taught me to do. They patted me—just on my back and shoulders. When I calmed down, Otis tried to convince me the message meant that Jane wasn't being hurt, not that she was dead. Odell called Sheriff Harmon.

I knew something else was wrong when Odell stepped out into the hall with the phone in hand. He closed the door behind him, and his words were too muffled for me to hear.

When Odell returned, Otis asked, "What'd he say?"

"Don't delete the message, but he says it will probably be like the other one. Sent from one of those freebie carriers like Hotmail or Yahoo! on a screen name created in a coffee shop. Not traceable." Odell frowned.

"What else did he say?" I asked.

"Said he's leaving the Jones crypt locked with new padlocks and that he put crime scene tape around it. It's sealed
off until Harmon decides whether he's going to get a
judge's order to open the casket."

"Open the casket?" Otis said. "We haven't even closed
it yet."

"Not Mr. Delgado," Odell answered. "The fifty-year-old
coffin in the crypt."

"Why?" I asked.

Odell said nothing, but he looked away from me, and I
knew he didn't want to tell me the reason. Surely Sheriff
Harmon didn't think Jane was in the casket. If he did, he
would have opened it without waiting for a legal order.

"What else did they find?" I asked.

"Nothing. Sheriff Harmon's just covering all bases."

"If he thinks Jane might be in that casket, he's wrong.
Did you tell him about the spiderwebs and thick dust on it?
I swept the remains of the casket spray off the top. It hadn't
been disturbed in years."

"I know that and you know that, but the sheriff says he's
playing it safe."

"To wait if there is any chance Jane might be in that box
isn't safe."

Odell didn't respond because "Old Rugged Cross"
sounded. He went back to his office to finish dressing. Otis
and I headed toward the front door to greet Little Fiddlin'
Fred's family.

Melena stood inside with Bone on one side and Andy
on the other. Directly behind her, Aaron Porter and the
other Second Time Around musicians were crowding into
the entry hall with the door still open. Behind them, the sun
seemed to have disappeared and left a gray, cloudy sky.
The widow looked sedate in a navy blue dress with a high
neckline, and all of the men wore dark suits.

"Whass up?" Bone said.

Melena interrupted before Otis or I answered his rhetor-
ical question, or, more precisely, his ridiculous greeting. "I
have a few questions," she said.

"Yes, ma'am," Otis said and stepped back. "Why don't you all come with me?" He turned toward me. "Callie, would you get coffee and some glasses of soda? Perhaps Mrs. Delgado and her friends would like something to drink."

"No, no," Melena said. "I don't want to take time for that. We want to see Fred before he's put on the trailer, and, like I said, I have some questions."

"Of course," Otis said, "follow me." He led everyone into Slumber Room A. Melena stood at the open casket for a moment, Bone holding one of her hands while Andy held the other. I had to consciously fight myself to keep from rolling my eyes. I should not have been feeling like I did. After all, Melena was a recent widow. On the way to her husband's funeral service. Who was I to be jealous that Andy was holding her hand?

Otis and I joined Melena and her two escorts when they walked away from the coffin.

"What concerns you?" Otis said.

"I want to be sure that everything is done the right way," Melena said softly. "I really want to do what's respectful for Fred. Do we close the lid before the visitation?"

"That's entirely up to you, Mrs. Delgado. Mr. Delgado is not disfigured, so open or closed is entirely your decision," Otis said in his Undertaking 101 tone.

"You don't understand. I bought the tux so he'd look good when everyone sees him at the church, but I don't want him riding all the way to Adam's Creek without anything over his face. It's clouding up. I think it may rain."

I stopped trying not to roll my eyes and switched to trying not to smile. Good grief. Did Melena think the casket would be open for a thirty-mile ride?

"We'll close the casket before moving Mr. Delgado outside," Otis assured her, "and should it begin to rain, we will stop and cover the trailer with plastic."

"But I want everyone to see how good he looks," Melena protested.

"We'll open the casket while Mr. Delgado is resting in the church," Otis said.

"I thought once you closed it, the top locked," Melena said.

"No," Otis said, "we won't lock it until after the service unless you tell us to."

"Okay. Now, about the graveside prayers down at the crypt," Melena began.

"I need to talk to you about that," Odell said as he walked up, fully outfitted in his midnight blue suit with necktie and shoelaces all neatly tied. "I'm sorry my brother let you think we could do that, but it will be much better if you and your friends leave from the church."

"You mean we don't have to go to the crypt?" Melena asked.

"It was my understanding that's what you wanted," Otis said.

"I thought we'd be doing something wrong if we left after the church part," Melena said and smiled. "I didn't really want to have to go down there to that dirty old place, but I figured it would be expected."

"Not at all, though as part of our service, Middleton's has cleaned the inside and outside of the mausoleum. Now, I really would like to see the arrangements you've made for the procession to Adam's Creek." Odell had taken over.

My mental picture was a grotesque vision of a band bus with a horse or boat trailer attached to the back. Maybe balloons and streamers or some other carnival-type decoration. I was wrong.

The Second Time Around bus had a tasteful black band around it, and the trailer was draped in black. The car in position behind them was not Cowboy's red convertible I'd expected but a sedate black Mercedes. Cars and SUVs were lining up behind the Middleton's stretch limo that Melena had decided to use to transport the ushers and pall-bearers.

Everyone gathered in Slumber Room A and watched as Otis removed the casket spray and closed the lid. The pall-bearers escorted the bier as Otis and Odell rolled it out to the back of the trailer, then lined up three to each side and lifted the casket to place it between low black railings that had been fitted to assure the casket didn't slide.

Odell decided to ride with the bus driver "to make sure he remembers that we must proceed at a slow pace," though I felt certain that the police escort in front of the bus would see to that.

I was assigned to ride with Melena, which put me in the front seat of the Mercedes with Bone driving while Andy comforted the bereaved widow in the backseat. I shouldn't say it that way. He just sat back there with her; there was no hanky-panky going on. Buh-leeve me. If there had been, I would have seen it because I stretched out my seat belt and turned sideways against the door so that I had a good view of the backseat.

Otis drove the limousine for the pallbearers, and the other vehicles followed on an hour-long, thirty-mile ride that seemed to take forever. Melena surprised me with her silence. Bone winked at me a few times, which didn't surprise me at all. Andy sat with a stony expression. We'd almost reached the church before Melena broke the solemn quietness in the car.

"Callie," she said, "can you think of anything I've overlooked? I keep telling myself that Fred has gone to a better place and that he didn't suffer, but I do want this to be a dignified celebration of his life and talent, not of his death."

"I think this will be a very nice service," I replied. "It's definitely going to be well attended." We'd reached the church. The parking lot was full and it wasn't even one o'clock yet. I recognized the names of some well-known bands on buses that had parked across the road from the church.

"Second Time Around and some of the other bands sent e-mails to everyone on their mailing lists telling them about the services and giving directions." Melena leaned forward and looked straight at me. "Do I look all right? I put on stage makeup so it would last through the day."

"You look fine," Andy assured her. He grasped the door handle, but I waved a no at him.

"Don't open the door yet," I said. "Melena stays in the car until Mr. Delgado is in the church. Then you or Bone will walk her to the front and sit beside her where people can pay their respects."

"I guess that should be Bone's honor, his being your brother and all," Andy said to Melena.

"Both of you," she said. "This is going to be difficult and having two strong men by my side will help me."

"I'm going up on the porch," I said to Bone. "When I nod, you and Andy bring Melena in."

The pallbearers lifted the casket off the trailer and carried it up the steps, where they placed it on an awaiting bier. Otis pulled at the front and Odell pushed at the rear. I watched from the porch as the brothers slowly moved the casket up the aisle. When they reached the chancel, they turned the bier in a three-point turn that placed the casket perpendicular to the center aisle. I've seen them do this thousands of times, and it never fails to impress me how smoothly they work together, especially considering how they talk to each other when no clients are present.

Otis opened the top half of the casket and peeked in to be sure Mr. Delgado hadn't shifted during his ride. Odell placed the fiddle-shaped casket spray at the foot. I nodded toward the Mercedes, and Andy assisted Melena out. With Bone on her other side, they entered the church and walked to the front. Melena appeared to be doing what I call the "bridal walk," but I could have been mistaken.

The next two hours flew by. I stood at the back of the church in awe as the people who sang and played on my CDs, on the radio, and on television showed up to pay their respects to Little Fiddlin' Fred. By three o'clock, the church was full, standing room only, with big-name stars spilling out onto the porch and down on the grounds around the building.

I didn't see the Baptist preacher nor recognize any of the other local pastors and wondered if Melena had brought in someone from out of town. Then Reverend Cauble, the preacher Otis hires for those with no pastor, walked down the aisle, stopped at the casket, and turned to face the congregation.

The man "intones." That's the only word to describe his voice.

"Friends," Reverend Cauble said, "I've asked Mister Otis and Mister Odell not to close this." He motioned toward Little Fiddlin' Fred. "Not to close this until later, because we want Mr. Delgado to know who came here today to show their appreciation for his talent and what he gave of his life to his first love . . . music. Not that he didn't love his beautiful wife here." He gestured toward Melena. "Oh, he adored her, but they both loved his music, and Mrs. Little Fiddlin' Fred has told me she didn't want me to preach a funeral sermon for this man. She asked me to lead us in prayer and then invite any of his friends who wanted to come forward to step up and say a few words about this fine musician and his contributions to the bluegrass world he loved so much."

I tuned him out. I always do that when Reverend Cauble speaks. His intoning becomes droning, and I don't listen. I looked around, each glance bringing recognition of yet another well-known performer. One by one, famous recording artists and musicians stepped to the pulpit and talked about Mr. Fred Delgado. I'd never heard so much laughter in a church, much less at a funeral.

Little Fiddlin' Fred's friends and colleagues had lots of stories to tell about him, and they were all funny. He'd been a classic prankster, constantly playing jokes on people. If I'd been the victim of some of the tricks they described, I wouldn't have thought it was funny at all, but now that he was dead, no one seemed angry.

A man behind me reached over and tapped me on the shoulder. When I turned around, he motioned toward the back, where I saw Sheriff Harmon beckoning me with a *Come here* gesture. I slipped through the crowd and followed him out onto the porch, down the steps, and over to his car. He held the front passenger door open for me, then walked around and sat in the driver's seat.

"Quite a crowd" was the first thing he said when we were both inside.

"I can't believe it," I said. "This place is full of internationally known performers."

"That must be why you've got that starstruck look. I hate to interrupt, but I need to talk to you."

"Jane!" My heart pounded. "Have you found Jane?"

"No, but I need to know if you have a key to her apartment."

"I don't have a key, but I know where there's one hidden over there. What do you need?"

"I want her hairbrush."

"DNA," I said before I lost my breath and couldn't talk at all.

"Yes, for DNA, but not because we've found a body that might be hers, so calm down."

"You've already got Jane's hairbrush," I said, and I couldn't help myself. I promise, I couldn't keep from smiling. Just a little.

"Where?"

"Wherever you locked up John's Winnebago. You didn't let us get our clothes and belongings before you impounded the motor home. Jane's hairbrush is the purple one lying on the counter in the bathroom." I reached over and touched his arm. "Tell me why you need her DNA."

"I'll tell you as soon as I can, Callie. Right now, you'd best get back in there to work and listen to what all those stars have to say."

"Aren't you going to stay? I figured you'd be here for the funeral. After all, Fred and Kenny were murdered. In the books, law enforcement officers always attend the funerals of victims."

"You and your mysteries!" Sheriff Harmon smiled. "I've got deputies inside and out here, both in uniform and in plain clothes, and I'll have officers at Kenny Strickland's funeral tomorrow in Greenville. The murders are important, but so long as there's a chance Jane is alive and can still be saved, I'm making that my top personal priority."

At least no one had found Jane's body yet, and her disappearance had become suspicious and more interesting to the sheriff. I couldn't give up on my friend, but I was more afraid for her as each moment passed.

Sheriff Harmon drove away when I got out of the car and walked back into the church. The pews were still full, and some big-name banjo player was speaking in tribute to Mr. Delgado. I tried to listen. I looked around.

I couldn't see the stars.

My eyes were wet with tears.

Chapter Thirty

Forty-five minutes. An hour, or an hour and a half tops, even for the up-and-down kneelers who have communion at funerals. A two-hour funeral that's not for some statesman on television is rare.

Little Fiddlin' Fred's service lasted *three* hours. My stomach was rumbling when Reverend Cauble closed with a final prayer after six thirty. My early lunch was gone, and I was past ready to leave. Besides, I wanted to stay with Melena so long as Andy was with her.

All of that is just to say that it was my turn to be teed off when Odell told me to stay at the church and ride back in the limousine. The pallbearers and ushers had decided to return to the campground in the Second Time Around bus.

After everyone was finally gone, which took forever—not really, but with all the talking and good-byes, it did take them another whole hour to load up and drive away—Odell, Otis, and I were alone in the church with Little Fiddlin' Fred and his flowers. Jake stepped into the back door.

"I got it, Boss," he said as he walked up the aisle.

Odell closed the lid of Mr. Delgado's casket, reached into his pocket for a crank key, and locked the top. He pushed the bier back so he could make a right turn to the center aisle and rolled Little Fiddlin' Fred to the back of the church. I hoped we'd finish with this soon. I didn't want to be messing around down at that crypt after dark.

I followed Odell and the casket out onto the porch and was surprised to see one of our funeral coaches backed up to the bottom of the steps. "How'd that get here?" I asked.

Odell growled, "I sent Jake for it during the service."

"Yes," added Otis, "Harmon won't let us put Mr. Delgado in the crypt, so we're taking him back to St. Mary. Help us put the flowers in the limo and the funeral coach."

The Baptist preacher seemed to appear from nowhere, but I realized he'd come from behind the chancel. "You folks about finished?" he asked. "We've got prayer meeting here at eight o'clock."

I checked my watch. After seven thirty.

"Oh, yes, we're leaving now," Otis said. "Did Mrs. Delgado take care of the charge for use of the church? She insisted she'd deal directly with you on that, probably thought the mortuary would get a commission on it."

"Her brother gave me a check. He also explained that Mrs. Delgado and Reverend Cauble were friends in high school and that was why she wanted him to officiate instead of me." The preacher looked at the casket. "Do you want me to help? The steps out front might be difficult without pallbearers."

We loaded everything, thanked the Baptist preacher for his help, and rode away as cars began pulling into the church parking lot for the Wednesday night service. Odell and Jake were in the hearse; Otis and me, in the limo. As we passed the graveyard, I saw the yellow crime scene tape around the crypt, shining beneath the rising moon.

"Otis, where are we going to put Mr. Delgado?" I asked. "He's not going to be like that body in North Carolina, is he?"

We both knew the story. A traveling carnival worker was killed in a fight. The man's father came and paid for embalming and said he'd be back to make burial arrangements and pay the rest of the money. The body was embalmed, but the father never returned. The local mortuary kept the embalmed carny for over fifty years and allowed people to look at the corpse.

"Oh, no," said Otis, "nothing like that. We'll just hold the body until the sheriff lets us back into the crypt." He smoothed his hair implants and patted them down on top of his head. "Mr. Delgado's planned expenses have already been paid in full, but we'll have to charge them extra for the round trip of returning him to St. Mary then bringing him back to Adam's Creek. If Mrs. Delgado changes her mind again and wants to have a graveside service when we place him in the crypt, she'll have to pay for that, too."

"What will you do if she refuses? Keep him at the mortuary like the guy in North Carolina?"

"Don't be silly, Callie. If we did that, we'd have to charge storage, which would rapidly add up to more than the fee for bringing him back in the funeral coach."

"That story's just an urban legend anyway, isn't it?" I asked.

"Nope," Otis said, "it really happened. It was in Laurinburg. They called the man 'Spaghetti, the Carny Mummy,' because his name was Italian and too hard for the locals to pronounce. Our father used to tell Odell and me about it. He went to Laurinburg to see for himself. Said the man looked pretty good, considering the corpse had been embalmed over fifty years by then."

"You're putting me on, aren't you?"

"Totally serious. Odell and I went up there in the nineties, wanted to see it for ourselves, but Spaghetti wasn't at the funeral home anymore. Some Yankee Italian congressman stirred up enough fuss that they buried him in 1972. The funeral home even donated a marker. Odell and I saw it. You can look it up on the Internet."

I didn't reply. I was thinking about Fred Delgado. What

would Otis and Odell do if Melena refused to pay? Not to worry. Knowing Melena, she'd find another ride to take her husband to the family mausoleum.

Lots of people don't realize there are CD players and radios inside most funeral coaches, family cars, and other mortuary vehicles. Otis pushed a button and filled the limo with classical music.

Otis hummed along with the radio. I wondered how Aaron Porter felt about attending his replacement's funeral. Then I thought about the other musicians. Two of their own had been killed in quirky ways with a tuning fork, a bass string, and capos. Was there a psycho out there with a vengeance against musicians? If so, were all musicians the targets or just bluegrass performers?

Chapter Thirty-one

Exhaustion or exasperation? I wasn't sure which was keeping me from going to sleep before the phone call that night. I was snuggled under the covers while Big Boy lay on top of the Battenburg comforter. He had his head beside me on the pillow and was snoring, but that wasn't what kept me from sleeping. I was used to my dog's nightly serenade. It reminded me of one of Daddy's old jokes. "Know why a woman should never complain about her husband snoring?" he'd ask. Then he'd laugh as he delivered the punch line, "If she hears him sawing logs beside her, she knows he's not lying up in some other woman's bed."

I'd heard that little story for years, and I always wanted to add a comment: "It only means he's not in some other woman's bed that particular night. Cheating isn't limited to evening hours. What about morning and afternoon delights?" I always thought it, but I never said it.

My exhaustion resulted from a long day of work and worry about Jane. The exasperation was because Andy hadn't called me. I'd given him my home number as well as the cell, but I hadn't heard a word from him since he climbed into that black Mercedes with Melena Delgado at the Baptist church. I'd thought tonight might be the time to shut Big Boy in the kitchen, the night to end my self-imposed period of celibacy. I was really fond of Andy, and the chemistry was fantastic, but instead of lying in bed with the Great Pretender, I lay in bed with my Great Dane.

My tossing and turning made Big Boy restless, too. He woke up several times and looked at me as though to say, "What is *wrong* with you?"

I'd showered after walking Big Boy when I came home from Middleton's, but after about the hundredth time looking at my bedside clock, I got out of bed. The digital numbers showed almost three in the morning. I decided a long soak in a warm bubble bath might help me stop thinking and get sleepy.

Gardenia is an old-fashioned fragrance, but I still love it. Besides, I had a whole basket of bath items in that scent, a gift from my brother John. I poured two capfuls beneath the faucet, then filled the tub with warm water, just a few degrees below too hot. In for a dime, in for a dollar—I pulled the gardenia-scented candle from the basket, lit it, and set it on the counter. I dropped my nightshirt on the floor and slid into the slippery water, immersing myself low enough that the only thing above the waterline was my face. That's when the telephone rang. If I'd chosen to take another shower, I wouldn't have heard it over the splash of the water.

Andy! Forget that it was the wee hours of the morning! I *knew* he was the caller. I scrambled from the tub, wrapped a towel around me, and raced to the bedside telephone just as the ringing stopped.

"Callie here. Talk." I heard my own voice deliver my greeting on the answering machine in the living room.

"Callie?" The voice wasn't Andy's, but it only took a second for me to realize this was a voice I'd rather hear than his.

"Jane!" I gasped. "Where are you?"

She ignored my question and continued talking.

"Jane," I kept saying, but she talked over me. In what seemed like only a minute, I heard the line disconnect.

Please let me remember exactly what she said, I thought as I listened to the dial tone, then punched in 911. I was fully prepared to insist that the dispatcher call Wayne Harmon at home and wake him, but when I said I was calling about the missing blind woman, the officer immediately transferred the call to the sheriff.

"Sheriff Harmon."

"This is Callie, Callie Parrish," I blurted out.

"You're the only Callie I know."

"I just had a phone call from Jane."

"Your friend, the blind Jane who's missing?"

"She's the only Jane I know."

"What did she say?"

"She said, she said . . ." My mind went blank. I couldn't remember her words. "I can't remember exactly but that she's okay and that we can stop looking for her. She'll be back soon."

"Are you sure she said that?" Sheriff Harmon asked.

"I can't quote her exact words, but that's what they meant." Suddenly, I remembered about the answering machine picking up. "She might have been recorded. The machine cut in about the time I answered."

"Listen to your recording."

"I can't. It won't play messages while I'm on the phone."

"Then hang up and go check it. I'm on my way to your place."

Lady Luck was with me. The machine had recorded the call.

I pulled on a pair of jeans and my Brissey Elementary School T-shirt from when I was a teacher, then listened through the message several times while waiting for Sheriff Harmon.

The first thing I said when he arrived was, "It's all on the machine." My second comment was, "I've got caller ID, but the call came in as 'Private Number.' "

We listened to the recording, both huddled over the phone, too excited to sit down.

> *"Hi, Callie, this is Jane. I know you had a vigil for me and put up posters, but I don't need any of that. I've just been feeling low and decided to get away for a while, like to 'find myself,' so you can tell everyone to stop worrying about me. I'll be back in touch later. That's the key to everything. And Callie, please tell Mom that I love her."*

Those were Jane's exact words but not precisely how they sounded because I'd interrupted several times asking where she was and demanding to see her, but Jane had totally ignored what I said and continued talking.

"That's a recording," Sheriff Harmon said.

Duh, I thought, but I said, "I know. My answering machine recorded the call."

"Does your recorder have a removable cassette?"

"No, it's digital."

He reached into his shirt pocket and pulled out a minirecorder smaller than a pack of crayons. "Play it again and I'll record it," he said.

We listened once more.

"Jane isn't talking in real time," Sheriff Harmon said. "That's a recording of Jane being played on your phone. Her voice never pauses or changes when you try to interrupt her. Is there anything strange about what she says?"

"Well, she said 'hi,' and that's not very Jane. She thinks that's Yankee. She says 'hey' or 'hello.' Another thing. Jane and I have talked about the old hippie days before we were born. Her mother described herself as a leftover hippie who was always soul-searching, and while Jane loves the retro clothing, I don't really believe she'd ever say she was going off 'to find herself.' Jane's as together as anyone I've ever known. The voice is hers, but the words don't sound like Jane."

"Somebody may have dictated the message and made her record it."

I confess I'd hoped the sheriff would convince me that Jane's message genuinely meant she was safe, but in my heart, I knew better.

"Or they told her what to say and Jane worded how she said it. If she did that, there may be clues in her words. Let's listen to it again."

I hit the button and we listened. This time, the last sentence grabbed me.

    ". . . please tell Mom that I love her."

"Her mother died when Jane was eighteen," I said, "and Jane didn't call her 'Mom' anyway. She always said 'Mommy,' even when I teased her about it sounding like a little girl."

"I think she's put some clues in that phone call," Sheriff Harmon said. "Let's write out the words and see what else surfaces." He looked at me. "Don't get your hopes up too high. We don't know when this message was recorded."

"I'm hoping it was taped right before the call," I said. "I haven't been to sleep, but I'm going to make a pot of coffee. Maybe the caffeine will help me think."

"Sounds good." The sheriff pulled out a pocket-size notebook and a mechanical pencil, sat down on the couch, and pushed the button to replay the message. I headed for the kitchen.

When the coffee drip started, I went back to the living room and asked, "What do you want in yours? Cream, sugar, Splenda?"

"Just black," Sheriff Harmon said. "And I sure need it. I haven't been home yet tonight."

"What were you doing?"

"Investigating."

"What did you find out?"

"Now, Callie, you know I can't tell you."

I stepped back into the kitchen, poured two mugs, and

put a mountain of sugar and some cream in mine. I carried the coffee in, set it on the glass-topped coffee table, and plopped in the recliner opposite Sheriff Harmon.

"You always say that," I said.

"Say what?" he asked and took a sip of coffee.

"You always say you're not supposed to tell me any-thing."

"Well, I'm not."

"But this case is about my best friend. If you tell me what you know, I might spot something significant that you'd miss because you don't know her as well as I do."

He nodded and took a gulp of coffee. "That makes sense, but most of the new information has to do with the homicides, not Jane."

"I think it's all related," I commented.

"I agree."

"So, tell."

"We have the autopsy reports on Delgado and Strick-land. Totally different deaths. Delgado died as a result of an A-pitch tuning fork being rammed up his nose. Crushed facial bones and forced fragments into the brain. I know he wasn't a full-size adult, but it didn't make sense that he'd be still for someone to do that to him. The autopsy showed that he'd been knocked out with an ether compound before the injury. Strickland's body has been released, too, and sent directly to a Greenville funeral home. His death looked like strangulation, and it was."

"Both of them were killed with common music equip-ment," I said.

"Yes, but what ties them together besides location and closeness in time is that Strickland's autopsy showed he'd been given ether, too, and I told you that tests showed Jane's cane had ether splattered on it." He drained his coffee mug and handed it to me for a refill. I took it and headed to the kitchen, calling back to him as I refilled the cup.

"But if whoever murdered Little Fiddlin' Fred and Kenny Strickland used knockout drops on them right be-fore he killed them and dropped the chemical on Jane's cane while trying to kill her, too, when would he have made the recording? It doesn't make sense that no effort was made to hide the first two bodies, yet Jane disappeared. The means seem different." I handed him his coffee.

"First, it wasn't knockout drops. Ether is a liquid, but the fumes are breathed in, not swallowed. We don't know if it splattered on the cane while being used on Jane or if it just spilled."

"But you do know that whoever killed Little Fiddlin' Fred and Kenny had this stuff and that somehow it got on Jane's cane, which Jane no longer has."

"That much is certain. What we don't seem to have is motive."

"Mom!" I squealed.

"Callie, what's wrong?" Sheriff Harmon looked at me as though I'd gone crazy. He's known me since I was born and knows that my mother died the same day.

"Mom. That's what Jane said. Mom. We've talked about the mystery and crime books I read, and she knows that MOM stands for motive, opportunity, and means. She's telling me something about one of those, or maybe even all three."

"It does make sense," Sheriff Harmon agreed.

"But what's she trying to tell me?" I wondered aloud.

The sheriff handed me the paper he'd written the message on. I read it over, but no ideas popped into my brain. He'd emptied his second cup of coffee and didn't bother to give it to me, just took it in the kitchen and refilled it himself.

"I went over to Happy Jack's Campground," he said when he returned, "and interviewed those musicians again after they got back from Adam's Creek. I understand they're heading out tomorrow morning." He looked at his watch. "Guess I mean in a few hours. They're going to Greenville for Kenny Strickland's funeral. I didn't learn anything from them that helps at all."

"What about Aaron Porter? Do you think he might have been mad that Little Fiddlin' Fred was taking his place?"

Sheriff Harmon laughed. "I considered that, but he vowed he was the one who decided to quit traveling with the band. The other members of Second Time Around all backed him up that they didn't fire him to hire Delgado. Porter's getting older, has arthritis in his hands, got a new grandchild. He wants out, and all of them seemed pleased that they'd found a good replacement for him, but they were sorry to lose Porter. It was definitely his idea to leave."

"Is Aaron Porter gonna stay with the band now?" I asked. After all, he could have changed his mind.

"No, he says he came to the festival because he wanted to be here to see Delgado's first time playing with Second Time Around. He says he'll stay with them another couple of weeks until they find someone, but he's eager to go home to Virginia and spend his golden years with his family."

"Did you talk to the Great Pretender?" I asked.

"Who?"

"Andy Campbell."

"Yeah, he was there. Seems like a lot of them went back over to Jack Wilburn's campground and were hanging out visiting and even playing some music."

"I'll bet Melena Delgado was there."

"As a matter of fact, she was, but her brother wasn't. Campbell was with her. Offered to take her upstate for Strickland's services, but she said she'd be staying with her brother for a while."

I don't know exactly what Sheriff Harmon said next. I don't even know what I said next. I was too angry. Not really angry, but jealous. The good Lord missed a great opportunity when he gave me blue eyes. They should have been green.

"Why don't you try to get some sleep, Callie? I'll let you know if anything comes up. We may be able to trace the call."

"I thought you had to keep the caller on the telephone to trace it."

"Not anymore. We've got all kinds of technology these

days." He went to the door and said, "Lock everything behind me," as he stepped out.

Why do the adult males in my life all tell me that? Like
I don't have enough sense to lock my doors. Then again, if
I'd locked up the Winnebago, I doubted it would have been
impounded.

Chapter Thirty-two

I felt like a thousand arrows were piercing my mind. Thoughts coming from all directions. After Sheriff Harmon left, I'd crawled back in bed beside my dog, but I couldn't get to sleep. I could blame it on the caffeine, but I didn't think that was the problem. The need to figure out any clues in Jane's message gnawed at me. I gave up and left Big Boy snoring while I made and drank even more coffee and played the recording what seemed like a thousand times. Listening, listening for some clue in the way Jane enunciated, a hint in her tone. I'd written out the words for myself, but if those words held a solution, I couldn't find it.

When Big Boy awoke, we went outside. I watched the sun come up while my dog hid behind a tree to tinkle.

"Come on, Big Boy, let's go in," I called to him, and he came nosing over to me. We were barely through the door when the phone rang. I dashed across the room so fast that I stumbled and fell onto the couch as I grabbed the receiver.

"Hello," I gasped.

"Callie," I heard. A wave of conflicting emotions washed over me—a flash of disappointment that the caller wasn't Jane and exhilaration to hear from Andy. "I just wanted to tell you we're headed back upstate." He paused. "In fact, we're on I-95 now."

"Thanks for letting me know," I said. "I was hoping you'd call last night." I tried not to sound irritated or like I was nagging.

"I wanted to because I hoped you and I'd get together, but Melena's been pretty broken up since yesterday, and it seemed I was the only one able to comfort her last night."

Puh-leeze. I wondered if he knew that "comfort" and "Southern comfort" were sometimes Low Country euphemisms for what I'd been tempted to do with him.

"Callie? You there?"

"Yeah, I'm here."

"Why are you so quiet?"

I tried, I promise I tried, but I couldn't keep the sarcasm out of my voice. "Maybe I'm quiet because I took my best friend to a bluegrass festival where two people were killed and my friend was kidnapped." My tone changed to sadness. "Maybe I'm quiet because the only good thing was I met someone I like, and it makes me feel bad that I won't be seeing him again."

"If you're talking about me"—he paused—"and I hope you are, you'll be seeing me again soon."

My world lit up a little. Not much, but a little. As much as it could with Jane missing. "Melena's not going with us to Kenny's funeral," Andy continued. "She's staying here with her brother. I'll be back in a week or so to talk to her about managing my career. She's planning to go back to college to become a bug expert, but she says she can just about guarantee that I'll be a huge success with the right management, and she knows all the ropes. I figured I'd call you when I get back, if that's okay."

"Yeah, sure, that's fine. Hey, your connection's breaking up. Call me later, okay?"

I hung up the telephone before hearing his reply. The signal had been loud and clear. I just didn't want to hear any more about *Melena*.

Dalmation! I felt like throwing something. I felt like kicking something. Or someone.

Big Boy rubbed his head against my knee. I reached down to pet him, thinking that at least my dog loved me. I guess he did love me, but I noticed he'd brought his bowl over to the couch while I was talking to Andy. He loves Kibbles 'n Bits, maybe as much as he loves me, probably more. I don't mean Andy loves Kibbles 'n Bits and he certainly wouldn't love me after knowing me such a short time.

I thought about calling Daddy and The Boys, but I just wasn't up to that. I dialed Rizzie's cell phone, but she must have been at home where I couldn't get the call through.

For years, anytime that I was really upset, I'd call or go see Jane. I couldn't do that now. What did Jane do to calm me? Lots of times, when I was all torn up about something, Jane fed me. I know that's not a healthy way to deal with emotions, but comfort food does comfort. That thought made me feel even worse. Andy had "comforted" Melena last night. I could eat something now, but the thought of my own cooking almost made me sick, and I'd already eaten the last Moon Pie my brothers had bought.

Music was calming. More specifically, playing my banjo soothed me. I opened the case and lifted out my Deering. Sometimes I played Daddy's prewar Gibson, but he wouldn't let me bring it to my place. Now he planned to sell it to start a reward fund for information leading to Jane's return. I'd miss that great instrument, but nowhere near as much as I missed Jane.

On the third song I played, I broke the first string, the high D. Banjo strings are numbered from the bottom, one through five, with the instrument in playing position. It was all I could do to keep my profanity on a kindergarten level. Luckily, I had an extra medium gauge steel high D in the case. Most pickers keep extra strings, but then, I'm not always as well prepared as most pickers.

I replaced the string and snipped off the extra length with the little pair of wire cutters from my banjo case before setting the cutters and excess string on the coffee table and playing another song. Picking wasn't working to calm my nerves. I put the banjo and my picks back in the case, placed it in the bedroom closet, and headed to the kitchen for more coffee. I saw the wire cutters were still on the table in the living room. I hadn't put them in the case where they belonged, and I didn't want to get that back out of the closet. I shoved the wire cutters into my jeans pocket and tossed the scrap of D string into the trash can.

I couldn't really think. I needed to calm down and analyze the message. I'd wasted hours. What would Jane suggest to clear my mind? The beach. Sand. Waves. Birds. Maybe even some dolphins playing in the water. I grabbed my cell phone, keys, and Big Boy's leash.

"Come on," I said to him, "let's go for a ride."

Big Boy trotted out to the Mustang and stood patiently by the passenger door. He knows that "ride" usually means no top. I soon had the ragtop down and Big Boy belted into the special seat belt I had installed for him.

When Big Boy and I reached the beach, we walked and ran for a while. The sky was clear, and it was a beautiful morning, but I was exhausted. I collapsed on the sand, planning to spend a long, peaceful time looking at the water. Thinking.

"Hi," Jane had said. Jane, who laughed that "hi" wasn't a greeting. I could hear her: " 'High' in Southernese means one has had too much alcohol or too much of some other good stuff that you don't approve of." She would giggle then and add, "Or should I say, of which you don't approve?"

We live on the coast, where "high" also refers to high tide when the waves are lapping into the beach, rushing up to cover the sandy play area. I pulled out the paper and looked at it again. "I've just been feeling low." Now, that wasn't a Jane thing to say, either. Jane would say, "I feel like poop," only she'd say another four-letter word for "poop" just to make me fuss at her.

"High" and "low." It seemed likely the message had to do with the tides, but what about them? And what about MOM? Jane meant for me to pick up on the tides. Was that connected with motive, opportunity, or means? For the hundredth time I wondered what she was trying to tell me. High tide and low tide didn't connect to motive. Were they related to means or to opportunity?

I read the words again.

What else was Jane trying to communicate? Definitely she wanted me to think of something hippie. "To find myself" was too sixties not to be a clue. Jane's mother was the only hippie I'd ever known. What about Jane's mother could be a clue? What did I even know about hippies? My brothers and I used to do a crazy dance that we called the hippie dance, but I doubt if leaping around flopping your arms up and down really had anything to do with the hippie phase of America's history. I wondered if Rizzie Profit knew much history.

I tried Rizzie's cell phone again. Still no service.

"Come on, Big Boy," I called, "let's ride." I couldn't just sit there. I'd drive to Surcie and look for Rizzie. If nothing else, we could walk around the island and look for Jane's other earring.

When we reached the car, Big Boy jumped in, and I buckled his seat belt. I tossed my cell phone in beside him, walked around the car, and reached into my pocket for the keys. Just then, my cell phone chirped, and I dropped the keys on the ground as I grabbed for it.

"Callie? This is Sheriff Harmon," I heard.

"Yes." The word came out as a gasp. "Have you found Jane?"

"No, sorry to say, I haven't. I called to see if you'd made any more sense of the clues in her phone call this morning."

"Not really." I picked up my keys. Thank heaven the lot

was paved and I didn't have to search through grass for them. Not that my keys ever stay lost for long since I got my SpongeBob SquarePants key ring. The yellow is as bright as crime scene tape and makes it hard to misplace my keys. I opened the door and sat in the driver's seat of the Mustang.

"I'm at a bit of a dead end here," Sheriff Harmon said. "I want to talk to Mrs. Delgado again, but I can't locate her or her brother. I hope they haven't gone to Greenville without telling me."

"Andy called. He said that Melena and Bone are staying here."

"The whole thing's getting stranger and stranger. You know, Callie, using ether makes the homicides premeditated."

"Sharpening the ends of that tuning fork makes it even more premeditated," I commented.

"What did you say?"

"I said sharpening the—"

"How'd you know that?" Sheriff Harmon interrupted me.

"Melena told us the tuning fork had been sharpened the first time I met her, back at the campground the day Fred was killed. Said she overheard you say it at the festival."

"That's not possible! I didn't know that myself until the autopsy report came back. We couldn't even tell the instrument was a tuning fork until it was removed by the medical examiner. You say Mrs. Delgado told you what the weapon was on the day of the homicide?"

"Yes!" I screamed so loud that Big Boy cringed. "That means Melena is the murderer."

"She probably has Jane, too."

"She can't have Jane. Melena was sitting by me in her lawn chair when Jane disappeared."

"I'm going to put out an APB on Melena Delgado, and, Callie, I want you to go to your dad's and stay there until I pick her up." He disconnected before I had time to disagree with him. I wasn't going to Daddy's. I intended to find

Jane. She'd given me clues, and it was my responsibility to figure them out. I pulled out the crumpled paper copy of her call and looked at it again.

"That's the key to everything," she had said. The message couldn't have been recorded the day Jane disappeared because she mentioned the vigil on the call. So . . . keys. Jane wanted me to think about keys. I pulled out of the parking area and headed for Surcie Island.

What kind of keys? Whose keys? Mine? I've had SpongeBob on my key ring for years. Jane went with me to buy a replacement when my keys were stolen.

What would SpongeBob have to do with any of this? Pineapple? SpongeBob lives in a pineapple. Nah. Starfish? SpongeBob's best friend is a starfish. Nah. Squirrels? One of the characters is a squirrel. Nah. I mentally ticked off places and things in the SpongeBob SquarePants cartoon as I drove.

My stomach complained that I'd skipped breakfast, and suddenly I realized what Jane would associate with the cartoon.

Food!

Jane loves to cook and is always interested in what's being eaten in books and movies. When I read one of those mystery books with recipes in them, Jane has me read the recipes to her. She brailles the ones that sound good so she can try them later. What's the food in Bikini Bottom, where SpongeBob lives? Krabby Patties. They eat Krabby Patties made at the Krusty Krab.

Bone had said he'd worked construction on a new crab restaurant that hadn't been finished because the owners ran out of money. Jane heard that when he said it. The restaurant was on Flower Island. What were hippies called? Flower children.

I screeched the fastest, tightest U-ee the Mustang has ever made. Big Boy ducked down and tried to put his head under the glove compartment. I hit 911 on the cell and told the dispatcher to send help to the unopened crab restaurant on Flower Island. Folks who live near the ocean usually know the approximate times of the tides. I knew high tide was approaching even if I didn't know how the tides were involved in Jane being held in a partially constructed crab restaurant.

The Mustang jerked to a stop in the middle of the unpaved parking lot. I jumped out without unsnapping Big Boy's seat belt. He howled, but I didn't go back for him. I ran to the restaurant door. It wouldn't open.

"Jane!" I screamed, hoping she'd hear me over Big Boy's howling. Hoping I'd understood the clues right. Hoping she was here and alive.

I looked through the windows. The place was empty. No people. No furniture. A good place to hide someone. I ran to the back where a patio had been built for outdoor dining. I was looking around for something to crash through the glass of the doors when I glanced at the dock. Someone was there, a woman in jeans. "Jane!" I shrieked over and over while I ran toward her, silently praying, *Oh, God, please let her be alive, please let her be safe.*

The woman lay across the dock on her belly with her head and arms over the water. Was it Jane's dead body? As I ran closer, I saw it couldn't be a corpse. The arms were moving. They were pulling on long, red hair that swirled in the water. I'd found Melena. With one hand, she pulled the red hair. With the other, she thrust her open bug jar toward its owner.

"Breathe it. Breathe it. You won't feel any pain. Just breathe," she shouted. "I don't want death to hurt you. Just breathe the jar."

When I got closer, I could make out Jane in the water and Melena trying to pull her head up by her hair while yelling for her to breathe from the container. I dashed to Melena and kicked the jar out of her hand. It rolled off the dock into the ocean. Melena ran back toward land. I grabbed Jane's hair. Her head wouldn't come up. I leaned over and saw Jane's face.

Duct tape. She had duct tape across her eyes and her

mouth. Her arms were taped behind her. A rope was wrapped around her neck and tied tightly to the dock support, so her head wouldn't rise any higher than it was. Waves lashed in at the exact level of her face, right where Melena had been trying to put the jar to Jane's nose. I dived into the water beside Jane and tried to untie the noose around her neck.

Got to get her loose, I thought. *Got to get her loose fast or the tide will be over her face. Got to get her loose fast or I'll never get her out in time.* I groped for Jane in the water and tried to pull the noose off. Pulling it was like trying to uproot a giant oak tree by hand.

I swooped underwater and shoved Jane up as high as I could. It wasn't far enough. She gasped air, but jerked right back down under the waves. My shoes and clothing filled with salt water, and I wished I'd kicked my shoes off. No way to do it now. I felt like someone had hit me in the chest with a hammer. I couldn't breathe. My head filled with a loud ringing. I pushed Jane up again, pulling at the rope and tape holding her down. I felt dizzy. I was losing it. My vision darkened at the edges as though I were going blind. Like Jane. Blind like Jane. Underwater. Drowning like Jane.

She kicked and struggled. Fighting for her life. The sound of my own heartbeat deafened me. Blind and deaf. I couldn't think. We'd both die right here. I couldn't untie the rope.

Suddenly, my mind flashed on something that seemed irrelevant: the broken string on my banjo. The new D string I'd trimmed with the wire cutters *that were now in my pocket*.

Wet, the jeans molded to my legs. I forced my hand into the tight pants pocket and managed to pull out the cutters. I struggled to open them, not knowing if they would cut the rope or not.

The blades parted, and I wedged one side under the rope. I squeezed as hard as I could. The rope split and the wire cutters fell. I pushed myself up out of the water, pulling Jane with me. I tore the tape from her lips. Her mouth opened and closed, opened and closed, but no sound came out.

I wrapped my arm around my friend and dragged her to the shore. By the time we were out of the water, I couldn't pull any more and was shoving her limp form onto the beach. I crawled up beside her and panted. I wanted to give her resuscitation, but I couldn't catch my breath. Jane gasped. She clutched her chest, then whimpered. It wasn't a good sound, not a strong sound, but she was alive and breathing.

We lay on the sand, side by side, desperately sucking in air. I pulled the tape from her eyes. I couldn't understand why anyone would tape over blind eyes, but I didn't like it. I rolled over onto my belly and tried to catch my breath as questions bombarded my mind. I seemed to float in and out of reality.

Where was Melena? Why hadn't she sedated Jane before trying to drown her? Why hadn't she given Jane the ether before tying her to the dock? Fred and Kenny had been unconscious before they were killed.

A shadow fell across Jane and me. Fear shocked me into reality. Was it Melena? What would she do now? I tried to get up, but it was all I could do to roll myself over and look up at the figure above me. A khaki uniform. Not Melena. Deputy Jim Smoak with his transmitter to his mouth. I could hear him demanding emergency medical attention *now!*

I managed to sit up by the time he reached us. Jane was still stretched out, but she rolled to her side and spit up. Her breathing was better. Not great, but better. Deputy Smoak used his pocketknife to cut the duct tape from her hands and feet.

Sheriff Harmon and the EMTs arrived simultaneously. I convinced them not to send me to the hospital, but Jane had to go. She had come too close to drowning and her body temperature was below normal. I followed the ambulance to the hospital in Beaufort, oblivious of the soaking wet clothes clinging to my body, hardly noticing Big Boy beside me.

Jane was back. She needed medical attention, but she was alive. Back and alive.

Chapter Thirty-three

Back and alive, but Jane wasn't okay. In addition to the aftereffects of almost drowning in cold water, the medical technicians said Jane had suffered a memory loss. They weren't sure how severe it was or how long it might last, but she couldn't remember anything since being in the band bus on Surcie Island before the storm.

A doctor I didn't know talked to me while I sat on the hard chair in the intensive care waiting room, but he wouldn't let me see Jane. The sheriff came by and took my statement. He returned two hours later while I was still sitting there.

"We picked up Melena Delgado," Sheriff Harmon said, "driving a rented Mercedes, speeding down I-95 trying to get to Florida."

"What did she say about Jane?" I asked.

"Nothing. She's not talking without a lawyer, and she's waiting for her brother to bring one."

"None of it makes sense," I said. "Why tie Jane to the dock post? All Melena had to do was make her breathe the stuff in the bottle until she was unconscious, then roll her into the ocean to drown."

"Melena must have been the one who kidnapped Jane," Sheriff Harmon said.

"She couldn't have. Melena sat by me from the time I walked Jane back to the bus until the storm came up."

Sheriff Harmon went to the coffee machine and brought back two cups. He remembered that I like sugar and cream, but it wasn't nearly sweet enough. I sipped it anyway.

"What about Dean Holdback?" The sheriff chugged a big swallow of coffee between words. "He seemed real interested in talking about Jane." He gulped from the cup again. "Could he and Melena Delgado have been in this together?"

"Anything's possible," I said, "but Dean was onstage right after I walked Jane to the bus and didn't come off until the storm began."

"My hinky cop feeling makes me like Melena's brother as a suspect. Maybe for both homicides and the kidnapping, but according to our notes, Jones was in front of the stage from the time Broken Fence started playing until Deputy Smoak interviewed him. He couldn't have killed Fred Delgado or put the body in the bass case."

"That's true. Bone was sitting by Jane and me when Kenny Strickland took his bass out and still there when Little Fiddlin' Fred's body was found. I *know* he was there because he kept making goo-goo eyes at me. Later that night, Bone was at parking lot picking when I arrived from the Winnebago. He was still there when Jane and Dean found Kenny."

"Melena was the one with the ether, but she swears she didn't get to the campground until after Broken Fence started playing. I'm hoping we'll get some answers when Jones shows up. Melena used her phone call to leave a message on his cell for him to get her an attorney. She'll probably clam up even more after she lawyers up. Right now, she only says she's been arrested for trying to save

Jane from pain. She was sobbing the whole time. That woman's cried more in the past hour than all the days since her husband's death added together."

"She's probably lied more, too," I said. Couldn't help it. I didn't like Melena Delgado even *before* I caught her trying to kill my best friend.

The sheriff patted my leg. Not the thigh, way down toward my blue-jeaned knee.

"Your clothes are still damp, Callie. Why don't you go home and change, then come back?"

"I'm not leaving until I see Jane. The doctor told me she's got some kind of amnesia."

"Yes, but it may be shock. I'm hoping in a day or so she'll be able to tell us what happened."

"Callie?" I recognized the smooth, mellow voice and looked up. Dr. Don Walters smiled down at me.

"Sheriff Harmon," the doc said and nodded toward him before looking back at me. "I checked on Jane the minute I arrived." Don knelt down in front of me and looked directly in my eyes. "She's stabilized and resting. I'll take you back for a minute to peek at her if you won't try to wake her or ask any questions." He stood and offered me his hand.

I walked with Don holding my right hand and the sheriff touching my left elbow as if I were an old lady. We went through a couple of doors, then behind a curtain, where Jane lay on a gurney with blankets pulled up to her neck.

She looked too much like the way Otis and Odell covered clients with sheets before bringing them to me at work. I blinked my eyes several times to hold back my tears. I didn't know if I'd ever go into my workroom at Middleton's again without seeing Jane in my mind instead of the corpse waiting to be cosmetized.

I've seen Jane sleep with her eyes open without it freaking me out, but thank heaven her lids were closed. Her hair was spread across the pillow, all tangled and matted, and she had oxygen prongs in her nose. Don noticed me looking at them.

"She's breathing fine on her own. The oxygen is just to keep her more comfortable right now," he said. He motioned toward the curtain surrounding Jane's cubicle. "You can come in for five minutes every two hours, on the odd hours. Her admitting physician plans to keep her in intensive care until tomorrow, so don't get upset that she's still here when you come back."

He looked at my well-inflated chest. "Callie, if you're not going home, I'll find a smock or something for you to put over that wet T-shirt."

Ex-cuuze me. You'd have thought my nippies were showing, but I knew better because my inflatable bra didn't have nippies, and my real ones were about two inches below my underwear.

"She's going home now—aren't you, Callie?" said Sheriff Harmon.

"Only if Don promises to call me if there's a change," I answered.

"I'll call you." A sheepish expression crept across his face. "And yes," he said, "I still have your numbers." Dr. Don Walters and I dated for a while and still went out occasionally, though not nearly as frequently as before.

I stepped forward and leaned toward Jane.

"Don't wake her," cautioned Don.

I kissed my friend lightly on the cheek, turned, and, as they say about Elvis: Callie left the building. Sheriff Harmon walked me to my Mustang.

"Where's Big Boy?" I panicked. "I left him in the car. He couldn't have gotten out of his seat belt."

"That was hours ago," the sheriff said. "I called your family to come get him. John and Bill took him to your daddy's house."

"Thanks," I said, waved good-bye, and drove to that dark Munsters house I grew up in.

Big Boy bounded out the front door and jumped up with his front paws on my shoulders when Bill answered my knock. Daddy and The Boys crowded around my dog and me, all talking at the same time, telling me how much it upset them for me to be involved in dangerous situations. "Where was your .38, Calamine?" Daddy said.

"In the drawer of my bedside table," I answered.

"I think we ought to talk to Wayne about getting Callie a license to carry concealed," Frank said.

"Wouldn't make much difference. Do you keep it loaded?" Bill said.

"It's loaded all the time except when I have company with children," I answered. "Then I unload it and put it on the top closet shelf."

"Let's just get off Callie's back and be glad Jane's all right," John intervened.

"But she's not," I said. "The doctors say she doesn't have any memory of what happened to her."

"That could be a blessing," John said. "Wayne told me you found pieces of her sunglasses in the Jones crypt."

"The last time he talked to me about that, he wasn't positive the pieces came from her glasses."

"But he also said some long red hairs were mixed in the trash that was swept out."

"So that's why Sheriff Harmon wanted Jane's hairbrush, to check DNA," I said.

"Yes, the results aren't in yet, but pink shades and long red hairs in the same place make it look like Jane was locked in that crypt until Melena decided to put Little Fiddlin' Fred's casket in there."

The thought of Jane being kept in that mausoleum with all those spiderwebs, bugs, and that fifty-year-old corpse made me shiver. Bill gently led me to the couch. Mike brought me a Coke, and Frank came from the kitchen a few minutes later with a sandwich. "Here, you probably haven't eaten anything today," he said.

I tried, I promise I tried, but I couldn't get the food down. It was egg salad, which happens to be one of my favorites, but I choked on every bite.

"Why don't you spend a few days here, Calamine?" Daddy asked.

"Thanks, but I really want to go home and take a bubble

bath. Try to sleep a little before I go back to the hospital to see Jane."

"Stay here and I'll give you the Gibson," Daddy said. That was tempting, but he always let me play it when I wanted to anyway. I shook my head no.

"You don't need to go to the hospital by yourself," John said.

At the same time, Daddy was telling Frank, "Go to the drugstore and buy Calamine some of that smelly bubble bath stuff."

"No, I want to go home," I insisted.

Big Boy gobbled the egg salad sandwich while Daddy and my brothers all offered their opinions about what I should do. After too much talk, we compromised. Big Boy and I would go to my place, but in an hour, John would come pick me up and drive me back to the hospital.

Bill insisted on walking me to the car alone. "I need a few minutes by myself with Callie," he said.

"No need to get all girly with sentiment," Daddy snapped. "Calamine's fine now that her friend's safe. Won't matter if Jane forgot some things. That girl's smart. She can learn 'em over."

"Sure, Dad," John told him, "but let Bill have his time with Callie. One Parrish man is enough to walk a lady to her car." He closed the door behind Bill and me.

At the car, Bill fastened Big Boy's seat belt, then came around to my side and checked mine. "Callie, I have something to tell you," he said.

"Don't tell me you're going to marry that Lucy." I said it as a tease, but it wouldn't surprise me. Bill doesn't always think much.

"No, Lucy's out of the picture. I'm back with Molly, and she wants me to tell you she's sorry."

"For hanging your underwear on the shrubs? If I'd put up with your shenanigans as long as she has and then you started running around all over town with another woman without even breaking off with me, I might have done a whole lot worse than that."

"No, for having a GPS tracker put on your car."

"*What?*"

"I used your Mustang a few times when you were at Surcie while John and Pa were gone in the truck. Lucy loved convertibles. Molly heard about it and hired a detective. Gave him a description of the car and your tag number. When you came back, the investigator was still sneaking and peeking for Molly. He spotted the car when you parked and grabbed the chance to place the tracker. He watched the whole fiasco with the cops and reported it to Molly. She says she's sorry. Do you forgive her?"

Bill caught the biggest eye roll I could muster. It's a wonder my eyeballs didn't pop out the back of my head. "She sure made a bad day even worse," I said, "but if you two are okay now, it's all right."

"She wants to know if you'll be a bridesmaid."

"I'm outta here."

As I drove away, I pictured another ugly dress to hang in my closet.

When I pulled into my driveway, it seemed like forever since I'd left my home that morning. So much had happened. I was grateful that my friend was alive and safe in the hospital. So she'd lost some memories. I wanted to see her, talk to her. I just wanted to hear Jane say, "Callie." If she never remembered what happened to her, it would be fine. I just hoped she'd remember me.

The red geraniums in the pots by my door drooped over the sides of the containers. They needed moisture, but Big Boy went straight to his dishes in the kitchen, so I topped off his bowls first. He noisily lapped up water.

I filled my watering can from the faucet and went back to the porch to give the plants a drink, too. I couldn't believe how tired I felt. When I patted my jeans and shirt, they felt dry, but the foam fanny in my panties was still wet against my skin.

Trying to consider the clues and analyze who might be

guilty of what was a waste of time. My mind wasn't working full speed. All I could think of was getting cleaned up, catching a few minutes of rest, and hoping Jane would be awake when John and I returned to the hospital. I hurried back into the apartment and passed the sound of Big Boy gobbling his Kibbles 'n Bits on my way to the bathroom. Apparently the egg salad sandwich had only whetted his appetite.

Two capfuls of bubble bath poured under the faucet refreshed the scent of gardenia in the bathroom. I turned on the water, adjusted the temperature, and let the tub fill while I went to the bedroom for fresh clothes.

At my closet door, I reached for a black work dress. If I sat at the hospital all night waiting to see Jane every two hours, I could go straight to Middleton's the next morning if Jane was okay by then. Thanks to Bill's comment, I couldn't help but glance at all the bridesmaids' gowns I'd worn in friends' weddings. I couldn't complain a whole lot because those same girls had ugly pink dresses they'd never wear again from my wedding.

Even my divorce seemed like longer ago than the few years it had been. I hoped my bridesmaids had donated the gowns from my wedding to the poor. Or burned them. Jane said she could tell how ugly those pink dresses were even though she was blind. Why had I put my red-haired friend in a pink gown anyway? Soon-to-be brides don't always think too clearly. Oh, well, if Molly selected a color that didn't go with my blonde hair, I'd just tint my hair a different shade. Again. I was about ready for a change anyhow.

I decided not to dress in work clothes. I'd had enough sadness the past few days and wasn't really up to the mortuary. I moved from the closet to the chest of drawers for clean underwear, jeans, and a shirt. I was putting my watch and earrings on the bedside table before taking my clothes off when I heard him.

His voice came from over my shoulder.

Chapter Thirty-four

"**W**hass up?"

The words were so unexpected that at first I thought I'd imagined them. I turned from the bedside table.

Pulley Bone Jones stood just inches behind me. Definitely in my space, and, for a change, not wearing a flirty expression. His face was a mask of rage, a rabid animal look.

"You couldn't stay out of it, could you?" he snapped.

"What are you doing here?" I demanded. "How'd you get in?"

"You forgot to lock the door, bouncing in and out watering your little plants on the porch, but don't feel guilty about your carelessness—I'd have gotten in if I had to break down your door."

"Why are you here? I thought you'd be helping your sister." I stepped back, away from him, with my behind against the table.

"That's what I tried to do, but you wouldn't let me take care of Melena." He stepped closer to me. Every word sounded as though it squeezed out of him through hate.

"Come on, Bone, I don't understand. What do you mean I wouldn't let you take care of Melena?"

"All her life my sister's been a loving person who hated pain. Couldn't even stand to think of an insect being hurt when she collected it in her killing jar."

"Killing jar?"

"Don't play stupid with me. You know what a killing jar is. It's that bottle she always has with her for capturing interesting bugs. Other collectors use fingernail polish remover with acetone in killing jars, but Melena didn't believe that was fast enough. 'Kill as quickly and painlessly as possible,' she always said, so she used carbon tetracholoride."

"Carbon tetracholoride?" I repeated after him.

"Yes, but then huffing carbon tetracholoride became popular with the druggies, and the stuff got so hard to get, she switched to ether compounds."

"That's ether like they used for surgery years ago?" I asked. "How does she get it?"

"Buys it from science supply houses over the Internet. She always wanted to be an entomologist. She had a science scholarship for college, but then she met Fred Delgado. She's spent half her life taking care of that man, looking after him. What did he do when he finally made the big time? Left her, that's what. I convinced her that Fred deserved to die so she could get his insurance money and go back to college. I thought we'd rig an accident or something. I had no idea that she'd take matters in her own hands and kill him such an odd way."

"Sharpening the ends of that tuning fork made it premeditated," I said, though I knew I should be keeping my mouth shut.

"Yeah," Bone said, "and twisting those capos onto the ends of the garrot makes Kenny's murder premeditated, too."

"Why'd Kenny have to die anyway?"

"He knew too much, but I didn't know Melena was going to kill Kenny until after she did it. Then, when she saw

Jane identify the flowers in that woman's bouquet by smell, she was convinced that Jane would recognize the scent of her cologne in the motor home after Kenny died. So Melena decided Jane had to die, too."

"Like someone could have recognized anything from odor in the Winnebago after Kenny's bowels emptied when he died." I smarted off.

"I tried to tell her that, but Melena was determined to kill Jane, so I took Jane to save her from my sister. I'd known Jane as Roxanne for a long time. I went to Broken Fence's bus after you took her there." Bone hesitated for a moment before continuing. "I guess I may as well tell you everything. You won't live to tell it anyway. I tried to talk Jane into doing some of the things Roxanne described, but she refused. Said that was just 'work,' as though Jane's better than Roxanne."

She is, I thought, but I didn't say it out loud.

Bone moved even closer. I turned sideways. He took another step, forcing me to lean against the bed.

"Jane ordered me to get out," he continued with his hot breath against my face, "but I'd swiped some of Melena's ether. I forced Jane to breathe it, and when she passed out, I carried her out of the bus and accidentally spilled the rest of my ether on her cane on the way to the inlet. I threw the cane down so the fumes wouldn't get to me. I carried Jane across the inlet at low tide and left her in an abandoned cabin. The storm hit about the time I got back to Surcie."

Bone's breath smelled like gin, but I cringed away from his words as much as away from the odor. "Later," he continued, "I didn't know a safe place to hide her, so I wrapped Jane up in duct tape and put her in the family crypt. I had no idea Melena would decide to have Fred's funeral in Adam's Creek and put him in the family mausoleum. When Melena did that I had to move Jane again. That's when I hid her in the food pantry at the unfinished restaurant on Flower Island."

My heart lurched. Rizzie had sworn she heard something

inside the crypt when we'd been in the graveyard. She'd heard Jane.

"How could you do that to her?" I yelled. "Jane is horrified of death and bodies. Being imprisoned in the crypt is probably what caused her amnesia."

"Amnesia?" Bone questioned.

"She can't remember anything."

"That's the roofies," he said. "After I dropped the ether, I gave Jane Rohypnol and kept giving it to her until I ran out. When she woke up, I made her call you."

"That's date rape drug, isn't it?"

"One of them. I gave it to Jane because I like her and didn't want her to be scared in the crypt. You know, in there with that old corpse. I figured she couldn't see that coffin, so it wouldn't much matter, but I had to keep her quiet, too."

"Did you rape her?" I spat out the words.

"No, I didn't, not even when I realized that Melena was right about Jane having to die. I couldn't kill her, couldn't bash her in the head or anything like that, and I didn't want Melena to think up some absurd way to get rid of Jane. I decided to let water kill her for me. Ocean water is sacred because salt is purifying. I've had an affinity for water since I realized as a little boy that whatever I held in my hand would point toward water."

"What about Jane's earring on the road at Surcie?" I asked.

"I planted it there to pull the searchers over to that end of the island."

"If Jane was unconscious from roofies, why was Melena on the dock?"

"I ran out of roofies and when Jane woke up, I made her record the call for you. Melena was hanging out at the campground. If you'd only listened, you wouldn't have to die now. All you had to do was drop the whole thing and believe that Jane had gone off on her own." He laughed. "Maybe think she'd run away to live the life of Roxanne."

"You and your sister are both crazy!" I shouted. I'm

grateful Bone was more interested in what he was saying than what I said.

"Melena e-mailed you that Jane felt no pain. She was sorry for you worrying so much. It's why she suggested the vigil, too. Melena thought doing something like that for Jane would make you feel better. My sister is really a caring person."

"Ex-cuuze me. I believe this 'thoughtful, caring person' killed two men and tried to murder my best friend."

"Melena wasn't trying to kill Jane at the dock. I was. When I told Melena that I'd tied Jane to the dock to drown at high tide, Melena went crazy because Jane was awake. She took her killing jar out to sedate Jane so she wouldn't suffer when she drowned, but the tide was already too high."

"How do you know?"

"I was inside the restaurant when you showed up to rescue Jane. I couldn't bear to watch Roxanne die, so I went inside to wait until time to go out and cut the body loose in the water. Melena came from the campground looking for Jane and threw a fit when I told her what I did. She had run down to the dock just before you arrived. I stayed in the restaurant until everyone was gone. Nobody even looked in there."

Bone looked down. Water was seeping onto the bedroom carpet from the bathroom. Not that it bothered me a whole lot to flood the avocado green shag that covered my floors. I'd been so intent on what Melena's brother was saying that I'd forgotten the bathwater was running.

"Now, Callie," he said, "I'm going to let water kill you since you stopped it from taking care of Jane."

"What?"

He ran his foot through the water. "I'm sorry, but it won't be salt water for you. I'm going to drown you in your own bathtub. Take off your clothes."

I didn't roll my eyes, but they must have bugged out, because Bone chuckled. "Don't be afraid I'll rape you. I admit I'd enjoy that, but this has to look like an accident."

Movement caught my eye behind Bone. Big Boy. I'd forgotten my dog was in the apartment. I focused back on Bone's face, so he wouldn't look behind him to see what had drawn my attention.

Bone reached for me. Big Boy lunged. His teeth sank into Bone's hand and pulled Bone away, forcing him to let me go. Bone kicked the dog. Hard. Big Boy howled while Bone swore obscenities and drew his boot back to strike again.

I yanked open the bedside drawer, pulled out the .38, and pointed it at Bone.

He laughed.

He stood there with a gun aimed at his chest and an amused look on his face.

Bone grinned. "You won't shoot me, Callie. Just like I couldn't bash Roxanne in the head, you can't shoot me." He put his hands out toward me and took another step, even closer.

My gun was ready to shoot. I wanted to empty the chamber. I gripped the revolver with both hands straight out in front of me.

Bone laughed again.

I pulled the trigger, and the room reeked with the fumes of burned powder. His eyes opened wide.

Lowering the gun barrel back to point at his chest while he looked at the hole in my bedroom ceiling, I said, "I pulled that one up on purpose."

Bone's expression turned to fear as he watched me.

I'd been shooting guns since I was a little girl, but never at a human being. I was taught *never* to point a weapon at anyone, even if it wasn't loaded.

"I *am* going to shoot you," I said, "shoot you where it will hurt, but not so you'll die."

Bone didn't believe me. I could see it in his eyes. Oh, he was frightened, but not that I'd shoot him on purpose. He was scared I'd pull the trigger accidentally.

"I want you and your sister to go to trial," I said, "to go to jail or be executed, but I don't want to kill you myself. If you'd murdered Jane, I might could shoot you dead, but I'd rather leave you to the state executioner. I just wish South Carolina still used Old Sparky."

At that moment, Bone must have convinced himself that I wouldn't shoot, because he rushed toward me. Then two things happened simultaneously.

My brother John crashed through the door.

I shot Pulley Bone Jones.

Chapter Thirty-five

Aromatherapy filled my nostrils. Puh-leeze, the odors did more than that. They filled my senses with a wonderful comfort. Smells of food prepared by folks who know how to cook.

Not Jane's famous lasagna. We weren't at Jane's apartment. I sat in a wooden chair beside Maum as she rocked in front of the burning logs in her fireplace on Surcie Island.

I opened the big kit of nail polishes and spread it in front of the petite lady. She leaned over and examined each one before pointing to the brightest red. As I continued Maum's manicure, we heard Jane and Rizzie laughing in the kitchen.

"How long is that going to take?" Rizzie called. "We'll be ready to eat soon."

"I've clipped her cuticles, and I'm filing the nails now. I'll polish them after dinner," I answered.

"Will you do my toes, too?" Maum asked.

"She can't do your feet unless you take off all three pairs of the socks you're wearing," Rizzie warned from the other room.

"I know that," Maum laughed, "but I told you before. Old bones are cold bones. I'll hold my feet out to the fire while Callie works on my toes."

The door opened, and Tyrone stepped in. "What's cooking?" he said.

"We've got lots of good stuff." Jane stuck her head around the kitchen doorway into the living room. "Rizzie's teaching me to cook Gullah. Next time, you folks can come eat at my place; and I'll show Rizzie specialties I learned from Mommy." Jane pulled her head back into the kitchen.

"What good bittle?" Tyrone asked.

"You don't fool me," Jane called. "Rizzie's been teaching me to talk some Gullah language, too, and I know 'bittle' means 'food.'"

"Exactly *what* do we have to eat?" the boy questioned. "It smells great!"

Rizzie named off, "Oxtails, yard greens, sweet potato pone, oyster mush, and tomato pie."

"*Ohhhhh*, I *love* tomato pie," Tyrone said and went into the kitchen. A moment later, he yelped and ran back to sit beside his grandmother.

"I thought Rizzie said that red-haired woman's blind," he said.

"She is," I answered. "What did she do to you?"

"I put my hand out to get a pinch of tomato pie and she swatted me with a wooden spoon."

"When I reach for a taste while Jane's cooking, she hits me with a stainless steel spatula," I said.

"That's not as bad as killing somebody." The boy's eyes widened. "Did you really shoot a man?"

"I did," I said and began buffing Maum's fingernails.

"Did he die?" Tyrone questioned.

"No, I shot him in the knee."

"Why?"

"Because he was bad. He tried to hurt my friend Jane."

"Did he kill those men on the other end of the island?"

"His sister, Melena, did that," I said and examined the

buffed shine of Maum's nails. They were almost too pretty to polish, but she wanted that bright red.

"Rizzie said one of the men was in your camper. Why?" Tyrone continued.

"Because Melena saw that I didn't lock the door, and she lured Kenny Strickland into the Winnebago by telling him she'd decided to pay him."

"Pay him for what?"

"Blackmail." I held Maum's hands up and inspected them again.

"What kind of blackmail?" Tyrone's questions seemed endless.

"Kenny had threatened to tell the authorities that Melena killed her husband. I saw Kenny arguing with Melena after the murder. Kenny knew how Fred got in the bass case and had figured out what Melena did."

Rizzie and Jane brought platters of steaming food from the kitchen, and Tyrone helped his grandmother to the table. We all sat. After Maum returned thanks, Jane asked, "How was Little Fiddlin' Fred killed onstage with everybody watching?" She laughed. "Well, everyone looking except me."

"Fred Delgado was a prankster, played lots of practical jokes on people," I answered as I spooned big helpings of everything onto my plate. "He planned a stunt for right after Broken Fence's performance. Kenny was in on it, and when he took out his bass to play, he intentionally threw the soft case to the back of the stage near the curtain. Nobody *put* Fred's body in the case. He climbed in." I took a bite of potato pone. Delicious!

"Fred was supposed to push the drapes out over the case," I continued. "Then he'd climb in and pull the zipper up as far as possible, letting the curtains flop back behind the case. At the end of Broken Fence's performance, Fred planned to leap out and surprise the audience. When Kenny opened the case, expecting to pull it forward so Fred could jump out after the prayer, Fred was dead."

"So Kenny knew Fred got in the case voluntarily?" Rizzie asked as she bit into an oxtail that was falling-off-the-bone tender.

"Yes, and Kenny figured out that Melena was the only person Fred would let help him into the case. He was also familiar with Melena's killing jar for insects and thought she'd used it on Fred after he climbed into the case. He knew she had come to see her husband's first performance with Second Time Around and to talk to him. But Melena lied about when she arrived—she got there early. When Fred saw Melena before the show, he told her about the joke he planned and asked her to help him get into the case, but he refused to talk about saving their marriage. Melena held the drapes so they covered the unzipped part of the case, then sedated Fred with ether from her jar after he climbed in. With Fred unconscious, jamming the tuning fork up his nose was easy."

I shook some hot pepper vinegar on my field greens and continued, "Kenny figured out Melena's part pretty fast and didn't tell the police anything about the planned trick. He was counting on sharing Fred's insurance money with Melena."

"How do you know all this?" Rizzie said.

"Melena kept her mouth shut, but Bone is a blabbermouth. After I shot him, he wouldn't stop talking. He wanted to help his sister, but he wasn't about to take the rap for two murders he didn't commit." I took another bite of potato pone. Even more delicious. If I hadn't given up swearing, I'd swear I'd learn to cook.

Tyrone opened his mouth and I expected another "Why?" Instead, he said, "I *love* tomato pie!" I tasted it and understood his enthusiasm.

"Speaking of love, what happened to that guy who went with us looking for Jane?" asked Rizzie. "There seemed to be some sparks between you two."

"Are you talking about Dean?" Jane said.

"No, she's talking about Andy. Dean helped search, but Dean's sparks were all for you."

"He's called me a few times," Jane said. "He'll be back

down here for the fall festival. He wants to see me then."
She frowned. "But he's still married."

"Andy's called, too," I said, "several times, but I don't
know if I'll see him again even if he comes to perform at
Happy Jack's next bluegrass festival."

"Why?" Tyrone asked around a mouth full of pie.

"Same reason that Melena killed her husband," I said.

"And why *was* that?" Jane said. "In those books you
read, the spouse is always the first suspect but is never
guilty. This time the wife killed her husband. What was her
motive?"

"Speaking of motive," I said, "I got the hippie refer-
ences in your telephone call, but did 'Mom' refer to motive, opportunity, and means?"

"No, 'Mom' was to get you thinking about flower children. Bone had told me where I was and what he was going
to do to me. I counted on your figuring out the 'key' reference to the crab restaurant Bone had talked about. 'Mom'
was supposed to get you looking for the clues in my message and also to remind you of Mommy, the hippie. Considering I was half dopey, I think I did great with the
clues."

"Sorry," I said. "I didn't mean to criticize."

"Okay, back to the point . . . Melena had opportunity,
and that bottle of ether opened the door to all kinds of
means," Rizzie said, "but do you think it was spur-of-the-
moment? What was her reason to kill her husband just as
he moved to a more successful band?"

"It wasn't in the heat of passion. She'd sharpened the
ends of that tuning fork before she came here. If Fred had
been willing to reconcile, that tuning fork probably would
have wound up in the ocean."

"If insurance money was Melena's motive, why would
getting back with Fred have stopped her?" Jane asked.

"Yeah, why?" Tyrone repeated.

"The insurance money would let Melena start a new
life, but that's not the real reason she killed Fred. He was
leaving Melena for another woman now that he'd made the

big time. She gave up her dreams to help Fred achieve his. Then, when everything was going great for him, he rejected her. That old saying about fury," I said. "No fury like a woman scorned. He wouldn't consider trying to save the marriage but still wanted her to assist him with his prank. Wanted her to help him like she always had. Melena killed Fred because he scorned her. She killed Kenny to keep him quiet, and she would have killed Jane because she was scared Jane could identify her by smell in the Winnebago."

"Have you ever been scorned?" Tyrone asked and helped himself to the last wedge of tomato pie.

"I felt scorned when Andy was sticking to Melena like glue while I had to load up all those flowers to take back to the mortuary after Fred's funeral service."

"Did the Middletons ever put Little Fiddlin' Fred in the crypt?" asked Jane. She still had no memory of being held there. I'd told her most of what happened but not about the fifty-year-old corpse who'd shared the space with her nor Sheriff Harmon's consideration of opening the coffin to be sure her dead body wasn't in it.

"Yes," I answered, "and we didn't even charge extra for it."

Maum placed her fork across her plate and looked at Rizzie. "When I die," she said, "I want my rocking chair put on the grave along with my spectacles and some quilts so I can rest in peace comfortably. Then I won't have any excuse to come wandering back to the house to haunt anybody unless you don't have my fingernails and toenails painted that bright pretty red I picked." She looked at me. "Callie, you will do my nails for me when I die, won't you?"

"I'll tell you what, Maum," I answered. "I've been thinking about quitting work at Middleton's and going back to teaching, but no matter where I'm working, anytime Rizzie calls, I'll come do your nails."

"Did you say you might quit Middleton's?" Jane sounded surprised.

"I've been thinking about leaving there," I said. "It doesn't matter how you spell it, there's no 'fun' in 'funeral.'

I like Otis and Odell, and I love making people look nice for their family and friends, but I'm tired of death and dying."

"Why?" Tyrone said for what seemed the hundredth time.

That's when I remembered the reasons I quit teaching kindergarten and went to work at the mortuary. I was tired of little boys and girls who had to tee-tee every five minutes. Children who wouldn't lie down for their naps, wouldn't listen, and most of all, kids who wouldn't stop asking "Why?"

"On second thought," I said to Maum, "Rizzie can find me at Middleton's anytime you want your nails done." I winked at her. "Would you like some red lipstick to match the polish?"

Maum laughed. "I sure would," she said, "unless you need it to catch that man."

"I don't want to catch a man who'll scorn me," I said.

"Andy wasn't scorning you," said Rizzie. "He's just young and was concentrating on his career and Melena's promises of success."

"You didn't see them together. That wasn't all she was promising him."

"How young is he?" Maum said.

"Quite a bit younger, like maybe twelve years or so," I said.

Maum spouted Gullah so fast I couldn't understand it.

"What did she say?" I asked Rizzie.

"She said, 'Play with fire, you might get burned. Rob the cradle, you might get pooped on.'"